A Vision of Loveliness

LOUISE LEVENE is a journalist, academic and one-time saleslady. She is currently the ballet critic of the *Sunday Telegraph*, and used to write and present Radio 4's *Newstand* among other programmes. She lives in London. *A Vision of Loveliness* is her first novel.

Praise for *A Vision of Loveliness*:

'Sparkly as a Babycham, dry as a Twiglet, and honest as a tinned pie – Janey James is the perfect hilarious, sexy, rude and clear-eyed guide to swinging London. I feel like I've been out on the tiles with her all night – and I'd happily do it all again' Helen Cross

'The plot is almost the least of the pleasures of Levene's enticing novel, whose glory lies in its author's exquisite mastery of period detail ... Like Flaubert's Emma Bovary, Jane's character is inseparable from her love of things, and like Emma, the things she loves turn on her in the end' **** Jane Shilling, *Daily Telegraph*

'Louise Levene . . . is a zesty storyteller and a master of the needle-sharp one-liner . . . For all the froufrou and fetishistic fashion vernacular, *A Vision of Loveliness* is a pointed indictment of a sexist, small-minded society' *Sunday Telegraph*

'A grubbily glamorous ride through a sleazy West End world of part-time modelling and full-time man-trapping' *Mail on Sunday*

'As light as a chocolate éclair' *Independent*

'Any first novel that earns a *Book at Bedtime* reading must have something going for it – and Louise Levene's *A Vision of Loveliness* has a lot, not least its setting' *The Times*

'Sixties Swinging London is beautifully evoked in this fine debut novel' *Choice*

'Hogarth would have painted this heroine's progress just as unflinchingly' *Sunday Times*

'If this debut novel were an item of clothing, it would be a sassy pencil skirt in nasturtium taffeta, wasp-waisted and exquisitely lined' Hephzibah Anderson, *Daily Mail*

'Exquisitely and often revoltingly detailed, the novel draws you into a world of tawdry glamour: of members only cabarets, mascara streaked sheets and mistress flats off Curzon Street' *Observer*

'An exploration of a bygone era's underbelly' *Financial Times*

'A delight – funny, sad and clever. For those of us who were young in the late fifties and early sixties, it's an uncanny evocation of our past. For today's young women, it will read like gender history – and I hope it makes their jaws drop' Barbara Trapido

A Vision of Loveliness

LOUISE LEVENE

BLOOMSBURY
LONDON · BERLIN · NEW YORK · SYDNEY

First published in Great Britain 2010
This paperback edition published 2011

Copyright © 2010 by Louise Levene

The moral right of the author has been asserted

Bloomsbury Publishing, London, Berlin, New York and Sydney

50 Bedford Square, London WC1B 3DP

A CIP catalogue record for this book is available from the British Library

ISBN 978 1 4088 0982 2
10 9 8 7 6 5 4 3 2

Typeset by Hewer Text UK Ltd, Edinburgh
Printed in Great Britain by Clays Ltd, St Ives plc

www.bloomsbury.com/louiselevene

For My Mother

You won't regret a single moment that you devote to becoming lovelier.

Part One

Chapter 1

> *Wear gloves whenever you can bear to;*
> *go without a handbag as often as possible.*

'Bag bag bag bag bag bag BAG.'

It was the old woman in the greasy tweeds. As she leaned towards Jane with the handbag, the hairy fabric of her skirt gave off an unmistakably nasty, *leaky* smell.

'You forgot your *bag*, duckie.'

It wasn't Jane's handbag. She wasn't even carrying a bloody bag. But she was flustered by the old woman's unexpectedly posh voice, by her sweaty yellow face as she loomed across the table of empties, holding the handle by one tobacco-stained hook.

'Your baaag, deah.'

Jane took it, too embarrassed to start explaining. They were about to leave the pub but Tony had gone to the Gents' and she didn't want to be stood in the street on her own. Not round here. She glanced down at the bag on her lap. It was an impressive-looking mock-croc affair and it clunked open expensively, releasing a delicious whiff of suede and scent and a glimpse of an Hermes label. Not mock croc at all. Croc croc.

Jane fidgeted the mirror from its special pocket and pretended to be admiring herself while she scanned the inside: handkerchief; comb; compact and a face: a face that gazed gorgeously out at her from a shiny black and white card. Jane's eyes batted between the mirror and the snapshot: pretty faces, late teens, dark hair, wide eyes; but the girl in the bag peered out with a look of such friendly, flirtatious glamour, such fabulous *finish*, that Jane wanted to run to the Ladies' and borrow a lipstick. Just behind the photo was a torn manila envelope. She clicked the bag shut.

There must have been a hundred quid in that envelope. Jane looked about her as if expecting the rightful owner to pounce but there was no one in sight who could possibly lay claim to a beautiful crocodile bag full of fivers. Jane and Tony had got to the pub just after it opened and there had been no one there then either. It must have been sat under the bench since lunchtime – more than likely, given the state of the floor.

The old woman was eyeing her nastily over her pink gin. Tony still wasn't back. Jane pretended to take an interest in the pub's *characters* – that's what Tony had called them. Loud-mouthed drunks more like.

The pub had filled up with Friday drinkers. By seven o'clock most of the 'swift halves' would have dried up, leaving the regulars to it, but for now the small bar was heaving. An optimistic little sales rep in a sheepskin jacket with dandruffed shoulders was telling a home-dyed blonde that he had a friend who took photographs. His showroom was always on the lookout for new models for the new models – if you took his meaning. Jane sized her up with a saleslady's eye. A large fourteen. She wouldn't stand a chance modelling anyway: too short; too top-heavy. The blonde, who would put up with a lot for a large gin and orange, stroked absently at her squirrel-fur jacket and patted her coarse platinum flick-ups. She didn't bother to listen. If she had, she would have heard it before. She was perched on a bar stool and the man patted her knee as he spoke. It wouldn't cost her a penny. She stared down at his paw resentfully but there was talk of dinner at the Regent Palace (paper napkins, but you couldn't have everything) and she decided to let the hand slither across the nylon and under the hem of her tight skirt.

A pair of regulars were squirming round her to the bar, smoothly borrowing a ten-bob note from a familiar face in the crowd as they passed.

'Who *are* all these people? Your pub's not your own. Where are they all *from*, for God's sake?' said one of them, a tall, fat man in a big black hat and a poncey pink Indian silk scarf knotted at his neck. And suede shoes. Poof, probably. Only poofs wore suede shoes.

'Streatham, darling. Streatham *Common*. I told you we should have gone to the Fitzroy,' drawled his friend, a rat-faced toff in a covert coat the colour of dishwater and a striped tie so horrible it had to mean something. You got them like that in the shop: debs' delights with frayed shirtcuffs and stiff collars: pricing cashmere but buying lambswool.

'Don't they have any fucking pubs in fucking Streatham?'

Aye-aye. *Lang-guage.* The smoky room was suddenly short of oxygen as drinkers on all sides sniffed disapprovingly. The landlord's face flickered a warning and the double act closed down, concentrating on their scrounged gins. Too bloody cold to go looking for another pub.

There were actually some very nice pubs in fucking Streatham. Proper pubs with saloon bars and carpet.

The smelly old woman had started up again.

'I *sa-a-a-aid*: You-wouldn't-like-to-buy-me-a-*Drink*, would you, duckie?'

Tony had fought his way through the bar and was signalling for Jane to join him at the door. She grabbed her coat from under the bench and slid the handbag down the side of her carrier, taking care not to crush her new outfit. The owner's name would be inside somewhere. She could sort it out tomorrow lunchtime.

'A *drink*, duckie.'

The woman kept her money in an old Oxo tin which she was now banging up and down on the table. The pub had only been open since half five but there were already four sticky dead glasses crowded in front of her next to the half-finished *Evening News* crossword and the tin ashtray was full. The Edwardian drawl had become loud and shrill, rising above the chinking hum of the bar.

'*Drink*. Deah.'

Jane stood up to go, lifting her carrier clear of the glasses as she sidled out from behind the table, her knees hobbled by the heavy little stools and snagging her already laddered stockings. The old woman lurched out of her seat and grabbed Jane by the sleeve of her sweater.

'The least you can do is buy me a Drink.'

She turned to address the room but the room kept its head down, afraid she might start on them. She rubbed Jane's sleeve between her twisted yellow fingers.

'Crocodile and *cash-meah* but she can't find the price of a gin. Mean little Bitch.'

Tony had been waiting for Jane by the entrance but the tide of fresh drinkers washing into the bar had forced him outside. His puzzled face appeared round the door.

'I'm sorry. My friend's waiting.'

Jane inched towards the exit, carrier bag on one arm, coat on the other. Men made a show of making room – 'Let the little lady through', 'Not going are you, girlie?' – but actually edged even closer, brushing against her body as she passed. She felt helping hands at her waist, on the small of her back, the inevitable pat on the backside.

'I'm sorry. I thought you were right behind me. Meet someone you knew?'

'Some woman wanted me to buy her a drink. Never seen her in my life. She was drunk. Do you often go in there?'

'It has a lot of Atmosphere,' said Tony, apologetically, as he helped her on with her coat. 'Augustus John used to drink in there.'

Did they really. What difference did that make? It was still a horrible pub.

'You sure you won't change your mind and have a bite to eat?'

Not on your life. If that was his idea of a nice pub she dreaded to think what the meal would be like. Foreign probably.

6

'I'm sorry, I can't. Aunt Doreen has tea on the table at seven. I'll be lucky if I make it. It's nearly half six.'

'Another night?'

Oh God. How to make him stop? Crew-cut, fifty-shilling suit, nylon shirt, body odour. Did she have to spell it out? She'd only agreed to 'one quick drink' as a thank you. Without Tony she wouldn't have the precious contents of her carrier bag: a Hardy Amies cashmere and wool dogtooth-check costume. *Buy the best suit you can afford.* Tony worked in the accounts department at the Savile Row boutique and told her that they were selling off that season's samples and misfits at an invitation-only sale on Friday lunchtime. Jane had got there on the dot with £10 from her post office savings. Hardy Amies suits retailed for nearly thirty guineas – six weeks' wages – and she wasn't sure what kind of discount she'd get. In the end the pricing was up to Tony who let her have it for a fiver.

She had spotted her suit straight away: short, exquisitely draped jacket, real horn buttons, pencil-slim skirt with a nice deep wrap at the back. She tried it on in the back room filled with half-naked size-ten salesgirls and under-buyers looking for a bargain. There was a really nice violet dress and coatee as well but she couldn't afford both and the black and tan dogtooth was more of a classic. The house fitter wouldn't leave off about Jane's stock-size figure. Not a single alteration. Jane could hardly wait to get home and try it on again.

'How about Monday?'

'Monday's my day off. Look, I'm sorry but I've got to get the bus. Thanks awfully for the drink.' *Awfully.* She blushed as she said it. What was all that about?

Tony insisted on walking her through Soho to the bus stop in Regent Street. The butchers, cakeshops and smelly delis were all shut up, blinds pulled down inside the windows. The coffee bars were quieter now that the pubs had opened. The usual warm, fatty whiff of roasting meat was already farting out of the back of the Regent Palace but it was too early for proper restaurants and it was far too early for the tarts – thank God – although Jane did glimpse one old trollop in a dressing gown pinning a card to the side door that led to her room above a chop-suey joint in Wardour Street: 'busty young model upstairs', apparently. Flat as a board she was. Imagine paying fifty bob for that. It was supposed to be more if they took their clothes off but it was hard to see why, looking at her.

It was a very cold, very aggravating walk, packed with opportunities for Tony to try and pin Jane down to a definite night. She tried talking about the miserable January weather but he kept a painful grip on the conversation, dragging it back to this date they were supposed to be having. He insisted on waiting in the queue with her, even though he lived in the opposite direction, but after only a minute the golden glow of Jane's bus swung round the bend and she ran up the stairs to escape the sound of his farewells, to escape the possibility that people might think he was hers.

It was lovely and warm on the top of the bus and she slid thankfully into a seat, enfolded in smoke. A man in an old, smog-stained Burberry sat down next to her although there were several empty seats further along. His thigh was pressed the length of hers and, although it couldn't really be helped on those skimpy double seats, some spark of unwelcome electricity, some unsmelled smell, told her that he knew what he was doing. Jane pulled her coat huffily round her and inched closer to the window, making herself as small as possible and opening up the tiniest crack of daylight between her thigh and his. He gave a faint grunt and immediately exhaled into the extra space. Jane flashed a cross glance at him: pale, sickly complexion, home-cut hair and an evil smell of Scotch and stale sweat.

The conductress had stomped heavily on to the upper deck, guarding the passengers' heads from her ticket machine with her fingerless-gloved hands.

'Any more fares please! You together?'

Cheek. Jane paid her fare and dug her book out of her coat pocket: *Lady Be Good.* As they reached Lambeth Bridge a huge drop of dark brown water landed splat on the page explaining how to tackle various hors d'oeuvres: *Want him to think you mysterious and sophisticated? Don't, whatever you do, order corn on the cob.* She looked up to see the whole tobacco-stained ceiling trembling with tarry, fat droplets of condensation.

The night was colder still by the time they reached Norbury and Jane huddled inside her coat as she tripped along the lightless windows of the shopping parade. Vanda Modes – *Vanda*, honestly, the woman's name was Edie. The huge walk-in windows were full of chipped, jazz-age mannequins dressed in snappy outfits, all identified with special labels (mis)printed on Vanda's little machine as if Vanda were afraid that Norbury wouldn't know the names for such clothes. Stylish gaberdine two-piece. Sporty ensemble. Casual jacket. Day-to-evening. Young seperates.

Jane had had a Saturday job with 'Vanda' as a schoolgirl. The windows might be full of winter fashions but at least a quarter of the turnover was corsets: slim pink boxes full of the things stacked in the light oak glass-fronted fixtures by size and length. White, pink, even black – service with a sneer here: either you were a slag or you didn't wash your underwear, both, maybe, but never neither. The decent pink and white ones were worn by straight-backed old ladies who had been taught to dress when they came of age and who saw no reason to give up Mr Marcel's waves, the tailor-mades, the smart little blouses and the figured rayon foundation garments they had worn as girls. The smart little blouses were also Vanda's bread and butter: lawn; rayon; Viyella. They were lined up in the window on fantastical wickerwork torsos, their rude pointy bosoms tilted up shamelessly at passing eyes.

Aunt Doreen used to buy corsets from Vanda (when she bought them at all, which wasn't often) but one year she was persuaded to try a new line in roll-on panty girdles instead. The scientific system promised 'twice the flattening, twice the flattering' and she couldn't really sit down in it. It rolled on all right but after a day of toast and biscuits and boiled sweets it was completely impossible to roll off. There had been a knock at Jane's door after everyone had gone to bed and there was Auntie Doreen in just her dressing gown, a porridge-coloured long-line bra and a gleaming white girdle. All Jane's fault of course – 'I only shop in the rotten place because you work there.' Jane had had to cut her out of it with the nail clippers, each careful snip increasing the V-shaped pillow of flesh until Doreen was finally scissored free. It was one of Jane's happiest memories. Doreen said she was going to take it back and complain but she didn't. Of course she didn't. She sewed it up and made it into a peg bag.

When Jane had started her Saturday job she didn't know dolman from raglan. She still had nightmares about her very first customer. The corset fitter had been off sick and Vanda and the proper saleslady were both in the fitting room seeing to a large order. 'Lovely woman. Difficult Figure,' mouthed Vanda as she dived back behind the curtain, tape measure slung round the neck of her tan jersey two-piece. So far Jane had done nothing but fold and box corsets. She approached the customer with exaggerated meekness. She didn't exactly curtsey, but her face did.

'Good morning, madam. Can I help you?'

'Last year . . .' No 'good morning'. Jane did not qualify. 'Last year I bought a very nice shirtwaister here. Peter Pan collar. Eau de nil self-stripe voile. Do you still stock it? I'd quite fancy another colour. Greige? Ecru? Or taupe?'

It was like Chinese.

'Sorry?'

No sale that time but Vanda had kindly sent her home when they closed that lunchtime with a carrier bag full of catalogues, a manufacturer's colour chart, Weldon's dressmaking encyclopaedia and a few old *Vogue*s and told her to get weaving.

The following Saturday a customer (right prat, Dulwich Village probably) demanded a peau de soie peignoir in cantaloupe and Vanda looked on proudly as Jane manfully tried to interest her in a peach rayon dressing gown. Jane revelled in the new vocabulary. Nothing would ever be green again. Emerald. Peppermint. Apple. Bottle. Chartreuse. Jade. Lime. Loden. Viridian. Moss.

Her last year at school, she spent the Easter holidays haunting fabric departments: fingering silks and worsteds, memorising the difference between chiffon and georgette, organza and tulle. *Crush a scrap of it* hard *in your hand. If the creases don't bounce out at once, keep looking.* She'd told her aunt she was just going into Croydon but spent whole afternoons in the West End stores at the daily fashion shows, sitting at the back while the real customers – groomed to death in natty tweed tailor-mades and three-string cultured pearls – killed time and wasted money: 'Paula is wearing Sherbet Sunrise, a sporty two-piece in lemon shantung with candystripe revers and simple self-covered buttons.' Paula looked like a right little madam.

Jane used to wander in and out of the arcades round Piccadilly gazing at antique china and twinfold poplin shirtings until one day she saw the little handwritten sign in the window of Drayke's Cashmere: 'Junior Saleslady Required'. She had been interviewed by Mr Drayke himself. Where had she worked? Who were her references? Could she speak French? Jane didn't expect you needed to speak French to fold up sweaters and make tea and take deliveries – which was pretty much all the junior was going to be doing. He was only asking her so that he'd have a reason to turn her down if the reference was no good. When she said she was doing O level French he immediately asked if she spoke Italian. Lot of Italian customers lately. What did she know about purchase tax? Foreign customers could claim back the tax – not something that ever troubled Vanda. But she knew he wanted her really because he gave her a Pringle catalogue to take home. Saddle shoulder. Batwing sleeve. Mock turtle. Geelong lambswool. Single-ply. Two-ply. Intarsia. Argyll. A whole new dialect. He rang at home to say she could start the day after she finished school.

'Who was that man on the phone? What did he want? Strange men on my phone.'

Auntie Doreen was not happy at the idea of a West End job. Jane fancied herself. Even the promise of forty bob a week for Jane's keep didn't really make up for it. Doreen couldn't remember the last time she went to the West End. What was cashmere anyway? Goats? No thank you.

Vanda was very disappointed. Mona was retiring next year and she had *hoped*. Particularly after she had taken the trouble to train Jane in the business. But Edie was a sweet woman really. She gave Jane a very nice reference – 'glowing', Mr Philip called it – and a blouse to start work in. A rather nice striped lawn to wear with her navy gaberdine. 'You watch out for that Mr Drayke. They can take advantage.'

The spiteful east wind flounced the length of the shopping parade and ripped easily through Jane's cheap coat – three-quarter-length flannel grey bouclé, Magyar sleeve, cape collar and showy red buttons the size of liquorice bootlaces. She had bought it – or had been sold it, rather – in the previous January's sale at Marshall and Snelgrove and regretted it the instant she got it home. It looked awful but it was still the warmest thing she had. The chill rose up from the pavement, freezing her knees, icing the bare tops of her thighs. She could feel her shoulders starting to curl up round her ears, sense her ribcage tightening to avoid breathing in the painfully cold night air. All wrong. *Walk like a princess! A girl who walks beautifully is one of life's thrills. Pretend two cords are tied around your ears, pulling you skyward. Your earlobes should be in a straight line with your shoulder.*

She swung her carrier bag lightly – only not so lightly. She remembered the handbag with a sudden twinge of guilt and embarrassment. Why hadn't she just handed it in at the bar?

You'd have had to get to the bar first of course. Never mind. She could take it back to the pub tomorrow and say there had been a mistake.

She had reached the avenue now. The stained-glass front doors glowed faintly all along the street. Occasionally a thin slice of light escaped from between the skimpy cotton curtains of an upstairs window but there were no matching lights in the downstairs front rooms. Everyone was home – it was gone seven – but they were all out the back having their teas. For two or three weeks each winter a Christmas tree (usually an everlasting affair of wire and tinsel) would twinkle tartily in the bay windows of the darkened parlours, unseen by their owners but only visitors or funerals or Christmas Day would ever make it worth opening and heating the front room.

She walked a few yards past the house so that she could perform a nice Paris turn: *Right foot forward, toes out slightly. Left foot across and in front with the weight well forward. Use the right foot to pivot you to the right, left leg straight. Pause fleetingly with weight on the left foot before moving off again on the right.* Jane had watched the house models doing it at the big-store fashion shows and she had practised with a book that had a pattern of little black and white feet for you to follow. She fell over the first time she tried.

She closed the front gate carefully. Her aunt had a horror of dogs (what dogs?) getting into the 'front garden', a crudely concreted patch with a hole left for a dusty hydrangea bush which was now wearing its winter wardrobe of dead brown blooms. It had once had vivid, Capri-blue flowers but Aunt Doreen resented the idea of having to feed it whatever it was that kept it blue and it had sulked back, summer by summer, to a dirty, tooth-powder pink.

The Christmas tree was back in the cupboard under the stairs and the gap in Doreen's elaborately swagged net curtains left a theatrical little space in the middle of the window sill for her treasured 'Royal Doulton' figurine, a cheesy Victorian miss in a fat pink crinoline. It wasn't actually Royal Doulton. The real Royal Doulton one (a wedding present) had been smashed by a six-year-old Jane (who had never been allowed to forget it). The replacement had 'foreign' stamped accusingly on its bottom and had come from a curio shop on the Streatham High Road.

Jane knocked on the door with the approved amount of force. It wasn't usually loud enough to penetrate the running argument that took place in Aunt Doreen's kitchen but if anyone rapped too hard there were more reproaches. Jane didn't have the key-of-the-door. Aunt Doreen took the words of the song entirely literally and wouldn't be letting Jane have one until she was twenty-one, two whole years away.

She knocked again, *fractionally* louder, and instants later a light appeared at the end of the passage and her aunt tore open the door, cheered up by a fresh grievance.

'Banging and banging like that! Anyone would think it was the bailiffs!'

What bailiffs? Jane doubted very much she'd ever seen a bloody bailiff. No hello. No nice day. No kiss my arse. Nothing.

'Your tea's on the table. Don't blame me if it's cold.'

Chapter 2

> Early man lived in the Croydon
> area but avoided Norbury.*

Only fourteen bombs had fallen on Norbury (by mistake: the Germans wanted Croydon – or thought they did). But one of them, a flying one, fell on Jane's happy, smiling mother and her shy, squinting father who had decided to go and see *Fanny By Gaslight* while he was home on leave in 1944. Both were killed instantly – funny how people always were killed instantly. Jane had been only three at the time and her image of her parents was based on a dog-eared snapshot of her mother, stuck for ever in black and white gingham, and one photograph of the two of them at Brighton in the boiling hot summer of 1939, sat on the stony beach fully dressed in floral flock and flannels with a nice tray of tea between them. There were no wedding photographs. Aunt Doreen had lost them – except the one of herself as matron of honour looking like Charley's Aunt in a huge crêpe dress and a neighbour's moth-eaten silver fox.

Doreen was in a nursing home expecting a baby (Kenneth Leonard Deeks) when Jane's parents were killed and so motherless little Jane and her two-year-old sister June were packed off to a war orphanage down in Kent somewhere until the Women's Voluntary Service could arrange to billet them on some unsuspecting old couple. Asked to point out her baby sister in the recreation room, Jane's three-year-old eyes passed over fat

* *Norbury: The Story of a London Suburb*, J.G. Hunter and B. A. Mullen, 1977

15

little June with her grubby frock and the cold sore that gnawed at her upper lip summer and winter and pointed, unhesitatingly, to a smiley-faced blonde in a pale blue polka-dotted sundress. The house they had stayed in had a lovely big garden with apple trees and a swing and a beautiful little Wendy house full of lovely old dressing-up clothes. Jane had enjoyed three months playing at sisters with that nice, friendly, pretty little girl who had followed her everywhere and who joined delightedly in all her make-believe.

It wasn't until Doreen turned up (reluctantly) to claim her nieces that the mistake was spotted and June was fished out of the orphanage (they hadn't been able to find anyone to foster her). Fortunately Doreen and the family had assumed it was all just a cock-up by the WVS ('interfering bunch of prats' was Doreen's verdict) but Jane was still teased mercilessly about leaving her sister to the horrors of an institution: cabbage; bed-wetting; saying grace before meals. June had had nightmares about it for years. She knew it wasn't the WVS's fault. Jane never saw the pretty little girl again.

The hall smelled. A nasty, stale, mumsy mixture of bleach and burned toast. Jane ran across the dusty lino and up the stairs. She stuffed the crocodile bag under her pillow and quickly hung her new suit from the picture rail – she couldn't bear to put it away but it did look funny against the wallpaper's grubby pink rosebuds. There was a knock at her bedroom door. June, Kenneth and Uncle George had all been trained to do this. Doreen would have just burst in, mid-complaint. It was June. Minus the cold sore but just as unappealing. She was seventeen and had been at teachers' training college since leaving school the previous summer.

'Auntie says your tea's stone cold.'

June was not Doreen's favourite; Doreen disliked and resented all the children equally, but June ran errands and told tales on Jane and there were rewards for this.

Tea was dished out in the ground-floor back or what Doreen liked to call the 'sitting-cum-dining room', an expression that was supposed to explain away the fact that they all had to sit and eat and watch television in one room while another perfectly good one was left empty at the front. You could barely move: table, six chairs, sideboard, three-piece suite in cut moquette and three leatherette pouffes all fanned around a huge teak-veneer telly. The TV aerial dangled over it from a hook in the ceiling that had been put there to hold up the Christmas decorations. There was a little bit of pink paper chain still stuck to it. You had to duck to walk under it but it was the only position where you could get ITV (Doreen liked *Emergency Ward Ten*). There was a blue glass bowl of plastic apples and oranges (Doreen had tried having real fruit but it only got eaten).

Tea was very cold indeed but as it consisted of gala pie and 'salad' (two quarters of tomato and Heinz tinned potato in salad cream) this wasn't really very surprising. There was a grey-green ring round the central disc of hard-boiled egg and a hard, glassy yellow jelly gluing the pink meat to the unnaturally orange pastry.

Aunt Doreen had learned her housekeeping with a ration book in one hand and a tin opener in the other. She had never really got the hang of – or even seen the point of – nice food or nice houses or looking nice and so what you got was food out of packets in a grotty back room served by a lank-haired woman in a dirty nylon housecoat. *Do try to greet their homecoming with smooth hair and a well-groomed, bright appearance. There is no excuse for moping about in 'any old thing' just because you are doing household chores.*

Doreen's idea of a really nice hot tea was a tinned steak and kidney pie, soggy King Edwards and Surprise dried peas – the surprise being that anyone bought them. Uncle George had other ideas. He would put up with the two veg but he quietly refused to go anywhere near meat pies – tinned or otherwise. His father had been a factory inspector and told disgusting,

Sweeney Todd-y tales of what passed for filling in the pie trade and young George was having none of it. Ditto sausages. And potted meat. And faggots. And mince. And fish fingers. Unless it was a recognisable slice of the animal Uncle George wasn't interested and so he got steak or a nice chop of an evening. Jane wasn't very interested in Doreen's repertoire of tinned pie, Spam salad and beans on toast either, and tended to shunt most of hers on to her spotty cousin Kenneth's plate while his mother banged the eye-level grill around, fussing furiously over her husband's special diet.

George and Doreen never called each other George or Doreen. When she spoke to him she didn't call him anything and when she spoke about him he was simply E or Im. He called her Reenie or Reen, both of which drove her mad. He probably knew this.

Doreen had been a 29-year-old mother of the newborn Kenneth when she first came to drag the two sisters back to Norbury. Kenneth was now a great big spotty kid of fifteen with a tiny bedroom full of model aeroplanes (although it was actually Uncle George who made these). Kenneth's real hobby was bus serial numbers. He would lurk at the bus stop for hours peering at passing Routemasters and noting them down in a little red memo book.

There had just been the three of them until eighteen months ago when, out of the blue, Kenneth's baby sister arrived. Doreen, who didn't want the children she'd got, let alone any more, was furious. Even more furious when people mistook her for the baby's grandmother. She did almost warm to it in the end – it had the lardy pink blonde looks she admired in a child – but nobody else liked it much. It cried whenever you took its dummy out and could only be kept quiet with rusks and Ribena. Its name was Georgette. Georgette Ann.

It turned out that Doreen had had two babies before Kenneth. Jane only found this out when she was seventeen because a letter arrived in the post for a Miss Mary Jane Deeks giving her

National Insurance number. Uncle George made Doreen a cup of tea and told them all that there had been a second Miss Deeks as well, born a year later. Both babies had died within days. Pity really. June wasn't much of a sister. It must have been rotten for Doreen, the babies dying like that, but when Jane dared to say as much her aunt looked genuinely surprised. What were their names?

'Mary Jane and Sally Ann. Not names I would have chosen but I had to call them something. I never saw them. E saw them. Said they were very pretty babies.'

Jane kept the National Insurance card and the birth certificates, often thinking wistfully of the missing sisters.

She never felt that way about the ones she'd got. Georgette was wet. Wet, smelly and uncomfortable. She spent large parts of each day in her high chair in a hand-knitted pink matinée coat and a pair of elasticated plastic panties. Doreen had potty-trained Kenneth with terrifying speed at the age of twelve months. Jane remembered it happening almost overnight. The next-door neighbour was busy training a new puppy at the time and the four-year-old Jane had really begun to wonder if Doreen, too, had just rubbed Kenneth's nose in it. And yet, since those no-nonsense days, Doreen had read a women's magazine (in the doctor's waiting room – she didn't waste her money on that rubbish) which had other ideas. As a result Georgette was still producing bucketfuls of shitty terry towelling and showing no interest at all in the shell-pink celluloid potty that Doreen had bought for her. The whole upstairs stank like scented sewage.

The family was sat round the gate-leg table for tea. No cloth. Tablecloths made work. So did napkins. There wasn't a napkin in the house although, funnily enough, there were lots of napkin rings: one set of silver plate and one set of pearly Bakelite. Doreen had got them as wedding presents and they lived with a family of silver fish in the bottom drawer of the sideboard.

'You're late.'

Still no hello or nothing.

'We had a late customer. Had half the stock out.'

The lie flowed nicely. Jane had once explained that she had gone for a quick drink with the girls after work (actually a rather pushy young man from the camera shop in the Arcade) but Doreen's envious fury had taught her to think better of it. Drink? When did she ever get a chance for a Drink?

'No consideration,' said Doreen, lightly spraying the table with food.

Doreen always talked with her mouth full, waiting until a fresh forkful had been shovelled in before starting up the next complaint. It was disgusting enough anyway but it also meant you got to see her teeth. Doreen had all her own teeth – no one else would have wanted them. She had resisted the mad rush for National Health dentures after the war, deciding that it was 'common'. Uncle George took one look at the gleaming white gum shields being knocked out by Mr Bevin's army of dentists and decided to make his own arrangements with a private man on Putney High Street. German Jew. Good craftsman. The result, artfully chipped and stained here and there, were a perfect fit and completely undetectable – or would have been if Doreen hadn't gone on about them all the time.

'Of course, I prefer raspberry jam,' she'd say in the queue at the self-service, 'but the pips get under George's plate.'

The family was still up to its knees in a row that had started at 'breakfast' (burned toast and marge with a scraping of damson jam). A small silver and white cardboard box containing a smashed slab of wedding cake had arrived in the morning post. No one had the least idea who it was from. Uncle George's mother had been the youngest of fourteen children (disgusting, Doreen said) and they'd all bred ferociously. The various grades of removed cousins had topped a hundred some years back.

'Well, whoever it was didn't ask us to the bloody wedding,' whined Doreen, squinting crossly at the little box's torn wrapper.

Not that they went when they were invited – not after the last time, years ago when Jane was about six. It meant Expense. Pop-up toasters. Hats. New clothes. Not likely.

June and Kenneth had been wrangling enthusiastically all teatime about who would get to eat the cake. Doreen solved the problem by shutting it up in a rusty biscuit tin with a rather self-satisfied Yorkshire terrier on it. 'Wedding cake keeps for months.' Not this piece, though. Doreen, who habitually thought of all foods in terms of reward and punishment, made herself a little present of the cake later that evening with a cup of tea. A nice cup of tea.

Jane was itching to finish the meal, wash up and get back upstairs. She refused pudding which always drove Doreen mad – 'You're skin and bone. You want to eat more.' Only Jane didn't want to eat more: *The cold fact is that you cannot possibly be fat and chic*. But Doreen ate more: much, much more. Kenneth had left the egg, June the meat and Jane the pastry of the slices of gala pie, thus making a whole extra helping for Doreen. It was as if she knew.

Later, when everyone was out of the way watching *Take Your Pick*, Doreen would get to work on the strangely abundant leftovers. Doreen wasted not. The larder was empty except for a few bottles of sauce and whatever was to be eaten that day. No one ever got more pie or Spam because there never was any. But there was always too much jelly or custard or blancmange, or spotted dick (puddings were the only thing she could be bothered with). Every night the remains of the dish would be whisked away 'for tomorrow' only to disappear into the softly expanding Doreen who would stand by the larder door, spooning them into her mouth straight from the Pyrex bowl as she gazed unseeingly at the fat, ripe peppers and aubergines that garnished the kitchen wallpaper. Vegetables she would never actually taste. Vegetables George would probably have liked.

Jane carried the plates out to the kitchen to wash up. Doreen didn't believe in rubber gloves (Jane bought her own). Fortunately

Doreen didn't believe in drying-up cloths either – *Germs*. That and the lazy-cow's tea her aunt had made meant there were only the plates to do (Uncle George had to do his own grill pan: a kind of penance) which could all be left on the slimy wooden draining board. Ten minutes later Jane escaped upstairs to her beautiful suit and the beautiful girl in the crocodile bag.

Chapter 3

> *Want to be a success? Look posh.*

Jane had the big room at the back. Kenneth had the box room. June had the small front room. Doreen and George had the large room at the front: bay window, twin beds (much good they'd been) and his-and-hers burr walnut veneer wardrobes. Georgette's cot had been in her parents' room at first but she made so much noise – even when fast asleep – that they had moved her out on to the landing. There had been talk of her sharing Jane's room. There had also been talk of Jane not rotten well putting up with it and finding a nice bedsit somewhere. Nice bedsit? Fifty bob a week for some bug-ridden box in Earl's Court? Don't make Doreen laugh.

Jane shivered into her room and switched on the one-bar electric fire. Hardy Amies's suit hung from the picture rail and there was a bulge under the pink candlewick bedspread where she had stuffed the bag. She used to try hiding things under the bed or under the mattress but, while Doreen had stopped making Jane's bed when she started at primary school, she still liked to nose about in such places. That was how she found poor Kenneth's dirty postcard (a black and white *Rokeby Venus*). That was how she found Jane's secret library: *Lady Be Good*, a pronouncing dictionary and *Anita Colby's Beauty Book* (*Let's make a star out of you!*). Doreen had a field day. Some people didn't half fancy theirselves. But she never actually looked inside the bed – she had enough to do without waiting on Jane – so everything was now tucked safely away under the eiderdown.

Jane wedged a chair under the door handle, sat down at the frilly dressing table and posted a penny into her flowery china pig: *A daily penny put away becomes 30s 5d in a year; buy two savings certificates and in seven years they will be worth £2.* She pulled the big mock-tortoiseshell slide from the back of her long brown hair. She brushed it hard then reached for her china pot of hairpins – *A present from Whitstable* – God knew who from: no one in the family had ever been there. She fumbled her hair on to the top of her head then dabbed on a bit of lipstick. Too much. *Outline your smile with a brush then blot with care. Try to give the outer edges a merry, upward flick. Never forget that a man will judge a girl's disposition by her lips.* Better, but it was still a rotten cheap colour. Geranium. She'd be better with Rose Satin or Raspberry Ice. Finally she slipped into the skirt and jacket, shuddering as the cold silk of the lining slid over her skin.

She put on her only high heels, a really smart pair of black suede stilettos that a customer – elegant little South American woman – had left behind in the shop still in their box and bag. They had hung on to them for a few weeks but she never came back. The senior salesladies had wanted them very, very badly but they weren't a three and a half double A and Jane was. She walked – *always leading with the thighs* – towards the mirror.

Next she practised sinking down on to the corner of the bed and pretending to tuck her legs into the passenger seat of an imaginary sports car, raising her knees slightly so that the skirt slid up, exposing her lovely young knees, all cobwebbed by her cheap, laddered stockings.

Jane tilted her head into her mirror face – three-quarter profile, sucked-in cheeks – and gave herself a snooty model-girl look. The hair wasn't right but it was a wonderful suit. Smiling with satisfaction, she perched on the dressing-table stool, crossed her legs – *high on the thigh so that they are absolutely parallel from the knees down.* Her reflection was deliciously rich and expensive, very 'Can I help you, madam?' She answered herself softly in her best elocution voice. A five-year scholarship to a convent school had given Jane lots of voices: dressy, casual and several grades in between.

'I'm looking for something to match this,' she said in her posh, world-weary whisper.

She passed the pot of hairpins to her reflection, smiling flirtatiously. *As you sit before the glass, pick up various small articles and pretend you are passing them to your reflection.*

Jane placed the magic handbag on her smooth, dogtoothed lap and began emptying its contents on to the glass top of the dressing table: handkerchief, envelope, compact, photograph, a tiny pair of nail scissors, a wallet full of hairpins, a pair of really good-quality stockings in a little cellophane bag (spares: very organised), a pair of gloves (*always carry extra gloves in your bag in case the ones you have on become impossibly soiled*), three keys (one Yale, two Banham) and a red leather purse – a very Norbury purse for such a beautiful Bond Street bag – with a ten-bob note and some silver. There was a tiny jeweller's brooch box and Jane was half expecting diamonds but there was only a pair of fluffy black false eyelashes and a tiny tube of glue inside. Two expensive twist-up lipsticks – one for day, one for evening – and a brown eye pencil. There was the mirror in its little pocket and – bit funny – the price ticket. One hundred and ninety guineas. Export Only. Blimey. A good saleslady usually took the price off in case it was a present.

There was nothing with the girl's name on it. No letters. No cheque book – you'd expect someone with a crocodile bag to have a cheque book. There was an expensive-looking diary covered in ginger pigskin that told you when to stop and start shooting things. The personal details page was blank but there were twenty, maybe thirty birthdays written in in the same colour ink – as if whoever she was had sat down in January and copied them over. Some of the other dates were circled (for fairly obvious reasons) and the next few weeks were peppered with mysterious meetings:

'Bergman's (day for evening) 10.30 5gns'; 'Earl's Court. West Door. 9am. Short sleeves.' There were some gin rummy scores on the inside cover – S, P and M – and a few phone numbers in the back – all men's names, all West End exchanges. But Jane could hardly ring some strange Dick or Harry (Regent 4121) and ask about a mysterious brunette and a crocodile handbag.

There weren't any cigarettes but there were two books of matches: one was from Carpenter's oyster bar, the other was the photographic kind they made at dances and had ready by the time you went home. The girl was sat on the lap of a middle-aged man in a dinner jacket. They were both wearing party hats. The man just looked old and a bit drunk in his but the girl, in her strapless satin gown, made the funny little fez seem larky and exotic. She was having a very good time – or knew how to photograph that way. *The more dress rehearsals you have with your make-believe audience, the better the real performance will be.* Jane threw her head back and laughed lightly at the mirror, dislodging some of the pins in her hair so that the whole lot fell down.

She brushed it all out again and hung the suit back on its hanger ready for the morning. It was far too good for work really but where else was she going to wear it? Shopping in Croydon? The shop closed at one on Saturdays. If the worst came to the worst she could always go back to that dreadful pub but she'd try the oyster bar first – in her suit. See if anyone could remember seeing the girl. She looked at the photograph again, unconsciously tilting her head to the same angle, smiling the same smile. They were bound to remember.

Chapter 4

> *Just remember that your personality*
> *isn't printed on you like a birthmark.*
> *It can alter for better or worse –*
> *and you're the girl who alters it.*

Jane's alarm went at half six, a strange soft sound from inside a sandwich of cushions – whoever woke Georgette had to change her and poke Ready Brek into her with a special pink spoon. Jane was most at risk (she got up a good hour before anyone else) but it was usually June who was unlucky. She was rather heavy on her feet but Jane suspected she did it on purpose. She liked taking the pram out as well. Creep.

Jane's stockings, underwear and quilted nylon dressing gown were already hanging over the back of the chair in front of the fire. She leaped out of bed, switched it on, drew the curtains then jumped back under the covers. A fancy lace of frost had grown on the window panes overnight. It was even colder today. A few more minutes in the warm and Jane was up, huddling into her dressing gown and slippers and tiptoeing along the corridor to the bathroom. Georgette had taken her time getting off to sleep the night before but was dead to the world now, grunting and snoring through some dreamland tantrum.

Jane met Kenneth just coming out of the bathroom, spots glowing after a good wash. Kenneth usually spent his Saturdays loitering at bus stops. But today he was off to Streatham bloody Garage – a lot of really important routes didn't come as far as Norbury apparently.

Kenneth had left the heater on but it hadn't even started to take the chill off the room and only ever really heated the ceiling. The bathroom was very bare (Doreen couldn't abide clutter). There was a bottle of medicated shampoo, a pale blue nailbrush shaped like a swan, a rack of curling toothbrushes and a yellow bar of soap with a label glued into the middle of it. Uncle George liked to keep the Steradent in the bathroom cabinet with the Elastoplast and the iodine bottle but his wife was forever taking it out and putting it in the middle of the glass shelf – in case anyone forgot. On the ledge behind the lavatory sat three wrapped bath cubes. June had once given Doreen a Mothering Sunday present but it wasn't a mistake you made twice ('I'm not your mother, thank Gawd' was the thanks she got). The bath cubes (Goya, Black Rose) had sat there unused and dusty ever since: 'they dry the skin'.

The Ascot water heater had a big red sign hung round it from the Gas Board pointing out that it had been condemned as unsafe to use. Doreen couldn't see anything wrong with it. All them water heaters made a noise. The notice was all curled up with age and damp. Either Doreen was right, or they were all living on borrowed time. *A smart female will earn enough (or marry enough) to live in a world where constant hot water is never a matter for comment or concern.* Jane was prepared to be hissed and banged at for her twice-weekly bath but managed the rest in cold. There was also the danger that the boiler would wake Georgette. She washed quickly with her own soap (Bronnley, English Fern) that she kept in a sponge bag with her shampoo, her face cream, her depilatory cream and a secret supply of tampons: *Smart young moderns choose Tampax. Nothing could be daintier.* Doreen called these 'pessaries' and said only married women could use them but that wasn't what 'Sister' said on the leaflet inside the box.

Jane reckoned it would be all right to wear the Hardy Amies if she wore her half-sleeve black twinset sweater under it. That way she could take off the jacket for work and still pass for Junior

Sales. She decided to risk her best pair of stockings (the only unladdered pair she had). She would wear the high heels on her way in but change into her everyday pumps once she got there. She wouldn't carry the bag (in case someone saw it) but she could put it in the same carrier – a really nice pale green Fortnum's one that a customer had left behind. Whatever happened, she wanted the thrill of walking along Piccadilly in the full rig-out. Pity about the awful grey bouclé coat but she couldn't not wear it in this weather. Pity about the hair as well. She wasted a good ten minutes fiddling about with it but she couldn't find a style that was smart enough for the suit but dowdy enough for work so she just wore it held back with the big brown slide as usual.

Even so, she caused quite a stir at breakfast. Doreen, thank God, had her Lie-in on Saturdays. She also had her Lie-in on Sundays and quite a lot of the school holidays. Uncle George got up extra early on Saturdays and was sat by the radio, soft black book of racing form on the table, drinking his third cup of tea when Jane sashayed into the kitchen.

Uncle George was all right. He thought of kind things to do and he found nice things to say. How he came to get humped up with a nasty, small-minded cat like Doreen Crick was enough to last the huge and very chatty Deeks family an entire wedding breakfast. She hadn't even been good-looking. Very much the ugly sister – like poor little June really.

'Don't you look smashing! Is it new? Turn round.'

Jane smiled and twirled.

'Nice fit. But then you've got a nice figure.'

He was the only person on earth who could say something like that without meaning something else. June might say such a thing but would really be saying 'a nicer figure than mine'. One of the senior salesladies might say something like it but only in a 'much good may it do you' sort of way. And Alan and Bill and Keith (was it Keith or Kevin?) and Tony wouldn't say anything about her figure without rolling their eyes over it. Compliments were like coupons that they saved up and stuck down until they'd got enough for what they really wanted.

The only person apart from Uncle George who could make a compliment a statement of fact had been the woman at the Trudi Morton modelling academy. Yes, Jane did have a perfect figure. Possibly a shade too short for photographic work but just right otherwise. But it would take work. The walk. The make-up. The wigs – models used a lot of wigs apparently. And that meant money. Twenty-five guineas for a two-week course and diploma. No point asking George and Doreen.

The Trudi Morton woman seemed really, really nice at first. Jane had gone to the academy in her lunch hour just after she'd started working in the arcade. The reception area had been quite crowded with two completely different sorts: girls who were models and girls who wanted to be models. The most obvious difference was that the models all had a dirty great canvas suitcase which Jane knew to be full of stockings, shoes, wigs, petticoats, scarves, gloves – all sorts of stuff you might need on a job. It seemed that the people you worked for only supplied whatever it was you were modelling: frocks, Hoovers, cat food and whatnot and anything else was supposed to be in your bag. Must weigh a ton.

The other big difference was that the girls who wanted to be models looked like they'd done each other's hair and make-up in the dark for a bet. Jane had her hair in its usual slide (she'd come straight from a morning's work) and wore no make-up at all. She hadn't time and besides she'd actually talked to Vanda about this. Vanda was no fool and Vanda reckoned that it was all about Potential and that they'd get a better idea from a bare face. Funnily enough, she was absolutely right. The Trudi Morton woman had said how refreshing it was to see a girl with her own natural complexion and was her bra padded? That was when she spent five minutes carefully taking Jane's measurements and that was when Jane went off the whole thing.

Jane had a cup of tea and an apple for her breakfast. It was all she usually had but at least on Saturdays there was no fat Doreen sat there telling her she ought to eat more. *Today's smart girl cannot possibly be too thin. Pay no heed to anyone who pretends otherwise. A slim figure is your most priceless asset.* She ran her cup under the tap, kissed Uncle George goodbye and put on her coat and gloves. She'd have to get a new coat from somewhere. She still had £15 in the Post Office. All that was left of her Vanda Modes money.

The walk to the bus stop was good practice with the high heels. They made her two inches taller and made the model walk much easier. She'd only worn them once before, to go dancing at the Locarno with a bunch of girls she'd been at school with. She wore them with a floral stripe California cotton frock: big blue poppies with sooty black centres. She had two net petticoats under it – one black, one white – and her black twinset cardigan over it.

She'd got the dress for half price in a funny little shop halfway in to Croydon. She'd only gone in there for dress shields. Vanda didn't sell these. Dress shields weren't Lingerie, they were Haberdashery, and Haberdashery was where Vanda drew the line. The shop's window had been full of creepy little woollen vests, tenderly laid out on brass T-shapes and draped with yellow cellophane to keep the sun off – as if it mattered what bloody colour the things were – but once inside, she was surprised to see a rail of gaudy fat sun dresses. The woman who ran the shop looked quite surprised herself. A salesman had been round and she couldn't resist the lovely flowers – like seed packets – but when she'd tried putting one in the window it looked all wrong somehow so they were left on the rail inside. Her regular customers just tutted at them or said they'd make nice loose covers.

Jane told her she worked at Vanda Modes and offered to re-do the window for her. Only took ten minutes. She put all the vests and elastic stockings in the side window and left just two frocks in the main one, one on each side, with a hand-written ticket: 'Perfect for dancing. Only sizes eight and ten remaining.' They were actually the only sizes the woman had got.

'He had bigger,' she confessed, giggling, 'but I can't see big girls wearing all those flowers, can you?'

She could if she went to the Locarno. The dance floor last summer had been heaving with size fourteens in yards and yards of waxed cotton begonias and peonies and sunflowers. Like a great big, sweaty municipal flowerbed.

Jane had taken the bus into Streatham and met her old schoolfriends outside as arranged. Two of them were engaged already – tiny little diamonds to prove it. The other two were working on it, slyly eyeing up the Brylcreem boys and spotty Herberts who stood round the edges of the room ready to make a move when the music slowed down. Couples were showing off their practised steps, plain girls were dancing with each other. It was yet another filthy hot night and the room stank of body odour and Evening in Paris.

Jane had pushed her way to the bar for an orange squash, and a man – quite old, thirty at least – had started chatting her up. He used the usual rubbish lines but differently somehow. As if he were taking the mick out of the whole thing.

'Now what, to coin a phrase, is a nice' – he put a lot of work into the 'nice' – 'a *very* nice girl like you doing in a place like this?'

He had a nice deep voice. Not Streatham at all. More Rex Harrison.

Jane selected one of her own smarter voices.

'I'm here with some old schoolfriends.'

'To dance? Or are you just on a man hunt?'

He had spotted the four of them, giggling and stealing glances at Jane's new friend in the blue suit. Hand-stitched lapels. Four proper working cuff buttons.

Jane crossed her legs – high on the thigh to keep the calves parallel – and his eyes slid politely down them to her black suede toes. *Nothing grabs the average male's attention faster than a pair of pretty legs.*

'Smart little shoes. But can you dance in them?'

Norma and the other three seemed about to muscle in for introductions.

'You bet.'

The band were playing 'C'mon Everybody' and the room had decided to jive to it. He looked a bit old for all that. A bit big, too, but he turned out to be a lovely mover. Twirling her and her blue poppies round him with just a flick of his strong wrists. People made room. They even had the spotlight on them for a bit. He watched her the whole time. She had twirled in the wardrobe mirror enough times to know how she looked: the smiling face; the flash of stocking tops under the lace and the tidy little black suede feet.

When it was over he led her back to the bar and bought her another orange squash (no funny business, just plain squash). Norma was hovering again. He spotted her approaching and everything happened very fast after that. He leaned down, placed a hand behind Jane's back and kissed her right on the lips. Not sloppy, but not a peck either.

'That was very, very nice indeed.' That word again. She could practically feel his voice between her legs. 'But, sadly ...' he looked at his watch (nice watch) and took his car keys from his pocket (nice car) '... I have to see a man' – he had timed it brilliantly – 'about a dog.'

He left just as Norma arrived, leaving this vague insult hanging in the air. Doreen always said that Norma must take Ugly Pills. She looked extra terrible that evening. She had looked better in her old school gymslip, quite honestly. Her mother helped her with her beehives, big yellow busbies of lacquer and backcombing with a bow on the back to match whatever outfit she had on.

Norma never went to the West End. If she wanted something really special she went to Croydon. *The plainest woman alive can find a man somewhere who will marry her and happily have intercourse with her.* Not in Norma's experience.

Jane went to the Locarno the next week and the next but she never saw the handsome stranger in the blue suit. Why would she? What would a nice man like him be doing in a place like that? He hadn't exactly spoiled her for the local talent but she couldn't even be bothered to dance with them any more. Norma said she was stuck up. She didn't dare say this to Jane's face but Jane could imagine her saying it just the same.

Jane was in the West End six days a week so she didn't really have a lot of time for Norma and that lot. Norma and Joy had gone to secretarial college and had got jobs in the council typing pool. Carol and Eileen were just killing time working in Woolworths until the Big Days in May. They talked about their Big Days all the time. Carol's mum, who'd had to make do with a hideous old borrowed frock and a pitiful little wedding cake made with powdered egg, wanted Carol to have four tiers and eight bridesmaids – her dad could afford them – but Eileen cried so hard they'd agreed to both have three and six. Carol's wedding was still going to be the biggest. Reception for two hundred at the Nelson Hotel; honeymoon at the Palace in Torquay.

Turned out that Carol had managed to pick Princess Margaret's Big Day so they were going to have to rent a television for the reception so no one would miss it. The happy couple would then be living happily ever after in an ugly brick doll's house on a brand-new estate just outside Crawley. Joy had never been to Crawley – none of them had except Carol and she'd only been for twenty minutes to look at where the house was going to be (semi-detached, own garage, picture windows, separate toilet) – but Joy was very snide about it: 'Very suburban'. Joy reckoned you hadn't reached the suburbs as long as the buses still said London Transport on the side – which let South Norwood off the hook.

Kenneth had already started scribbling down bus numbers when Jane got to the stop. A couple of his buddies were there with him and they were all laughing at some joke Kenneth had just told them. She didn't know he knew any jokes. He looked different suddenly: smiling, relaxed, almost handsome – apart from the spots. Like a younger, skinnier version of Uncle George. He seemed to shrink when he saw Jane, when he saw his mates looking at her legs in their Bear Brand 15-denier. He didn't say hello and nor did any of the long line of familiar faces in the tidy little queue. She tried it once but they all looked at you like you were trying to sell them something. The buses weren't too full at that time on a Saturday and she managed to get a seat downstairs. She decided she'd better change into her old black pumps on the bus. You weren't allowed to wear stilettos in the shop anyway – it knackered the parquet. Customers did enough damage. The whole floor was pockmarked with the traces of their spiky heels. 'A woman in stiletto heels,' as Mr Philip kept on saying, 'exerts the same pressure as an elephant standing on one leg.' He'd read it in the *Daily Express*.

It was a bit tricky getting the shoes on and off but the man next to her was very nice about it. Skinny dark-haired bloke. She'd seen him somewhere before. He worked in a shoe shop in Bond Street. Jane had a funny feeling he was a poof but she didn't mind that particularly as long as they kept themselves to themselves. Doreen minded very much although Norbury didn't give her much chance to show it except on Sundays when the *News of the World* sometimes served up a nice scoutmaster.

The shoe-shop man was speaking.

'Lovely courts. Nice low vamp.' Definitely queer.

'Aren't they? They're yours, aren't they? I didn't buy them myself, to be honest. A customer left them in the shop and never came back for them. I was the only one with feet small enough: three and a half double A.'

'Sample size. Tell you what, we're having a sample sale next Monday after the shop shuts. You're welcome to come if you like. Only ten bob a pair. There won't be many of you. A few really, really special customers and friends with small feet.'

'Ooh. Yes please. That would be super.' *Super*. Doreen should hear her.

New shoes. And no annoying little thank-you drinks to pay him back.

'My name's Jane, by the way. I work at Drayke's. Jane James.' She had been Jane Deeks at school to make life easier for everybody but Uncle George had never got round to adopting her so it still said Jane James on her cards. It sounded better anyway.

Chapter 5

> *Don't, whatever you do, forget that the girl behind the counter is a human being too. She has feelings just as you have.*

The Arcade still had the gates up but they were pulled open a foot or so at the Bond Street end to let the sales staff sidle in. Jane had hoped to be first into the shop so that she could sneak out of her coat and jacket without anyone noticing but Bennett was in early. Bennett's real name was Brenda but she'd been ten years in Young Separates at Derry and Toms where the manageress had been a Brenda. Something had to give and it was Bennett.

Bennett had a choice of two trains from Catford and she liked to play safe with the early one and then do her face in the mirror of the basement showroom in the belief that the unflattering light was helpful. *Have a powerful, shadeless light over your glass. Fool your audience, but never fool yourself.* In fact, it just meant that she put on far too much make-up and the distorting colours of the fluorescent striplight meant that she never noticed the tide mark where the Honey Velvet of the foundation met the Dove Grey of her neck.

'Let's have a look. You're a bit done up, aren't you, for a Saturday morning? You after that job at Hillson's?'

There was an 'Experienced Saleslady Required' notice in the window of a rival knitwear shop in Bond Street. Not such a bad idea, actually.

'I'm going out for lunch.'

'Ooh! Get her! Out for lunch in her –' she peered at the jacket's label on the hanger. 'What make is it? I can't see without my glasses.'

Bennett was always saying this but the plain truth was that she couldn't read at all. No one else seemed to have tumbled but Jane was wise to all her tricks because she had an aunt – George's sister – who was the same: always forgetting her glasses or complaining that the print was too small.

'It's a Hardy Amies.'

'Hardy Amies? Where did you get that kind of money? Hardy Amies! You can't be on more than a fiver a week – if that.'

'Sample sale.'

'All right for some.' Bennett was a size eighteen. She had eaten a cheese roll and a doughnut for elevenses every day for twenty years and the evidence was all held in place under a huge whalebone and 'power elastic' foundation garment that was supposed to take five years off you in five seconds flat. Twenty-three separate measurements tailored to fit every inch of her lumpy, fat torso. You didn't catch Bennett bending. If something got dropped on the floor it was gone for ever as far as she was concerned.

'Let me see the skirt. Mmm. It fits you all right but then they're always a very funny shape, those Hardy Amies showroom numbers. The house model – Yvonne? Yvette? Eva? Evadne? Sonia? – name like that. Lovely girl but she's got a very peculiar figure: hollow back. What is it? Cashmere and wool? The seat will bag out if you're not careful. You ought to have a higher heel than that. It just looks frumpy with those.'

Jane left her to it. No sense giving her the satisfaction. Poisonous old crab.

Once Jane had escaped from Bennett's clutches she began straightening the fixtures. She was supposed to replace any colours that had been sold with new garments from the stockroom. This took all of ten minutes. The last week in January was completely dead. The sales were over (not that the Arcade's shops ever had anything as common as a sale), there were no tourists and the rush of post-Christmas exchanges had dried up ('So *sweet* of him but it just isn't my colour'). Saturdays were even quieter if anything, because any English people with money would be in the country for the weekend. What you did get were time-wasters. Overdressed ladies from places like Stanmore and Rickmansworth who liked to spend the morning swanning in and out of smart shops before they had to decide whether to go for the set lunch at Debenham and Freebody or blow six bob on an 'Elegant Rarebit' in Fortnum's – twice the price of the inelegant kind. The Welsh weren't elegant enough for Fortnum's apparently.

The proper salesladies took it in turns to patrol the ground floor. You weren't allowed to read or smoke or look as if you were deep in conversation. No. You must either be folding or generally fiddling with the stock or just mooch about ornamentally, waiting for a customer to come in and give your life a meaning.

There were days in January when the door didn't open at all and, rather than stand about sniping at each other, the senior sales used to take it in turns to man the shop while the others retreated downstairs to read magazines or play gin rummy. This didn't affect the all-important pecking order. If a customer should cross the threshold, Bennett might do the 'Good morning, Madam, can I help you' lark but she would then hand over to Brigitta straight away. Bennett had the knack of sounding like a snotty manageress as she explained that Madam would like to see something in lovat blue with a short sleeve but it was still Brigitta who got the commission. By rights, Jane was Fourth Sales which meant that she seldom saw a single customer at this time of the year. If ever. Brigitta had been known to serve as many as three customers at once. Made a party of it, as if they were all out shopping together.

Jane had taken all the cashmere shirts out and arranged their polythene bags into tidy rainbows with each shade blending into the next like the colours on a cinema organ: primrose, moss green, lovat green, bottle green, brown, camel, natural, white, pink, camellia, tartan red, claret, black, navy, Dior blue, Sandringham blue, lovat blue, powder blue. She then somehow shoehorned the slithering pile back into its fixture. She'd polished all the mirrors – why did people touch mirrors? – and stood with her back to the stock gazing out at the arcade through the window display where the coloured cashmeres were suspended on their glass shelves like fully fashioned tropical fish.

Bennett kept up a merciless running commentary on the passers-by as they bustled along.

'Have you seen these two?'

A pair of identically dressed girls dashed by: very 'with-it', very Chelsea, with red woolly tights and matching red berets on top of their shiny bobbed hair which was cut in hard lines round their faces like the hair on a cartoon character. They wore A-line flannel coats well above their knees with big shiny red buttons – like a really, really embarrassing school uniform.

Brigitta looked out of the window as she tripped past on her way back down to the basement after her tea break. She was Dutch but she could bore you to death in six languages. Her saving grace was that she swore all the time. She would never have sworn in Dutch, but she picked up dirty little scraps of English like a tramp rooting through a dustbin. It was a miracle she didn't swear at the customers really.

'Whoever cut those fucking jackets should cut another jacket and then be shot.'

She'd got that one from a little Jewish alterations tailor and she used it a lot.

You didn't call her Brigitta to her face. You called her Mrs Taylor. Brigitta had been married very, very briefly to an Englishman she met nearly ten years ago while they were both working in the same department store. Bennett always reckoned it was just one of those friendly arrangements to get a work permit and that the split was all very amicable but Jane knew what really happened. Brigitta had had three Dubonnets and four glasses of punch at the Christmas party (table for twenty at the Cumberland Hotel) and had cornered Jane and explained that Mr Taylor had expected to be able to put his dirty great thing into Mrs Taylor whenever he felt like it.

'I told him to stick it up his arse,' said Brigitta and Jane said that would be a good trick if he could do it and Brigitta shot Dubonnet straight out of her nose.

Brigitta was, technically, still married to Mr Taylor but a week after the honeymoon she'd moved back into the salesladies' hostel behind Marshall and Snelgrove, a miserable great barracks of a place where a girl could find refuge. Anyone with a gentleman caller had to wheel her bed out into the corridor. No gentlemen ever called. Mr Taylor was now living with his common-law wife in Carshalton Beeches and Brigitta eventually got herself a two-room flat near Clapham Common.

A very large woman in a mink coat had parked in front of the window.

Bennett pulled a face.

'Oh no, Madam. Not in that size, Madam. Please!'

But Madam came in anyway. Very, very loud voice. Pointed to a baby-pink batwing-sleeved number in the window.

'I'd like to see that in nigger brown in a size 48.' No 'good morning'.

'I'm not sure if we still have that shade, Madam. It's been a very popular line. But if you'd like to step downstairs one of our ladies can show you what we have. Mrs Taylor? Perhaps you could show Madam something attractive in nigger brown?'

Jane could hear the suppressed giggles and the whispered 'Sidney Poitier' but fortunately the customer didn't. Brigitta hadn't much to go on but she soon set to work persuading

Madam that what she wanted was not a nigger brown, batwing-sleeved boat neck but a duck-egg blue, edge-to-edge cardigan. Unfortunately even the largest size didn't allow edge to meet edge over Madam's enormous tits. *The most 'generous proportions' can be made to appear attractive when allied with perfect posture – look at the Queen Mother.*

'This style does run very small, Madam,' said Mrs Taylor's voice, apologetically. 'I'll just run upstairs to the stockroom and get you the next size.'

Brigitta stopped when she got to Jane and Bennett and immediately snipped the size labels off the 48 in her hand before pulling the cardigan as wide as it could possibly go. Cashmere can be any size you want. After the cardigan had had its nice little 'schlap', she folded it, put it in a bag and slipped back downstairs.

'Oh yes, that's better. Mind you the sleeve seems a bit short.'

You could hear the faintest sneer in Brigitta's voice. 'Short? Oh NO, Madam. *Bracelet* length.'

Whether or not they made bracelets big enough for those dimpled pink wrists Madam didn't say, but she looked nice enough in her new cardigan and she knew when she was beaten. She even allowed Brigitta to sell her a bottle of Woolite and a D-Fuzz-It. After that, the shop went quiet for nearly an hour. Jane flicked furtively through a copy of *Vogue* on the counter. *Why go to Yucatan?*

There were no prices in the window. Prices were vulgar and, besides, once they'd plucked up the courage to come in and ask, there was always the chance the customer would be too embarrassed to scuttle straight back out again and admit that a twenty-guinea three-piece was more than their husband earned in a week and you could just shame them into buying something.

The door pinged open. Mousey woman in windowpane checks.

'How much is that cardie in the window?'

Bennett had started humming a tune. Jane raised her voice slightly.

'The anthracite bolero, Madam? That model is six guineas, Madam. It's pure cashmere.'

'Oh.' Her little fat face fell. 'Do you have the same thing in Orlon?'

Uh-oh. Bad sign. Mr Philip couldn't abide man-made fibres. Cheap and machine-washable, they were a threat to his whole way of life. His contempt was infectious. Did they have the same thing in fucking Orlon? No, Madam. Or Ban-Lon. Or Acrilon. Or Courtilon. Or Nylon. Or Brilon. Or Draylon. Or Vilene. Or Terylene. Or bloody polythene. Orlon *cardies*. Peasants.

'Or what, madam?'

As she scuttled out by the far door the other one dinged open and suddenly there were two men in the shop. They didn't seem to know it but they looked nothing like customers. One wore a leather car coat, the other had a big sheepskin draped over his shoulders. Both were wearing silk socks – wide boys always did. The beadles had already spotted them and were now stationed at either end of the arcade, on the lookout for a passing copper.

Bennett was on the attack at once.

'Good morning, *gentlemen*. Can I help you?' She turned to Jane. 'I shall be busy looking after these *gentlemen*, Miss James. Perhaps you could tell Mrs Taylor and Miss Williams and Miss Stent and Mr Keating they're wanted in the showroom?' She made the last two up.

Jane kept her eyes on the two men and felt for the electric bell on the side of the stairs and pressed it three times. The card-players nipped swiftly up the stairs and took up their positions near the other two doors.

'You got any intarsias, love?' They didn't bother with 'good mornings' either.

'Yes, sir. We have some beautiful designs at the moment. What size was sir looking for?'

He looked nonplussed and opened his jacket. Bennett kept a completely straight face.

'About a forty I should say, sir.' She slid back the glass, pulled a single pullover from the top fixture and spread it on the counter further down while Jane smoothly came in behind her and slid the glass door back in place. Bennett shook the sweater from its folds. It was gorgeous: sooty black cashmere with exotic sprays of fuchsia, camellia and violet flowers scattered across it.

'Would Sir like to try it on? We have a nice private fitting room downstairs, very discreet,' said Bennett in a horribly understanding way. The man was a nice shade of camellia himself. His friend was trying not to laugh but keeping an eye on the door.

'No. I meant that diamond pattern. You know.'

'Ah! Sir means Argyll, I think. Not this one then?'

She and Jane went into their little dance, Bennett folding and bagging the garments while Jane worked the glass doors. Bennett moved down to the Argylls and her fingers hesitated a moment in front of the pigeonhole.

'Same sort of colours?'

There wasn't much left in that range. Jane had had to fill up the whole fixture with the brown and camel colourway.

'Er. Brown?'

Bennett peered at the toffee-coloured pile in the fixture.

'Oh dear. That's the one colour we're out of, sir. But we are expecting a delivery much later this year. Or early next.'

Jane opened the door and joined Bennett in a sort of pincer movement as they ushed the pair of them out of the shop under the watchful eye of the beadle.

A saleslady's radar could recognise shoplifters immediately. She also had a sixth sense about messers. You got the same ones coming in again and again. Something about their clothes, about the angle of their feet (were they heading for the door?) told you that it wouldn't be worth your while getting half the stock out.

Jane had spotted one of them outside looking at the window display. A painfully thin, miserable-looking woman with dyed black hair and a slightly sticky-looking beaver coat. A regular. She spent time but never money and nobody wanted to be prevented from serving a proper customer by getting bogged down with a time-waster. Jane tried to take evasive action but she was too slow off the mark. The other salesladies had begun tidying fixtures the moment she stepped through the door, leaving her to Jane. She always asked if she could take things home 'on appro' and always tutted when she couldn't. She would then disappear into the fitting room and start amusing herself, putting together rather clever ensembles and walking up and down. She probably looked OK in certain lights but the crude strips and spots in the basement took no prisoners. She was even thinner than she looked – *Over-zealous slimming leads to scrawniness, salt cellars, flat chests, bad temper and even (if you read your daily newspaper) suicide.* Also, Jane soon realised that her trim figure was all spare parts: shoulders, bosom, even hips, were all little bits of wadding attached to her bra and corset. Tailored clothes hid all these bits and pieces but she looked very lumpy in knitwear.

Today Madam wanted to see something in vicuna, an animal so soft and fluffy and delicate that you practically had to kill it to get the silky brown wool off its back. They were running quite low on vicuna. So was Peru. Madam quite liked it but wasn't sure about the brown. Did they have the same in a Saxe blue? Or a turquoise? Jane imagined Saxe blue and turquoise vicunas scampering across the Andes. No, Madam. Not in that style. Ignorant old bitch.

The only other customers that morning were a matching pair of Americans in his-and-hers camel overcoats, tartan trousers and cashmere scarves. Mrs Taylor, who had no conversation in real life, oozed professional charm. Not a very nice time of year for their trip, was it? London not at its best. Were they here on business? etc. All the while laying plans to sell them the entire shop, fixtures included. It was warm and slightly airless in the basement showroom and the cashmeres were cosy and soft and the pair could suddenly think of nothing nicer than a whole new wardrobe of knitwear plus the mix and match tweeds to go with them. They had already picked out over £200 worth of things when there was dangerous talk of lunch and coming back on Monday. Brigitta wasn't going to let her commission get away that easily.

'Miss James here can pop out and get you a nice smoked-salmon sandwich if you're peckish. You still need to decide on a skirt length.'

'Sure, honey. Let's get it done today,' said the husband, good-temperedly. 'Just one skinny old English sandwich and then we can have a good lunch at that roast-beef place.'

Jane hurried into the coat room to put on her jacket and gloves and slip into her smart shoes. She walked the length of the arcade freezing to death but warm with pride at her reflection in the shop windows. She could sense the loafing shirt salesmen moving nearer the doors to watch her pass.

One of the regular buskers had taken the pitch at the end of the arcade. He was an old man with a tiny mandolin. He couldn't play it but would stand there plink, plink-a-plinking away until one of the shopkeepers gave him half a crown to clear off. Jane preferred the old tapdancer with the wind-up gramophone and the suit made of Union Jacks. She'd once tried dropping a penny into the mandolin man's case and he'd thrown it right back at her, calling her all the names. He wouldn't take coppers: it was sixpence or nothing.

It was warm and spicy in the grocer's. A few fussy old ladies were being served one at a time by young men in starched Holland overalls, scaling the high walls of shelves for tiny jars of orange blossom honey and stem ginger. The sandwich counter was right at the back under the skylight. A funny misshapen little man was making a right meal of a ham salad on white, tenderly buttering every slice from scratch as if the order for each sandwich came as a terrible surprise. He would then layer on the sugar-baked ham – 'muthtard?' – and tuck in the hospital corners of lettuce with the flat of his knife once the top slice had gone on. All the time in the world. Jane raised her head and looked about her a trifle impatiently – the way customers did – and a wide-awake young man in a morning coat and striped trousers magically materialised.

'I'm sorry to keep you waiting, Madam.' Madam. Not Dear. Not Miss, Madam. 'Can I help you at all?'

She smiled. *Charm every single person you meet. It's more than a skill: it's a fine art.*

'Yes you can, actually.' *Actually.* 'I'd like a smoked-salmon sandwich please.'

'Certainly, Madam. Brown or white?'

She raised her eyebrows in slightly pained surprise. He very nearly apologised.

'Brown?'

'Brown.'

He may have graduated to spongebag trousers but he must have served time in overalls because he definitely knew his way round a smoked-salmon sandwich and had knocked one together – lemon and pepper included – before the old bloke next to him had finished mummifying his in greaseproof paper. And then he was out from behind the counter, ushering her down to the cashier and holding the door open. He was rather good-looking. Bit like David Niven.

'Goodbye, Madam. See you again, I hope.' Nice posh voice, too.

She rewarded him with another smile – *never underestimate the power of your smile* – then swung her brown paper carrier bag all the way back to the shop. Brigitta had moved seamlessly on to sportswear by this time. The Americans put out their cigarettes and nibbled gratefully on their sandwich.

'What a neat suit! Isn't that neat, honey?' They really did say 'honey', both of them. The wife turned to Brigitta for guidance. 'Do you have those here?'

Jane felt herself shrivelling with awkwardness. That, as Mr Philip would say, was why it was so important for the staff to wear their uniforms. The salesladies got four different outfits a year (although Junior Jane only got two) to be worn to work whenever humanly possible: 'You girls must be my Living Advertisements.'

'Might I have a word, Miss James?'

It was Mr Philip himself.

'Uh-oh. He's seen the suit,' hissed Brigitta, happily. 'He'll have your guts for garters.'

Mr Philip was the younger son of the man who founded the business in 1928. Mr Drayke senior now lived in the south of France on his share of the profits. Januaries might be dead but it was still a very good business, especially the mail-order department which was run by a terrifying old stick of a woman in butterfly glasses who used to tint the front of her blue-grey bouffant to tone with that day's ensemble. She never wore green, sadly.

Mr Philip spent most of his time up in the office, checking off the huge stock book and drinking Scotch which he kept in an old cough-mixture bottle in the safe along with the takings and the luncheon vouchers. He was a difficult person to talk to. Partly because you were trying not to react to the whisky breath and partly because, perched on the top of his head, like a friendly forest creature, was a glistening, nut-brown toupee. He'd obviously got a whiff of a Big Sale and had been lurking on the basement stairs proprietorially and overheard the unwelcome compliment.

'That is a nice suit, Miss James.' His clever, rag-trade fingers automatically reached out to price the tweed. 'Very nice. But it is not a Drayke's garment, Miss James. You girls are my Living Advertisements. You are not paid to advertise' – he ran an expert eye over the sculpted waist, the hand-covered buttons – 'Mr Hardy Amies. You've got your uniform, why don't you wear it?'

'I've not been here long, Mr Philip. I've only got two outfits and I can't wear the same thing every day. I washed my navy twinset last night but it's still drying. It did say "dry away from direct heat" on the swing ticket.' *Sweaters are called sweaters for a reason. Stay fresh and never fall victim to underarm fustiness.*

'Well, well, we'll see if we can't find you something upstairs.' He had a whole cupboard full of samples and oddments most of which supplied his family's Christmas presents. 'Come and see me on Monday and we'll dig something out.'

'It's my Long Weekend.'

'Tuesday then. I don't ever want to hear a customer say that to you again. Nice-looking girl like you. You should be a real asset to the firm.' He looked at her again. 'I hope you aren't thinking of leaving us?'

Guess who else had seen the sign in Hillson's window?

'I'm very happy here, Mr Philip.'

Which was no answer and he knew it.

Brigitta was now at the till with a vast pile of sweaters, swatches and order books. Jane and her suit disappeared downstairs to tidy away the stock. She didn't mind. The basement was warm and nicely smelly with traffic wax and the faint scent of burning fluff from inside the Bakelite wall heaters. Mirrors covered every inch of wall space that wasn't taken up by shelving. The counters were elbow-deep in cashmere. It was Brigitta's style to pull out all the different shades; that way the voice in the customer's ear saying 'Why not have both?' seemed almost reasonable when they looked at all the colours they could have had. Jane folded and bagged, folded and bagged until she had finally dug back down to naked rosewood. Ten minutes to one. Please don't let there be a late customer.

Jane finally looked up from her last bit of folding and saw her reflection, flushed from the basement heat. She did her best to smile a warm, winning, crocodile-handbag smile.

'The wind'll change and you'll stay like that.'

Bennett was like a portable Doreen, a whining voice in her ear to drag her back down to earth.

'A young man called for you with a delivery while you were out getting that sandwich.' She produced a large Hardy Amies bag from the stock room. 'He said the fitter thought you might like it. No one bought it in the end. Can't say I'm surprised. It's a horrible colour and the zip's broken. I had a quick look. I knew you wouldn't mind.'

It was the violet dress and coatee.

'He seemed very disappointed to miss you, your young man. Rotten suit he was wearing.'

The bell was being rung by the beadle and she could hear the happy sound of the doors being locked and blinds being pulled down. Jane stuffed the last pile of three-button cashmere shirts into their cubby-hole. They fitted easily now – the American couple played a lot of golf.

'How much did they spend in the end?'

'Two hundred and sixty quid,' said Bennett glumly.

They both silently calculated Brigitta's two per cent. More than a week's wages for Jane.

Chapter 6

> *Just follow this simple, practical advice*
> *and you, too, can evolve into a charming*
> *and attractive woman. A magnet to*
> *any single man and the natural focus*
> *of attention at any social gathering.*

It was only when she was actually walking out of the shop that it dawned on Jane that finding Miss Crocodile might not be as easy as all that. Why hadn't she just taken the bag round to the police at Vine Street? It was too late to take it in now and, anyway, the more she thought about it, the more she worried about the price tag and that envelope full of tenners – she hadn't dared to count it.

She walked along Piccadilly but carried on right past the side street where the oyster bar was. Instead she headed for the department store on the corner. She slipped off her coat as soon as she got inside, folding it round to the plain black silk lining: that was better. She swanned over to the perfume counter, swinging the Hardy Amies carrier with the violet dress and crocodile bag inside it. The salesgirl sprang to attention. She was thinking of changing her scent. Did Madam have anything in mind? Madam sniffed pickily at several before putting a big cold squirt of Joy on her wrist. *The costliest perfume in the world*. That was probably the only reason people bought it. It was a bit sickly, tell the truth.

'I won't buy it today, if you don't mind. I need to get someone else's opinion first.' The saleslady smirked understandingly. They were used to people killing time. They got through six bottles of Joy a month: five for the browsers; one for the saleslady.

Jane faffed around playing shops and being madamed a bit more before finally putting her coat back on and heading off for Carpenter's.

You could see into the restaurant from the street. It was nearly half past one but the place looked pretty dead with only a handful of old bachelors slurping down a few dozen oysters at the brass and mahogany counter. There was a rather lively little crowd in the bar next door but they could hardly be waiting for tables.

Jane stood by the door pretending to study the menu but looking in through the lumpy yellow glass panes. Bingo. There in the middle of that laughing group, lit by the lamps that dangled above the bar, was the girl in the photograph.

She was sitting on a high stool apparently in the middle of telling a funny story. She was wearing a shortish, short-sleeved dress in peacock-blue ribbed silk with a bubbling bib of black and blue beads. Her legs were crossed (high on the thigh, natch) and they dangled temptingly over the edge of the stool.

Jane opened the door and slipped inside. The funny story was in full swing and the girl was telling it brilliantly. She had a delicious voice – like an actress but more natural. The accent had golden touches of Army and In-ja all gingered up by a spicy vocabulary that she used almost innocently, like Brigitta swearing in a foreign language.

'So. The chap says, "Fifty quid! That's a hell of a lot of money. What's it made of?"' She giggled a little. 'Now you mustn't blame me for this. It was Dickie's story so any complaints and you know where to go.'

She took a tiny sip of her gin and tonic, looking at them saucily over the rim of her glass, making them wait.

'Anyway. The man trying to sell him the wallet says, "It's made from elephant's *foreskin*."'

She said it in a shocked stage whisper and the bar was already yelping with laughter. There were four men and two other women, older. The men wore tweed jackets or blazers, the women smart weekend clothes and just-set hair.

' "Well, I'm sorry," says the chap, "but fifty quid's still a lot of money just for a wallet." "Ah, yes," says the other man, "but if you rub it, it turns into a suitcase." '

Mayhem. One of the women – black and white striped suit and hair the colour of bottled orange juice – had a laugh like an air-raid warning.

'Trust Dickie to teach a girl a story like that.'

The girl seemed very pleased with the success of her joke and had another taste of her gin. One of the men – handsome, curly dark hair, mid thirties – moved in to offer her a cigarette from a smart silver case. She took it and leaned forward to find the flame. It was beautiful to watch her raising her eyes to his as she sucked the cigarette alight. Jane knew how to do this (she'd practised in the bedroom mirror when everyone was out) but she'd never actually dared put it to use. The girl looked so sexy doing it. It wasn't a trick to waste on any old Tony.

Jane edged closer to the laughing group. The girl saw her first and smiled expectantly at the mousey little person in the funny grey coat but it was the dark man who spoke.

'Hello, young lady. You looking for someone?'

It was like being on stage. They had all turned to look at her. She stammered over her lines: 'I think, I think one of you might have lost a handbag.' She pulled it free of the carrier. 'I found it yesterday.'

The girl's eyes lit up. They were bright blue. Lobelia blue.

'You absolute *darling*!' She could say something like that and not sound stupid. 'I didn't think I'd ever see it again. At last I can powder my nose.'

She was wearing quite a bit of make-up, Jane reckoned – powder; rouge; eye pencil; mascara; lipstick – but it didn't look tarty, just brighter somehow. Her nose didn't seem to want powdering but she slipped down off the stool and put her arm through Jane's and whisked her up the wide staircase to the Ladies'. It didn't have a sign saying Ladies or WC or anything, just a silhouette of Alice in Wonderland on the door. There was a knave of hearts on the Gents'.

It was lovely inside. All mirrors and armchairs and big boxes of tissues and cotton wool and hairspray and tidy piles of hand towels embroidered with pale-blue oyster shells and a wonderful slot machine that gave squirts of different scent for a shilling.

'It was really super of you to bring it back. Luckily I had a spare set of keys but it was still a huge pain. However did you track me down?'

She sank down on to one of the little chairs and reached into the bag for her compact. She didn't even look to see if the money was there. Jane sat down beside her and peeped at herself in the mirror.

'Just lucky really. There was your photograph and some Carpenter's matches inside. I thought I'd come here first. I only work round the corner and I didn't fancy going back to that pub.'

The girl pulled a face – a pretty face, but a face.

'Not your local then? Don't blame you. Anyway I can't thank you enough. You're an absolute darling. Take your coat off now you're here. You must stay and have a drink. What a divine coat and skirt!' Oh my dear, 'coat-and-skirt'. Get her. Lady Muck.

She examined Jane with her head on one side as if sizing up the mismatch between head and body.

'You really ought to wear your hair up.'

'It only falls down.'

'Not if you backcomb a bit underneath and then pin it right. Come here.'

She took the pack of hairpins out of the crocodile bag and, without even asking, began to twist and spray Jane's hair into a neat chignon.

'French pleats are nicer,' she said, checking her own smooth profile in the mirror, 'but your hair's a bit long. Want to borrow a lipstick?'

It was wonderful. More wonderful than the suit really. Jane could have sat there all afternoon just looking at herself. The girl stood next to her, smiling, obviously waiting for Jane to smile back so Jane pulled her lips into a grateful shape.

'That's better. Do you not have a bag?'

'I can't afford a really nice one so I just keep my purse in my coat pocket.'

'Tell you what. You borrow this one. I'd look bonkers carrying two.'

She handed Jane a black suede pochette she'd been carrying. Just right with the shoes.

'You can give it back to me later.'

She finally took a proper look at the inside of the crocodile bag and took out the envelope. She still didn't actually count it.

'This'll come in handy. I think this calls for a little celebration.'

Jane left her coat and carrier bag hanging on a hook and she followed the girl downstairs.

'We haven't introduced ourselves. I'm Suzy. Suzy St John.'

'Jane. Jane James.'

'Good name. Your own? Mine isn't.'

They reached the bar where some of the life seemed to have leaked out of the little group.

'Everybody, this is Janey James who has brought back my lovely crocodile bag and all my lovely winnings. Janey darling, this is Madge and Sylvia,' Madge was the one with the laugh, 'and this is Derek, Reggie and Bob and this disreputable-looking creature is Alpaca Pete.'

Pete took Jane's hand and sized her up with his dirty brown eyes.

'Peter Benson. How do you do?'

It was a posh voice but probably dyed rather than natural (Jane should know). He wore cavalry twill trousers, a lemon-yellow alpaca cardigan and a paisley silk cravat. Doreen would have had him down as a poof but he was just a man in a yellow cardigan.

They hadn't looked at Jane when she came in but she wasn't invisible now. They made room at the table while Suzy organised her little celebration.

'I think we'd better make it a magnum, don't you, Ted my darling?' She crackled two of the crisp blue fivers and waved away the change. 'Have a drink on me, Ted,' she whispered. Flash.

Ted swerved out from behind the bar in his dapper maroon mess jacket and little black bow tie. He had a huge ice bucket in one hand and a bouquet of champagne saucers in the other. Jane knew about these, mainly from her etiquette books but also from Doreen's sideboard which contained an odd pair – both pinched from the one and only wedding reception she'd agreed to go to. Jane used to drink cream soda out of them when Doreen was out. Cream soda was actually nicer, she thought, as she sipped the sour, icy bubbles.

There were lots of nice things to eat on the table. A mixed plate of smoked salmon and fresh crab sandwiches (on brown) and a huge glass dish divided into sections for Twiglets, Cheeselets, cheese straws, cheese footballs and green olives with red stuff inside. The glass ashtrays were printed with a picture of the Walrus and the Carpenter eating oysters. Similar prints covered the walls of the bar, as well as some grimy brown oil paintings showing silver trays heaped with lobsters and prawns and glassy-eyed fish. Jane sat there smiling over her champagne glass and nibbling shyly at a crab sandwich. She hadn't said much but that probably wouldn't matter. She looked nice, that was the important thing.

'So what do you do, Janey?' asked one of the men. Reg? Bob?

'At the moment I'm working in the Albemarle Arcade, at Drayke's.' People always said 'at the moment' as if they were about to switch to something much, much better.

'Ah, indeed,' said Pete, 'home of the alpaca cardigan.'

'Done any modelling?' wondered Reg. They were starting to sound like the awful man in the pub but Suzy joined in too, looking approvingly at Jane's carefully casual pose.

'You should, you know. Perfect for it.'

'Suzy does modelling, don't you, darling?' *The great advantage of this line of work is that you need only* be *a model. You don't ever actually have to* do *any modelling to qualify.*

'Bits and pieces. Ooh, did I show you my composite Dickie made for me?'

Suzy reached into the bag and dug out the card with her photos on it. 'He wants twenty guineas to make up three hundred but I'm not sure I really want photographic work. You have to get up too early. I'd much rather stagger around a showroom in a pretty frock for an hour or two. Money for old rope, darling,' she said this to Jane.

The restaurant had finally given up hope of any more customers and the champagne was disappearing fast. Pete leaned over and stroked Jane's best stockings appreciatively.

'So! Are we all heading over to Dougie's flat? You going to join us, Janey? Glass of Chablis. A few oysters? Spot of lobster?'

He nodded meaningfully at Ted the barman who disappeared through a side door, returning moments later with a huge parcel, beautifully wrapped in brown paper with drawings of oysters and carpenters printed all over it in navy-blue ink.

'Mr Carter has made up your order, sir.'

He didn't wink exactly but his voice seemed to be winking. No money changed hands.

'Do come. It'll be fun.'

Suzy was being helped into the blue sack jacket that matched her dress. Over that she wore a fingertip-length black Persian lamb coat: shawl collar; three-quarter-length sleeves (bracelet length) and long black leather gloves.

'You look like a million dollars, Suzy my darling,' purred Pete. 'Very smart for a Saturday morning.' Everyone thought this was very funny.

'Susan always dresses so well,' smarmed the woman called Sylvia.

'Yes,' muttered Pete, 'and so *quickly*.'

Jane got her bag and her rotten grey coat from upstairs but couldn't bear to put it on. Suzy seemed to sense the problem immediately.

'Tell you what, darling,' she whispered. 'I don't think that those buttons Do. You. Any. Favours. At. All. Do you?'

Quick as anything, she had pulled the nail scissors out of her bag and in the time it took the others to get their coats on she had snipped off all six of the big red plastic lumps and the stupid great half-belt thing at the back.

'That's *miles* better. You can hold it together edge-to-edge with the pockets.'

It did look better, a lot better. But she should have asked just the same.

Pete led the way to a big brown car parked outside.

'We'll all fit in the Rover, won't we? It's not far.'

Pete drove and the rest piled in after him, the girls perched on the men's laps. Jane got Derek who had one hand on her knee and the other round her waist the whole way. He had a friend who was a photographer – funny the way they all did.

Chapter 7

> *Most parties can be improved by*
> *having a few pretty girls around.*

'Dougie's place' turned out to be a big luxury flat up behind Selfridges somewhere.

'Mrs Simpson used to have the one on the first floor.' Suzy's voice was slightly distorted by the fact that her mouth was stretched wide as she reapplied her lipstick in the mirrored wall of the automatic lift. 'Dougie's old mum says there used to be Secret Service men all over the place whenever the Prince of Wales popped round. Never saw the same milkman two days in a row.'

Jane had read about 'luxury' flats in the *News of the World*. She'd never been quite sure exactly what they meant by 'luxury', but she now decided it must mean white wall-to-wall carpet, central heating, glass coffee tables, two bathrooms, a real bar with little stools and every drink you could possibly want. It also meant a great big painting of a girl with no clothes all done in blues and greens and purples as if she was covered in bruises. Jane had a good nose round when she went off to the toilet. Lavatory. *Lavatory*. She opened one door but it was a cupboard full of beer and wine and whisky and Dubonnet and boxes of chocolates and great big tins of Twiglets and cheese footballs. The bathroom was wonderful: thick, thick carpet; fat pink towels on a hot chromium-plated rail and matching pink toilet paper – *lavatory* paper – with a spare roll hidden under a great big dolly in a yellow lace crinoline.

There were already people at the flat when they arrived, all sat drinking in the vast, L-shaped sitting room. There were a couple of men (who brightened up no end when Jane and Suzy walked in) plus a fat platinum-blonde called Connie who was still wearing last night's cocktail frock. She said she was 'going on somewhere afterwards' but you could tell from the state of her hair – which looked like a lacquered bird's nest – that she'd never actually made it home. Next to her on the gold brocade settee was a very, very thin dark-haired woman in a turquoise suit. She looked like the Duchess of Argyll with a headache and her lipstick was all stuck to her capped front teeth. Her name was Iris and she was divorced. Her face sank like a failed sponge at the sight of Jane and Suzy.

'Iris, *darling*,' lied Suzy. 'Cheer up, sweetie. It may never happen.'

'Lovely woman, Iris,' she explained later in an undertone, 'give you anything: smallpox; syphilis . . .'

Iris liked to give as good as she got.

'And who's your little friend, Susan?'

Cheek. The volume in the room had dropped, ready for a bit of theatre. Iris could be very good value once she got warmed up. Jane picked out a nice ritzy voice.

'Jane James. And you are?'

'Iris Moore.'

'How do you do, Mrs Moore?'

It worked really well. The 'Mrs' definitely took the wind out of her sails. Aged her ten years for a start.

Dougie was an old army pal of Reggie's: a posh old lech with a handlebar moustache and wandering hands. He was wearing a Sexy Rexy double cashmere cardigan, a checked Viyella shirt and a cravat. What Doreen would call a right ponce. Dougie, who had begun life with a two-gin start on the rest of the world, had been drinking solidly since just after breakfast but, drunk or sober, he was a good host and stepped in at once with offers of drinks and more drinks. It wasn't really his flat; it belonged to his mother who was installed in the corner. Dougie managed to keep up appearances cravat-wise but he actually had his digs over a laundrette in Paddington.

Dougie had swelled with pride and happiness at the sight of Jane and Suzy. He had resigned himself to spending the afternoon with his 75-year-old mother and the dry, sour prospect of Connie or Iris for a bit of slap and tickle later (Reggie said they usually came across after a few stiff drinks and a bit of help with the gas bill) but this was much more like it. Or failing that there was always Good Old Madge.

'Hello. Ladies, ladies, ladies. Hello, Madge old girl. Just what the doctor ordered. Got to look after myself, you know. I said to Reggie just now, "If I'm not in bed by ten o'clock, I'm going home." ' Shrieks of polite laughter from the sofa. Dougie leered happily in Jane's direction. Nobody seemed to mind her gatecrashing.

'What's your poison, my love? We can cater for your every whim here, you know. Little drop of fizz?'

'Super.'

Jane had taken up a pose on the sofa, her crossed legs revealing a couple of inches of firm, young thigh. Alpaca Pete was out in the kitchen shelling lobsters and Madge and Sylvia – who always pulled their weight – cut up the flesh and arranged it on some toothpicks they found in a little novelty holder on the bar. Jane helped herself to a bit of the lobster. Very nice. Much nicer than crab. Or whelks. Not that they ever had whelks in Norbury. Doreen said they were common but they were actually just far too chewy for a woman with all her own teeth.

Dougie returned with a crystal saucer full of bubbles and perched his cavalry-twilled arse on the arm of Jane's sofa, the better to leer at her bust. He didn't actually twirl the ends of his moustache but he looked as if he might.

'Very, *very* glad you and your little friend could drop by and help us celebrate.'

Jane set her eyelashes to 'stun'.

'Oh Dougie!' *Dougie*, honestly, she'd only just met the man. 'Is it your birthday?'

'No. Good Lord no. Never have birthdays. No actually it's Mother's.' He had his arm along the back of the sofa and was telling Jane what a trim little figure she had and how she was like a French film star he'd once met.

'Really?' Whoops. It came out as 'reel-y'. She'd have to watch that. 'I must go and wish your mother many happy returns.' *Heppy* returns, that was better. 'Will you intra-juice me?'

He couldn't very well not.

'Mummy, this is Janey, er, Janey, friend of Reggie's. Janey, this is my mama, Frances Pillman.'

Jane shook hands firmly (but not too firmly). 'How do you do?' *NEVER 'Pleased to meet you'*.

Dougie's mama was sat in state in a Chanel suit on a little gold throne thingy. She was seventy-five going on thirty-six. She bestowed one of her brisk, downward-turning smiles on Jane. Her mother had taught her to smile that way to avoid crow's feet but a lifetime of sour half-smiles seemed a heavy price to pay for smooth cheeks. She might have had a nicer life if she'd looked like she was really enjoying herself.

Her hair was dyed exactly the colour that Doreen's hydrangea used to be. Would all those fat artificial curls go back to being toothpowder pink if you stopped feeding her the special stuff? She wore it in a fancy, heavily lacquered bouffant (either she kept a hairdresser in the wardrobe or she slept sitting up). Her face was thickly smoothed with peach Pan-Cake, her eyelids were a pale silvery blue, her cheeks rosy with Bewitching Coral and her lips painted Lilac Rose which was already seeping into the sphincter of cross little lines that fanned out from her mouth. Her teeth were a sort of dirty Daz white and beautifully made –

like Uncle George's, only smaller. Her weedy grey eyebrows had been overwritten by new ones drawn on neatly by her maid who lived in a funny little warren of box rooms on the eighth floor under the roof. She usually managed to get them symmetrical but they were never the same twice. Today she looked very, very surprised and slightly annoyed.

Mrs Pillman had eaten a cheese football when she first sat down which had stuck to her plate and taken a lot of shifting so she'd been keeping to liquids ever since and had now clocked up four glasses of champagne which had done her temper no good at all. She'd taken an instant dislike to Connie and Iris who had ignored her after the first brief gush of introductions. She was itching to share her feelings.

'Do you know those women?'

'Not really.' *Rarely.* That was more like it. 'I think they're friends of Reggie, the chap over there in the blazer.'

'I shouldn't have anything to do with them if I were you, my dear. Have you ever had an abortion?'

Jane nearly choked on her Veuve Clicquot and blushed a charming Bewitching Coral herself.

'Of course not.'

'Exactly. Well those two harpies have talked of nothing else since they got here. They must think I'm deaf. The skinny one with the bad teeth is arranging it apparently. Can you imagine discussing such a thing *in public*?' This seemed to bother her even more than the thought of the operation itself.

'I should give both of them a very wide berth if I were you. A young gel like you needs to be very careful about the company she keeps. They're tramps, both of them. I pity that poor child.'

She nodded in the direction of Virginia, Iris's nine-year-old daughter, a skinny, serious-looking girl with big brown eyes and a bulging forehead exposed by her velvet Alice band. She wore a Buchanan tartan kilt, a bottle-green cashmere twinset, matching woollen tights and black patent-leather shoes (Iris had a friend who was an under-buyer in Harrods' children's department). Dougie's mama didn't have a lot of books but Virginia had found one that was keeping her occupied. It was the Kinsey Report on *Sexual Behavior in the Human Female*. Only Dougie had noticed but he didn't want to draw attention to it so Virginia sat there, round-eyed, boning up on impotence and vaginismus while the grown-ups got loud and drunk. One hand held the book while the other worked back and forth between her mouth and the cocktail snacks. She made short work of the Twiglets and Cheeselets – she liked those – but there was still no sign of a proper meal so she set to work on the cheese footballs and finally she was down to the olives. Bitter, vinegary things. She didn't like them at all – they were an Acquired Taste, Mummy said. They were so sour they made her wink but she ate them anyway. Eventually, after a whole tray of nibbles and four glasses of Tizer, Virginia found that she wanted to be sick. But by now the room had filled up with noisy, boozy grown-ups smoking and eating lobster and Mummy was flirting pathetically with a big bald man in a blazer. Suddenly, Virginia spotted a lovely pineapple-shaped ice bucket. Perfect. She fitted the lid back on neatly afterwards and rinsed her mouth with a sip of Tizer.

There was a huge television in the corner, boxed away to look like an antique chest of drawers. A man in an Argyll cashmere slipover was watching *Grandstand* and trying to get his bookmaker on the phone.

'What do you mean "no each ways on this race?" All right. Thirty bob to win. Bastards.' He growled as he put the phone down and sat back for the race.

Reggie asked Jane to put another record on to drown out the sound of Peter O'Sullevan. There was a big teak gramophone unit with dozens of records racked in wooden compartments. Jazz mostly. She'd never heard of any of them so she chose the one with the prettiest cover. All the others had coloured men on the front.

'Jazz fan, eh? Girl after my own heart.' Reggie put his hand round her waist and pulled her against him for a dance. His other hand was behind her, stroking her cashmere and wool backside. He smelled of brandy and cigars and dirty twinfold poplin. This was all too much for Iris. No one was stroking Iris's backside (not that she had much to stroke) and she wanted an explanation.

'Reggie! I need to ask you something!' Jane escaped and had a bit more lobster and a sip from the wine glass Dougie had given her. Lobster was lovely. Chablis wasn't so lovely but it was what you had with lobster, apparently, so who was she to argue.

Suzy was now sat on Pete's lap telling the other men the elephant's foreskin story which went down a storm although Iris's daughter had to be patted on the back when Tizer went down the wrong way. Suzy left 'em laughing and got up to pour herself a drink at the dinky little bar. Jane watched her do it. She tonged a few ice cubes from the ice bucket (this one was shaped like a beer barrel) and tipped up the gin bottle as if pouring herself a good strong measure – only she hadn't taken the top off. She then filled up the glass with tonic water. She caught Jane's eye and pulled a sheepish smile.

'I'd get pie-eyed otherwise but they hate it if you don't keep pace. Ted the barman at Carpenter's looks after me as well – holds the glass up to the measuring thingy but doesn't push. What are you up to this evening, Janey?' *Janey*. It was nice. Janey.

'Nothing special.' Or, more probably, *Dixon of Dock Green* and *Billy Cotton's Band Show* followed by half an hour pulling faces in the dressing-table mirror.

'I'm going out for dinner with a friend of mine but he could easily get a date for you if you like and we could all go dancing.'

Why was she being so friendly? What was she after?

'I'd have to go home and change.'

Girls do wear their daytime skirts and jerseys in smart restaurants but they will need to be extremely pretty to pass muster. Jane thought glumly of her only evening dress: full-length chartreuse velvet. She'd bought it in a panic for the firm's Christmas party. It was a swine. Doreen said she looked like a streak of snot in it.

'Where's home?'

'Well. I'm living with an aunt in Norbury at the moment.'

Life with Doreen sounded a lot better put like that. And it sounded suddenly, miraculously, temporary.

'Oh God, that's miles. Look, I've got stacks of evening things you could wear. And the flat's ankle-deep in shoes. What size are you? That's amazing! Glenda used to model shoes but she's gone to Spain with the boyfriend. Bit of a spiv, but he paid three months' rent in advance and she didn't have to take a stitch with her. You can sleep in her room if you like. Come on, let's go. I've had about enough of this.'

'Who's going to help Dougie clear up?' worried Jane. There were empty glasses everywhere.

'Oh don't worry about that. Iris does it. It's the only reason she gets asked. That and the cabaret. Ooh look. Here we go.'

Iris had started. The eighth gin had done it.

'They're all parasites, Dougie. You just don't see it: drinking your drink, wrecking your mummy's beautiful flat. They make a lot of noise but really your life is empty, Dougie. Empty. Like mine.' She squinted sorrowfully into her empty glass of gin but perked up at the sight of Jane and Suzy.

'And look at those four tarts! Suck you off for the price of a dinner at the Caprice. You deserve better than them, Dougie my darlin'.' Iris's accent was slipping down and her skirt was riding up, showing the tops of her scrawny white thighs and the grim, net-curtain grey of her nylon panty girdle. *Research tells us that seventy-five per cent of women never launder their corsets.* Little Virginia saved the day.

'Mummy. I'm really sorry, Mummy, but I think I'm going to be sick.' Iris magically pulled herself together and reproachfully bundled little Virginia off to the bathroom.

'We've got to go, Dougie,' said Suzy, kissing him firmly on both cheeks and letting him cop a quick farewell feel as he helped her on with her coat. 'A man's coming to cut my hair at half five. Crew-cut. Very Zizi Jeanmaire. What do you think?'

Jane came next. 'I've had a wonderful afternoon. Such a nice surprise.' A big smile. A bit of work with the eyelashes. Like shooting fish in a barrel.

'Oh it's pretty much like this every Saturday – give or take poor Mrs Moore. Sorry about that. You must come again.'

She let him have a brief grope. It seemed rude not to.

Alpaca Pete called out his goodbyes from the telly – he had a £5 yankee going.

'Cheerio, girls. Don't do anything I wouldn't do.'

'That doesn't exactly narrow it down!' Screeches of laughter.

They finally got downstairs. Suzy lived 'near Cavendish Square' she said. Jane knew the West End inside out. She had one of Kenneth's bus maps and she used to pore over it, working out the best route from Derry and Toms to Swan and Edgar (9) or from Gamages to Selfridges (8). Jane was still running through possible bus routes in her head – 159? 13? where was Kenneth when you needed him? – when Suzy hailed a taxi.

'Bourne and Hollingsworth please.' She'd gone very Celia Johnson all of a sudden.

The streets were already dark and the taxi hurtled along Wigmore Street and on towards its destination. Suzy pulled the cabbie's window to one side.

'We don't really want Bourne and Hollingsworth *as such*, darling. If you could take the next right, St Anthony's Chambers is first on the left.'

It was nowhere near bloody Cavendish Square.

'Have you really got someone coming round?' Jane sensed that Suzy didn't always tell the exact truth.

'Oh yes. Big Terry.'

The taxi driver, who'd been eyeing up the pair of them in his rear-view mirror, raised his eyebrows.

'Why's he called Big Terry?' wondered Jane.

You could see the cabbie straining to hear Suzy's whispered answer. She passed a handful of silver through the window.

'Keep the change,' she said then looked him right in the eye. 'And none of your business, cheeky.'

Chapter 8

These tiny details of personal grooming might appear mere trifles when taken one by one. But add them together and they can make the difference between rich and poor, married or single, happy ever after and a miserable broken home.

If Bourne and Hollingsworth had been a bit of a let-down after the promise of Cavendish Square, St Anthony's Chambers was a serious kick in the teeth. It was a large mansion block built of dirty red bricks with no lock on the street door and stone stairs that smelled of piss. Although there were lights on each landing, most of the bulbs were missing and you had to feel your way up the wrought-iron banisters in almost total darkness. Suzy's flat was on the second floor. It wasn't a luxury flat.

There were, or had been, about six locks on the front door which was scarred with the screw holes of old bolts that hadn't quite made it.

'Used to be burgled nearly once a week – the trouble some people will go to for the thirty bob in the gas meter – but Glenda met this very obliging locksmith. Banham deadlocks, steel plate, the works. Like the Crown Jewels, darling and very, *very* reasonable. I only moved here last summer. It's a bit of a dive but it's only four quid a week for the three of us and *so* central. I can be in most of the showrooms in half an hour from a standing start.'

She twisted the third key in the lock and the door swung open, releasing a terrible smell of dry rot, wet nylons and Chanel No 5.

'Sorry about the pong. Glenda smashed a bottle of scent on the kitchen lino.'

The pay telephone on the wall of the passage had been ringing the whole time she was unlocking the door.

'Can you smell gas, darling?' sniffed Suzy, striking a match and lighting a fresh cigarette. 'God, it's cold in here. Do put the fire on. There should be some shillings on the chimneypiece.' *Chimneypiece*. Swank.

Suzy slipped out of her Persian lamb coat just as smoothly and foxily as if she were trying to sell you what was underneath. She hung it up carefully on a wooden coat hanger marked Trust House Forte which was dangling from the picture rail. The phone rang on while Suzy kicked off her shoes and switched on a few lights. Finally, finally she picked up the receiver.

'I don't think so.' She said this in a strong South African accent. 'She maht be upstairs. I'll jist chick.'

She left the phone hanging off the wall and disappeared into the kitchen to fetch a glass of water.

'Ah'm sorry. Miss Saint John is still not beck yit.'

She smiled at Jane as she hung up the receiver.

'No one's ever actually seen inside the flat so you can say what you like: "I think I saw her go out into the garden" or "She may be downstairs in the billiard room" – anything. No one's *ever* in, by the way: always check who it is first or run your eye down the list.' There were men's names written in lipstick and eye pencil on the wallpaper by the phone. 'Oh, and if the Dreaded Arnold rings I've just got a job in Hong Kong and you don't expect to see me back. Ever. Ghastly little man. Canadian. Do get the fire on, sweetie. Big Terry will be here in a minute and I need to ring the boyfriend. Have you got any pennies? It's all very grand saying "keep the change" all the time, but you never have money for the telephone.'

Jane scrabbled in her purse for fourpence and Suzy hooked the receiver lazily over her shoulder and dialled the number, watching herself in the full-length mirror on the opposite wall – *Hang a looking glass by your 'phone so that you can keep an eye on your expression.*

'Hello, my darling. Yes of course I am. But listen, I have a lovely, but *love-ly* little friend staying and I hate to leave her at home alone with nothing but the Black and White Minstrels for company.' A pause while he spoke as Suzy batted her eyelashes at her own reflection. The naked lightbulb in the passage cast big, smutty shadows across her powdery cheeks. 'You've got a very dirty mind, Henry Swan. Now then, the question is do you have an equally *love-ly* friend who might like to join us?' More chat his end. 'No,' she eyed Jane thoughtfully, 'no I don't think so. Not yet anyway.' Another pause. '*Extremely*. Good. Well bring him along and we'll expect you at around nine. Me too.' She purred the last two words. A voice that Jane didn't yet have.

Suzy hung up the receiver then skipped off to the kitchen while Jane found another fourpence to ring Doreen. They'd only got connected a couple of years ago. Doreen had almost been tempted by a white wrought-iron telephone seat she'd seen in the Green Shield Stamp catalogue but she decided that would just run up bills. Instead the phone was perched precariously on the arm of the hall stand so you had to answer it stood up in the draughty front passage. Doreen was very suspicious of the telephone, often not saying hello at all until the person on the other end had spoken. God help anyone who had dialled a wrong number. This time she was more forthcoming as Jane had caught her in the middle of the wrestling and if she stayed away from the set too long Uncle George would switch over to *Robin Hood*.

'Wot?'

'It's me, Jane. I'm over at Joy's and she's asked me if I want to stay overnight so I said I would if that was all right with you.'

Doreen just grunted and hung up, the quicker to get back to the telly. Suzy had stepped back into the corridor so Jane carried on talking, pretending to be having a normal conversation with a normal bloody human being.

'Oh I expect I can borrow a nightie. All right, Auntie. See you tomorrow. Bye.' She even blew a kiss. And then hung up the dead phone, ready for the grand tour of the flat.

The sitting room had bare floorboards covered by a peculiar offcut of carpet that had been woven with a fancy monogram of Ps and Hs (when they redecorated the Portland Hotel the landlord had done a deal with one of the carpet fitters he'd met in a local pub after finishing the job). The only furniture was a three-legged chaise-longue propped up on a pile of old *Vogues*, an armchair and a row of six red plush tip-up cinema seats. The dingy striped wallpaper had half a dozen clean, gaily coloured patches where pictures had once been. A naked light socket hung from the chipped rose in the middle but there was no bulb in it. Instead Suzy zipped round the room switching on three lamps with pink nylon shades on stands made from old dimple whisky bottles. There was only one electricity point in the room and the long flexes had all been crudely spliced together with fluffy black knots of insulating tape. The three plugs all met in one corner in a terrifying tangle of wires and two-way adaptors.

The only ornaments on Suzy's huge old plaster *chimneypiece* were a row of blue china elephants linked together by trunks and tails and a Moët and Chandon ice bucket full to the brim with ritzy little matchboxes. Jane selected a Claridge's bookmatch and crouched down to light the gas, waving the flame along the bottom row of charred white mantles until the whole thing stopped hissing and *woomfed* scarily to life.

'Would you like a glass of water?' called Suzy. Jane wandered out to the kitchen. It was a largish room about twelve feet square with a utility dresser, an old stone sink, a grimy gas stove and a huge, gleaming white roll-topped bath tub.

'Mad, isn't it? Not all the flats have got one. Most of them head off to some cosy bath-house place down in Soho. You know, special occasions: Jewish holidays, Queen's birthday, Grand National, that sort of thing. The lavatories are all down on the half landing. There is one for each flat but it's still a frightful pain. We usually wee in the bath, quite honestly. Quite hard finding anyone to share. Most of them just curl up and die when they see the kitchen. Glenda just used the place as a wardrobe really and we only got Lorna by dropping her rent to a quid provided she did all the cleaning and washing up. Which worked brilliantly for about a fortnight but as you can see . . .'

The bath was the only clean thing in the room. The kitchen floor was covered in black and blue fake marble lino tiles but the blue ones were almost black with grime, except for a cleanish path polished back to their original colour by passing feet. Doreen kept a pretty hairy kitchen floor but she did at least run the mop over it occasionally.

'I could clean the floor if you like.' Jane wasn't sure she could face stepping barefoot on to that filthy old oilcloth. Beetles, said Doreen, *Germs*.

'Don't be daft, sweetie. Life's too short. You can put some newspaper down, if you like. There's even a bathmat somewhere.' Which there was. It said Grand Hotel and there was dried blood on one corner.

The sink was overflowing with coffee cups and glasses, the gas stove was brown and sticky with long-forgotten fry-ups and the walls, which had once been painted a sort of school-corridor blue, were encrusted with strange little yellow worms, each about two feet long. Jane picked at one of them very, very cautiously.

'Spaghetti. You can tell it's cooked when it sticks to the wall – so Lorna says. Bit of a dark horse, Lorna. Works in the British Museum, sensible shoes and all that but she spends most of the week shacked up with one of the Egyptologists in his rat's nest in Gordon Square. He goes home to the family on Friday nights but the wife and kids have gone to her mother's in Reigate so

Lorna's off to Brighton for a nice dirty weekend. Let's hope she brings back a new bathmat.'

Suzy began running herself a bath, pouring a large slug of swanky bath essence into the trickle of water from the boiler, filling the foul kitchen with the treacly smell of carnations.

The cupboard was nearly as bare as Doreen's – but in a much tastier way: a jar of powdered coffee; a box of cornflakes; a long blue paper tube of spaghetti; a large box of Fortnum's chocolates (unopened); a packet of Ryvita; a box of Biskoids; three tins of Carpenter's lobster bisque; a jar of stuffed olives and yet another huge catering tin of Twiglets; Cheeselets and cheese footballs (someone, somewhere was obviously very generous with these). There was no fridge but two bottles of Veuve Clicquot and a waxed carton of milk-machine milk were sat outside on the window sill.

A heavy knock on the door meant Big Terry had arrived. He wore tonic trousers, a red Carnaby Street shirt, a navy-blue Crombie and suede shoes. He was about five feet four.

'Terry, thank God.' Suzy, now down to bra and panty girdle (*No girl is ever too thin for a girdle*), planted kisses on both cheeks. 'This is Janey, by the way. Please say you don't mind doing both of us. We have to do something about her.' Like it was nothing to do with Jane.

'We're not doing fuck all about fuck all until I've had a bloody drink. God. God! What a day! One ugly bitch after another, all wanting miracles.'

He threw his overcoat on the chair and flopped down on the sofa so hard that the leg made of magazines slithered dangerously sideways.

'Have you got any Scotch?'

Suzy pulled a face.

'Glenda drank it. Is it cold out?'

'Of course it's bloody cold out. It's bloody cold in *here*.'

'Then we've got some nice cold champagne. It's that or instant coffee, darling.'

'God, girl, you are just so piss-elegant. All right, champagne it is. Now what are you two tarts after? At least it'll make a change from those trolls.' He put on a sort of Iris-type drawl: ' "I need a new *image*. I was thinking a sort of Julie Andrews." Julie Andrews! Eamonn Andrews more like.'

Suzy eased the top off the champagne bottle and filled three mismatched pub wine glasses. She opened the tin of cocktail snacks. All of the Twiglets had gone.

'Bottoms up, dear,' said Big Terry and he and Jane followed Suzy down the steam-choked passage to her bedroom.

It was more like a dressing room really. The bed, a small single, was pushed into the far corner next to the chest of drawers. The only other furniture was a huge old enamel-topped kitchen table with a big three-part mirror lit by a pair of desk lamps and a long piano stool to sit on. A dirty great chrome dress rail with one wheel missing completely filled with coats and frocks ran the length of the left-hand wall.

'We found it in the street one evening. Perfect, isn't it? Now sit down and let Terry look at you.'

She pushed Jane down on to the piano stool in front of the table and tweaked all the pins out of the makeshift chignon so that her hair dropped down below her waist.

'My God, girl! Are you growing it for a bet?'

Terry was enjoying this more than Jane, who looked glumly at herself in the brightly lit mirrors. The borrowed lipstick had worn off and she looked very plain suddenly. Very Norbury.

'Cheer up. Soon sort you out. You know what, my love,' said Terry, fingering the last few feet of her hair, 'it's not bad stuff. Not bad at all. And the colour's strong all the way down. Could have a very nice piece made with it if you like. Then you could pin it in when you wanted a bit of glam.' He drained his glass and got his scissors out of his back pocket. 'OK. Let's get weaving. I haven't got all fucking night.' He whipped a pink cotton cape out of his kit bag, brushed her hair hard and began shearing it off, carefully laying the cut pieces side by side on the table.

By the time Suzy came back from her bath, Jane was seeing how it felt to flick her hair from side to side – something she hadn't done since she was about six. The towel on Suzy's head said 'Dorchester' and the one round her body said 'His'.

'That's better! I've left the bathwater. You'll be finished by the time my hair's dry.'

Terry was extracting a hand-held hairdryer from his bag. It looked like a huge, ointment-pink revolver. He looked warily at the wonky Bakelite socket in the corner.

'Now where can I plug this in? I don't want to fuse all the fucking lights like last time.'

It was a funny sort of bath. Open your eyes and you could be in Doreen's back kitchen but close them and it was like the time Jane had begged for all the buttonholes at the cousin's wedding and sat there tickling her nose with asparagus fern and going giddy on the scent of the fat white flowers. She wrapped herself in yet another big white towel and carefully cleaned the bath with Liquid Gumption as the water ran out.

Suzy's hair was all dry when Jane tiptoed back into the bedroom – *Walk about on tiptoe whenever you can. It will lengthen your line, improve your balance and work on ankle puffiness and falling arches.* She sat beside Suzy on the piano stool while Terry decided what he was going to do. It was only when she saw the two of them in the mirror without make-up that Jane realised why the old drunk in the pub had given her the crocodile bag. Terry looked interested suddenly. Chances were he really did have a friend who was a photographer.

'Mmm. Bookends. Very kinky. Are you going to dress the same or do you want to go for a contrast?'

Jane didn't dare say what she wanted but Suzy seemed to have tossed a coin in her head.

'I think a twinset would be a giggle, don't you?'

'Well don't blame me if you get asked for a sandwich, that's all I can say,' said Terry, bafflingly, as he set to work backcombing and spraying Suzy's hair into place.

'You can have Glenda's room, Janey. It's a bit of a tip but there should be some clean sheets in the green holdall just inside the door.'

Glenda's room looked like someone had picked it up, changed their mind and dropped it again. The sheets on the bed were greying and covered with make-up and coffee stains but the clean sheets were very clean indeed. They were still in their cellophane packet: brand-new Egyptian cotton; king size.

'Are you sure about these sheets?' she called across the passage. 'They're doubles.'

'Are they? Damn. Oh well, never mind. Just do the best you can.'

'But you could take them back and change them if you've got the receipt.'

Suzy giggled.

'Mmm. Rather you than me, darling.'

Jane made the bed and neatly paired off the shoes – all three and a halfs – that littered the floor. Glenda's dresses and coats had all been hung neatly from the picture rails but sweaters and stockings and smalls were thrown around anyhow. Glenda sounded a bit of a slag, what with the spiv and Spain and everything. Jane stuffed all the dirty sheets and clothes into the green holdall, hung the violet dress that Tony had given her on one of the hangers and switched out the light just as Terry – who was a very fast worker – was putting the finishing touch to Suzy's hairdo: a lick of gold pencil along a single strand of hair running from the parting to the immaculate French pleat. From the back it looked like the chocolate brazil in a box of Black Magic.

Suzy shoved along to the edge of the stool so that he could give Jane the same treatment. While he worked, Suzy drew her face back on, transforming herself from fresh-faced teen to starlet with a few strokes of sponge and pencil and carefully gluing back the fluffy nylon fringes of eyelash to create all those killer glances. Next, she whizzed along the line of frocks behind her, picking out two dark blue dresses with full, ballerina-length skirts, square necks and low, low backs: one in grosgrain, the other in velvet.

'If you can keep completely still, Janey darling, I can do your face for you in five minutes flat.'

'Oi,' said Terry. 'Fill my glass first. I'm dying of thirst here. God this place is a dump, Suzy. That last place in Onslow Gardens was a dive but this is a fucking slum, girl.'

'It's four quid a week between three and it's only a five-minute walk from the White Tower.'

'Suzy, babe, a girl of your calibre' (he pronounced it to rhyme with fibre) 'doesn't walk to the fucking White Tower. I shouldn't think you even know the bloody way from here. Why don't you get wise and get one of your gentlemen friends to find you something a bit more chi-chi?'

'We'll see. I might be moving this week, as a matter of fact.'

Jane saw her own face fall in the mirror even as Suzy was powdering it. She'd been thinking of what she could do with Glenda's room. Get rid of all her rubbish. Buy a nice big mirror second-hand somewhere. Paint it, even. But she didn't really fancy staying on in the flat on her own with some strange Lorna living in the box room and doing the washing up.

'Chin up, Janey. I need to do your lips. Janey might be moving too. I only met Janey today. You remember that lovely crocodile bag I got?'

Terry pulled a funny face. 'Yes, duckie. One of your more memorable adventures.'

What adventures? But Suzy gave a little frown and shook her head. Subject closed.

'Anyway. I left the bloody thing under a chair in that ghastly pub Dickie always goes to and Janey found it and then found me and gave it right back. Two hundred quid in cash, the lot. I'm not joking, Janey darling.' She looked straight at Jane in the mirror. It was like talking to her reflection on the dressing table after work, paying herself compliments. 'I'm really not joking. I don't know a single soul on this earth who wouldn't have taken the money and kept the bag for themselves. Not a single soul.'

'Well it's no bloody wonder with that crowd. God! I had that Madge in the salon this morning. No normal person wants their hair done at half eight.'

'I wondered where she'd been. Did you dye it that colour just for a lark?'

'Not likely. You don't pull strokes like that with Madge, babe. She'd break your fingers. No. She actually bloody chose it. With her figure and that striped number she looked like a fucking Belisha beacon. There.' He stood back to scowl at his work. 'That's the best we can do, I suppose.'

He'd got one French pleat going clockwise, the other anti-clockwise, and there was a long curl escaping down on to the shoulder – opposite shoulders. Jane thought it looked a bit contrived but they seemed pleased enough.

'Get your drawers on, girls. I haven't got all night.'

He put away his gear then sat on the stool smoking a smelly French cigarette while they dressed.

Suzy hung her towel over the top of the door and quickly wriggled into stockings and suspender belt. No panty girdle this time. And no panties. Then she stepped into her dress.

'You are a very, very dirty little girl – you know that?'

'Just shut up and zip up, Terry Thomson.'

And there they both were. Like bookends.

'Not bad. Not at all bad. You ought to have another word with that Dickie. You could probably get quite a lot of photographic work with a gimmick like that. Especially bras, with your Advantages.'

'No thanks. Do lingerie and you never do anything else. Look what happened to Gloria.'

'Eight guineas a day and a nice little flat in St John's Wood? You should be so lucky, dear.' Terry wound the flex round his hairdryer and tied Jane's spare hair in a knot held in place with a hairclip.

'Do you still do Gloria? What colour is she these days?'

'No idea, duckie. She started wanting her bush and her poodle dyed to match and that's not really my scene. She's got an arrangement with young Rodney. Remember Flash Rodney? Always did like dogs, Rodney.'

Suzy and Terry were making for the front door but Jane just sat there looking at herself in the mirror. Her make-up was perfect and her hair was all sprayed into a shining brown cone.

She could hear Suzy seeing Terry out: 'No I insist. There were two of us, for Christ's sake! And you've got Janey's hairpiece to see to. I've got nothing smaller, anyway. No really, darling. Take it while I've got it. I'll probably be asking for credit next week.'

'Just you try it.'

Noisy, dry kisses on cheeks.

'Bye, babe. Take care of yourself. Ta-ta, Jenny!'

She shouted goodbye but she couldn't tear herself away from the mirror. Suzy stepped briskly back into the room.

'Now then, sweetie. You look the business. Let's see if Glenda's got an evening coat you can wear. Glenda used to have a very nice silver Furleen number. Here it is. Super. Now then. They'll be here in half an hour. You're not going to show me up, are you? Can you do French?'

Jane looked up suspiciously. She could only think of those dodgy little cards in the window of the post office on the high road: 'French lessons offered by strict disciplinarian'; 'Lost: a ring inscribed "I love Dick" '. What kind of a date was this?

'I've got an O level.'

'No no, darling, not that *plume-de-ma-tante* nonsense. *Proper* French. Restaurant French. Can you order a meal?'

Jane knew the sample menu in *Lady Be Good* off by heart.

'I think so.'

Suzy seemed unconvinced.

'So. What will mademoiselle have to start?'

'Saumon fumé.'

'Get you! Very ritzy. OK, salmon's off.'

'Er. Pâté maison.'

'And to follow?'

'Entrecôte.'

'How would madam like it cooked?'

'Er. Grillée?'

'No, darling. Oh dear. You are funny. You've got the outfit, you've got the walk but the rest is all theory, isn't it?'

Jane wanted to cry. Cow. Laughing at her. How was she supposed to know? She wasn't being wined and dined in the West End every night in her Persian bloody lamb. You try learning about menus when you lived on tinned pie.

'Oh my God. Don't start crying whatever you do. I'll have to start the whole face from scratch. No, honestly, it's really rather sweet.'

Sweet. Patronising bitch.

' "How would you like it cooked?" means "How long do you want it cooked for?" Just say "medium". Oh, and don't for God's sake hold your knife like a pen. OK, here's your bag: lipstick; comb; tissues; rubber Johnnies – only kidding.'

A car hooted in the street but Suzy just pulled a face and carried on getting ready. She put in a pair of pearl earrings and found Jane some clip-ons.

'Why don't you get them pierced?'

'Don't fancy it.'

Doreen had pierced ears. A cousin had pierced them with a pin and a potato in about 1922. The holes had gone through crooked and Doreen used to make Jane put her studs in. You had to wiggle the flabby white flap of flesh around between finger and thumb to find the hole in the other side. Doreen had taken Jane and June into Croydon to have their ears done hygienically as a treat one Christmas just after the war – 'Ears pierced while you wait'. June was thrilled but Jane ('ungrateful cow') had screamed the place down every time the woman came near her with the hole-making machine.

Uncle George, who never said a word about such things normally, had said, when it was being talked about over tea the night before, that he did rather think that piercing little girls' ears was just a bit, well, *common*. All hell broke loose.

'Common?' Doreen had screamed. 'Common! *You!* Telling me what's common? Your mother,' she shrieked, 'your mother – (Old Flannel Feet) – had *four-teen* kids. What the bloody hell do you know about common? Common! *Fucking* cheek!' (a word Doreen never used – it was common). Her rage carried on bubbling up for weeks afterwards. He'd say something – 'that's nice, dear'; 'good morning'; anything – and she'd look at him, face like a bag of spanners, and start all over again: 'Common!'

The doorbell rang this time.

'That's better,' said Suzy, tickling a drop more scent behind each ear. 'OK, darling. Party time.'

Chapter 9

A diner in the smart London eating places is in the kingdom of snobbery.

Getting down the stairs was a nightmare. Only one of the lightbulbs worked and Jane had to cling to the handrail all the way down to be sure of not turning on her new heels: dyed-to-match satin stilettos borrowed from Glenda's little shoe department.

A door opened on the first floor and a little old lady in a wraparound paisley overall and a curly yellow wig stuck her head out.

'That you, Suzy darlin'?'

'You shouldn't open your door at this time of night, Annie. There are some very strange men about.'

'Chance would be a fine thing,' she cackled. Annie didn't trust dentists. 'Need any washing doing?'

'Ooh, yes please, Annie. I'll bring it all down tomorrow. This is my friend Janey. She'll probably have a few bits and pieces as well. Will that be all right? I'll give you another two bob.'

'Whatever you like, Suzy-Sue. What Ever You Like. Pleasure to do it, lovey.' She turned to Jane in the half darkness as if sharing a wonderful secret: '*Lovely* little bits she's got. I'll hold the door open till you get all the way down. I got that caretaker geezer to put a new bulb in but those two tarts in the basement nicked it.'

'Goodnight, Annie darling. See you tomorrow.'

Suzy and Jane carried on down the stairs.

'Annie's marvellous. She does all my stockings and smalls for half a crown a week. It beats scrubbing away at the sink – especially our sink. You'd have to do a week's worth of washing up before you could even get near it.'

The street was almost completely dead. Even the pub on the corner closed at weekends. Suzy's date was vrooming his engine to show how busy he was but he leaped from the driving seat as soon as he saw Suzy and opened the nearside passenger door. Big man. Cashmere overcoat.

'Janey James, this is Henry Swan.'

'How do you do, Miss James? Suzy's told me a great deal about you' – no she bloody hadn't – 'I've brought an old friend of mine along for the evening. I hope you don't mind. I'll manage the introductions properly when we get to the restaurant. Mirador all right, darling?'

'Mmm. Super.'

Mr Swan's friend stayed put in the front while Henry Swan got Jane into the back of the car before ushering Suzy round to the other side. Nice manners. The car was nice too. There was a nice, pricey, leathery smell, like being inside a great big crocodile bag. An armrest had been folded down between Jane and Suzy like a big fat square of fudge and each seat was as wide and comfy as an armchair – comfier. Comfier than Doreen's cut moquette anyway.

Henry was speaking. 'Hard to be sure in this light of course but you are both looking exceptionally pretty. Aren't they, Ollie?'

' 'ceptionally pretty,' drawled Ollie in a cashmere slipover-y, Tattersall check-y sort of voice.

Ollie was old too. Early forties. Balding slightly. 'British Warm' overcoat, brown trilby. He didn't smile much but there was a funny clicking sound whenever he did. Not a raspberry jam man, Jane suspected.

As the huge car pulled up outside the restaurant Jane could feel her stomach beginning to tighten. Suzy seemed up for a good time but it was just one big obstacle course as far as Jane was concerned from the moment they got inside. Even the blowsy old blonde who looked after the coats seemed to be pricing every armful. The Persian lamb went down all right but there was the trace of a sneer for Jane's borrowed Furleen which was a bit rich coming from someone who lived on the shillings left in a saucer. God only knows how she'd have reacted to grey bouclé. Spat on it, probably.

The head waiter was terrifying too. Waiters, like salesladies, knew exactly how to make you feel small and out of place which was mad really. They trekked in and out of steaming hot kitchens carrying plates all day and they lived on tips. Waiters at the Savoy didn't get paid any proper wages at all, Uncle George said. What kind of job was that for a grown man? Skivvies, Doreen called them. Remembering that made Jane feel better. There was nothing to worry about anyway. The dear-me-no look on the maître d's face dried up when he saw Henry Swan. They'd known each other since before the war. Long enough to be friends. Only he wasn't a friend, he was a waiter.

'Captain Swan! Such a surprise to see you here on a Saturday! I have in my book "Mr Henry" and I say to myself, "Mr Henry? I don't know any Mr Henries." '

He buttonholed a passing plate-carrier and hissed at him, 'See to Captain Swan's table at once,' and turned back with a professional smile, well-oiled by decades of prudent over-tipping.

'Is Philippe in the kitchen tonight?'

The head waiter's world came to an end right there and then. 'I'm afraid not, Captain Swan. We don't usually expect to see our regular customers on a Saturday but the grills are all excellent this evening.' It was more of a warning than a recommendation. 'Your table is not quite ready, I'm afraid, but perhaps you will have a drink at the bar with my compliments?'

'Why not?' Henry Swan knew full well that the man was just buying time while the flunky hastily upgraded him from 'Mr

Henry's' poky table near the door to Mr Swan's usual one in the upstairs window. This involved hustling a middle-aged couple through their pudding and palming them off with free coffee and liqueurs in the bar and a handful of petits fours. The man grumbled a bit and wangled a second liqueur.

'Champagne cocktails all right for everybody? Splendid. Four champagne cocktails it is. Thank you, Adolphe. Now then, Miss James, may I present Oliver Weaver? Oliver Weaver, Jane James.'

Jane shook hands while Ollie eyed her up approvingly. He kept hold of her hand, stroking the skin with his thumb like young Mr Drayke fingering a quality tweed.

'Well Ollie,' boomed Henry, 'I reckon we're very fortunate to have the company of two such remarkably beautiful girls. Cheers, everybody!'

Jane sipped suspiciously at her drink. It was like champagne, only worse, but she didn't let it show, gazing shyly up at Ollie over the rim of her glass.

The two girls were side by side on bar stools, legs crossed by the book. Henry was offering cigarettes from his solid gold case and Suzy took one and went into the usual act but this was obviously a command performance. The 'O' of her pretty red mouth round the cigarette; the fingertips steadying his hand; the sucked-in cheeks; the upward glance and suddenly drooping eyelashes. As she drew in the first delicious puff of smoke the fingers tightened their grip just a little on the hand that held the lighter. The first breath out was like a sigh of relief – or ecstasy. It was a work of art, really. Jane decided not to take a cigarette. It was too hard an act to follow.

Their progress through the restaurant caused a bit of a stir. Jane and Suzy weren't the only young girls in the room but they were by far the prettiest and best-dressed – and a matched pair to boot. People actually turned to look.

Suzy seemed to see someone she knew in a far corner and gave a cheery little wave. They waved back – who wouldn't? – but they didn't come over to the table afterwards. Was it just part of the act? Jane saw someone she knew too. It was the skinny customer with the false hips now tricked out in last year's French mustard brocade. The woman didn't recognise Jane. Probably hadn't even looked at her in the first place. She looked at her now though. Jane saw her mechanically registering the Savile Row suits, then checking Jane and Suzy over, looking for cheap shoes, laddered stockings, stray bra straps: some tiny crumb of comfort for not being pretty and glamorous and young. Not a hope. She went back to her duck à l'orange with a face like a squeezed lemon.

'Jane – is it Jane or Janey? – what will you have to start?'

Here goes. She'd barely had time to glance at the huge tasselled menu but everything she'd learned appeared to be present and correct – all except the prices. Ladies' menus didn't have any, it seemed. She shook out her napkin. *Do not be intimidated by a swan or water-lily concoction.*

'Do call me Janey.' Do. Doooo. She nearly blushed at herself.

'Have you chosen yet?'

'Saumon fumé, please.'

'Smoked salmon over here. And then?'

'Sole grillée.'

'Then the grilled sole.'

'Would madam like it on or off the bone?'

'Janey?'

'Oh, off, I think.' Sounded safest. She took care to address her wishes to Henry who then passed them on to the waiter (*A lady never gives her order directly to the waiter*). Funny rule that. As if she and Suzy only existed in Henry's imagination.

Suzy went for pâté maison and entrecôte grillée which she wanted *saignant*. God knows what that meant (it wasn't covered in the book) but it seemed to surprise and rather excite Henry.

'You and I seem to be having fish, Janey. Chablis all right for you?'

Well no, actually. She'd much rather have lemonade or gin and orange.

'Super,' she heard herself saying but she barely drank any. When Ollie disappeared to the Gents' (must have a weak bladder) and Henry was busy discussing vintages with the wine waiter, she topped up her Chablis from her water glass. No sense getting tight. She'd only be sick.

Smoked salmon was nice and easy to eat. Once you'd squeezed on the lemon you couldn't really go wrong. A bit salty but much nicer than tinned. Pâté would have been trickier. Lot of knife and toast work with pâté. And besides, Uncle George had given her a healthy dread of meat paste, whatever fancy name you gave it. Ollie ordered pâté but looked rather surprised when it arrived – it looked like dog meat with a tiny tassel of gherkin on top. He made no attempt to eat it. Ollie had had two champagne cocktails but they were only to keep the whisky and sodas company. He thought Jane was very, *very* pretty and she seemed to grow prettier all evening. Ollie ordered sole too – on the bone – but after a few half-hearted stabs at the fish on one side he lost interest and concentrated on the Chablis instead.

He was quite nice-looking, really, with greying blond hair and the dregs of some kind of boyish charm. He did something in the City and said, sadly, that his wife – who was super, don't get him wrong, super girl – did not understand him. Jane thought she probably did but didn't say so. She didn't say much all told but she looked nice and listened politely so she seemed to get away with it. *A measure of wide-eyed admiration can work miracles.* Suzy was a different story. She listened, she flattered, she flirted – like mad – but she told funny stories too. She was telling Henry a joke about a man whose wife had died. His friend at the funeral is very sympathetic but reassures the man that he'll get over it and eventually find happiness with someone else.

' "I know, George, I know," sobs the widower, "but what about *tonight*?" '

Henry's laugh turned heads in the restaurant. Jealous eyes scanned their table: beautiful girls, rich men, funny stories. Only it wasn't a funny story. Not Jane's idea of funny. But she laughed prettily enough.

Even Suzy's fibs could make them laugh.

'So, Suzy,' said Henry, after ordering another bottle of Chablis, 'what were you up to this afternoon? I telephoned a couple of times but no joy at all. Not even the lovely Lorna.'

Suzy lied beautifully, taking a tiny bit of truth and embroidering it all over with eye-catching rubbish.

'Oh my God! Don't ask! Janey's Uncle Dougie wanted us to go over to his flat and meet his fiancée and her little girl. He knew her back in Gibraltar – was it Gibraltar or Malta, Janey?' She rhymed them both with a funny northern accent as if she was imitating the imaginary woman.

'Gibraltar. The Mary woman was Malta.' Life with Doreen taught a girl to lie nicely.

'Anyway. I think he wanted her to meet people. Iris, her name is. She's had a rather terrible life, you know. She was telling me while you and your uncle were fixing the drinks. She moved to Gibraltar after her first husband committed suicide. They found him laid out on her bed, wearing her favourite turquoise suit in full make-up and one of Iris's wigs. The little girl, Virginia, found him. Poor mite.'

Jane needed to powder her nose. Fairly urgently. And it seemed that, even at the Mirador, girls didn't powder their noses alone so Suzy tailed her into the Ladies'. As they sat giggling on the armchairs they heard distinct sounds of retching coming from one of the cubicles. Moments later the customer with the false hips emerged, looking slightly flustered to find them there.

'Er. Don't have the duck,' she said before hastily rinsing her mouth under the tap, repairing her lipstick and heading back to her table.

'You don't expect to find food poisoning in a place like this.'

'Not food poisoning, darling. They do it on purpose. How else do you think she keeps that sylph-like figure? Bridge lunches with the girls, tea at Fortnum's, business dinners with hubby. She'd be two-ton Tessie if she kept all that down.'

'Do you think Iris does that?'

'Bound to. Oh my God! Poor Iris. And her poor dead husband! I've met her husband actually. At the races. God! He tells some stories. Do you know she wouldn't let him smoke in the house? They had this poky little service flat on the Brompton Road and he used to have to go and stand out on the balcony in the rain whenever he wanted a fag. No wonder he never went home.'

'Ollie's wife doesn't understand him.'

'You won't have any trouble with Ollie; he's too drunk for one thing. But we might have to find you a dancing partner later. Shouldn't be a problem.'

They stood up and checked the fall of their skirts in the big gilt mirror on the far wall.

'Don't we look gorgeous? I think Terry's right: we should see about getting some snaps done. Maybe Monday.'

Back at the table Ollie had obviously been told to smarten up his act. They'd hardly all sat down again before he started showing a polite interest. *Most women have no desire for serious debate on the topics of the day. They far prefer what is known as small talk: what they did that day, a hat they admired, what they had for tea.*

'So what do you do, Janey?'

Jane had expected someone would ask this question. 'I'm a junior in a madam shop' was probably not the right answer.

'Well, I've been living with an aunt down in Surrey since my parents died but I'm hoping I might be able to get some modelling work.'

The 'aunt down in Surrey' was a masterstroke. Doreen was suddenly installed in a detached house on the outskirts of Dorking: fruit trees; odd-job man; pastel twinsets with mix-and-match tweeds. She'd have hated it. The trick was always going to be putting just the hint of tragedy queen in the 'since my parents died' part so that it sounded too recent and too painful to talk about. What you didn't want was the bit that went:

'Oh dear, I am sorry. When was that?'

'1944.'

Jane managed to sound like a plucky young creature with her living to earn.

'I shouldn't think you'd have any trouble modelling,' said Ollie, who had managed to get outside an entire bottle of Chablis on his own and was now trying to hold her hand. 'You're a very, very, very pretty girl.'

It was like having dinner with some great big, balding talking doll. He must *have* other conversation. He couldn't very well sit about in the City all day saying that to people.

Suzy and Henry's chat had reached the whispers and giggles stage and he was stroking her tiny white wrist as he spoke. She was leaning across the table with her pretty face propped on her other hand, smiling into his eyes and occasionally lowering those big, fat false eyelashes as if everything he said was utterly fascinating. Which it wasn't, quite honestly, not what Jane could catch. Mind you, she did hear the words 'Curzon Street' and wondered if this was the promised flat. *That* would be fascinating.

She returned to her duties with Ollie. *Talk about fashions, home life and people the man has not met are utterly boring to most men.*

'Do you live in London, Ollie?'

'I've got a bolt hole in St James's but the family live out in Wiltshire.'

Out of the corner of her eye Jane could see Henry Swan wincing then laughing at Ollie's idea of a chat-up line. Poor Ollie wasn't really cut out to be a ladykiller. Family in Wiltshire. It was pitiful, really.

'Oh Wiltshire! How lovely!' Which one was Wiltshire? She tried to dredge up a long-forgotten piece of geography homework. Wiltshire was mauve. Or was it yellow?

'Do you have a big garden?'

'About ten acres, I suppose.'

Jane tried to picture an acre. She thought hard about those little tables on the backs of red exercise books: rods, perches, furlongs, fathoms. Biggish garden obviously. Big gardens just made work, Doreen said.

'What flowers do you grow?'

Doreen actually disliked flowers. Cut flowers especially. It was just a vase to wash as far as she was concerned. The front room was full of virgin vases with cobwebs inside. But she hated garden flowers too: 'They only die off. Make the place look untidy.' The back garden in Norbury was little more than a long straight lawn, a few evergreen bushes and a lot of completely bare earth – she had George out there with the hoe most weekends. There were wooden trellises here and there but nothing grew on them. She had a horror of climbing plants. God alone knew why.

They had all had crêpes Suzette for pudding which involved setting fire to pancakes on a trolley in a rather flashy way but they tasted quite nice. So did the liqueurs Henry had ordered. The only other time Jane had ever had liqueurs was one Christmas when she was about nine. She had bitten into a chocolate only to find some kind of nasty medicine inside. But this was nice. Orangey. Took away the taste of the coffee anyway.

Meanwhile Ollie was still trying to remember what he grew in his garden in Wiltshire.

'Don't know much about flowers. Angela looks after all that side of things. Wonderful woman in many ways.'

He had hold of Jane's hand again and was sandwiching it between his. It wasn't a romantic gesture at all. Just something to fiddle with while he talked.

'Angela used to be a very, very pretty girl,' and suddenly the idea that veh, veh pretty girls should end up like Angela seemed too unbearably sad. *If a man wants to make a hit with the opposite sex and is not as happy as he might be, he should endeavour to keep this to himself.*

Henry pulled him back from the brink.

'You up for a spot of dancing, Ollie?'

But Ollie was like a dog with a bone.

'Used to go to a lot of dances with Angela. Met her at a dance in fact.'

Henry tried again.

'I'll bet you're a fabulous dancer, Janey.'

That rather depended. She'd spent some of her Saturday wages from Vanda on a course of dancing lessons at a funny old place in Thornton Heath a couple of years ago. Doreen thought dancing lessons were swank so she had to say she was listening to records over at Joy's house. Uncle George had been a very good dancer but Jane only found this out when a rumba came on the Light Programme one Saturday breakfast time and the pair of them were suddenly gliding round the kitchen. Doreen went to her room with Her Headache for the rest of the day.

Jane could rumba, she could waltz, she could cha-cha and she could jive (she learned that at the Locarno) but she had to quit the course before they got to the slow foxtrot – let alone the valeta and the Boston two-step. She had tried to get the basics from a book she'd got out of the library but the black and white footsteps made no sense at all, let alone 'hovering' and 'feathering'. She had enough trouble with the Paris turn. But it didn't matter. Only old people did those dances anyway – apart from on telly. The only dances Doreen had ever managed were the conga and the Okey-Cokey but now that her whole self weighed over thirteen stone she was reduced to sitting on the sidelines making unpleasant remarks about other people who were having a better time than she was.

'I rrr-rumba,' said Jane. She managed to say it in a slightly teasing voice.

'I'll bet you do,' said Ollie, loosening his tie.

Chapter 10

> *Master the art of smiling even
> when you're not smiling.*

'So. Where to, girls?'

Henry suggested Edmundo Ros in Regent Street and Ollie also seemed keen.

'Good spot for a rrrr-rumba,' growled Henry, encouragingly.

Suzy wasn't convinced. They were probably only suggesting it because there was no chance of either of them bumping into anyone they knew. Suzy wanted the River Club – Henry was a member – but Ollie had obviously been there with Angela. They finally settled on some members-only cabaret joint in Beak Street.

Henry drove and was annoyed when he couldn't park right outside. There wasn't a table, either. Nor was there likely to be now that Ollie had decided to take charge. Henry was obviously good at handling waiters: friendly, clubbable, gracious, grateful. Ollie wasn't. Ollie tended to stick to restaurants where he was known: his own club in St James's or some little place in Jermyn Street (he could crawl home from there). Sober, he was too self-conscious to catch a strange waiter's eye. Drunk, he was tense and toffee-nosed and generally made waiters want to spit in his soup (which they quite often did).

He had started giving the maître d' the full my-good-man treatment which was being met with a completely dead bat (*No one will think you a man of consequence if you incessantly bully the waiters*). Ollie then added insult to injury by tucking a ten-shilling note in the top pocket of the man's dinner jacket saying he was sure he'd be able to find them a nice table near the band. The maître d' took the note out and looked at it as if it were a currency he didn't normally accept and put it in the cloakroom lady's saucer. What he really wanted was for another foursome to come in so that he could show them straight to a table and put this public-school berk in his place. You could see him keeping his eye on the door, hoping. Instead the next best thing happened: he spotted Suzy.

'Ah! Mademoiselle!' All smiles suddenly. Hand kissing. She was looking very lovely this evening. No idea that the gentlemen were friends of mademoiselle. Coats were whisked away and they were led through the maze of tables to a semi-circular booth near the band. There was a delicious smell in the room. Like someone sneaking a quick fag while frying a steak in the perfumery department. A 'Reserved' sign magically disappeared.

Again the thrill of heads turning. Jane was almost giddy with it. It was fabulous. Like Miss United Kingdom walking past the judges' table in evening wear. Every eye on her: admiring her face, her figure, her legs. Marking her out of ten. All they needed was clipboards.

Ollie slumped ungratefully into a seat and ordered champagne. The waiter brought sweet instead of dry but Ollie was too depressed to send it back and besides, the girls seemed to prefer it. Suzy took a happy sip from her saucer then decided that it was time for a bit more nose-powdering and the two of them filed out to the Ladies'.

The mirrored room was packed with what looked like hundreds of women straightening seams, fixing straps, re-gluing eyelashes – like the emergency ward in a dolls' hospital. A girl in embroidered organdie sat with a broken zip, grubby pink deceivers spilling out of the front of her bodice, black tears snaking down her face while Elsie, the attendant, who had already clocked up over ten quid in half crowns, stitched up the back of her dress. All of them had had far too much to drink. One little gang of tarts were out for a good time with a bunch of loud-mouthed old northerners in town 'on business' (they were actually down South for the weekend to service the weighing machines at a sweet factory in Lewisham). Jerome wouldn't have let them in as a rule but a nice crisp fiver bought them a table by the kitchen door.

'What's yours like?'

'Hands all over the place – talk about Bolton bloody Wanderers.'

Two shrunken-looking women of thirty-odd made a beeline for a pair of vacant stools. Both were wearing greasy old gowns in tired duchesse satin. They'd managed to get the zips done up but only just and there were great fat folds of back bulging out over the top. They sat dabbing listlessly at their strawberry blonde perms – hard to know why, as every strand had been lacquered to a standstill. You could see nasty poultrified bits of razored armpit every time they moved. *It always offends the eye to see a thicket of hair under an upraised arm.*

One of them slyly eyed Jane and Suzy but then forgot to put her mirror face back on before looking away and got a sudden, terrifying glimpse of her own vinegary expression. Not just older. Older was bad enough. She looked suddenly panic-stricken. Was that what she looked like when she wasn't looking? Did all that envy and bitterness show through on the outside? You could see the trouble she had getting her face in order: chin up; eyebrows slightly raised to take up some of the slack. The possibility of a smile. Anything to lose the ghost of the sour old bag she had just seen.

'What a lovely dress!' She very nearly said 'dear' but swallowed it in time. 'Dear' would have widened the age gap still further.

'Thank you.'

Jane found a smile and turned back to the face that Suzy had made: the neat lick of eyeliner; the smart eyebrows; the bewitching sweep of long black eyelashes. Wasted on Ollie, mind you.

'Was that a man?' a posh, bored voice was wondering.

'Was what a man?' Her friend had peeled off her stocking and was putting a fresh corn plaster on her little toe. You could smell her feet.

'That tall one with all the feathers.'

'Don't be silly, Vanessa. She had a *huge* bosom. Jerry couldn't take his eyes off her.'

'So? Jerry never looks at their faces, darling. Looked like a bloody man to me.'

'God I hate the West End on Saturdays. Talk about Nescafé society.'

'No choice, unfortunately. Jerry's Swedish clients always make this sort of trip at the weekend so they don't lose a minute in the office. Bloody Lutheran work ethic. Are you going to that charity canasta party Monty Manafu's doing?'

'Never even met the man, darling.'

'Yes you have. You must have. At Audrey's. That wine-tasting evening she had for the spastics. Little fat chap. At Christ Church with Roger.'

'No, honestly I haven't.'

Vanessa wasn't letting go.

'You *do* know him. Little fat poof. Lot of gold teeth.'

'Vanessa. I'd *remember*.'

'You *do* remember. Little fat poof, darling,' she lowered her voice, 'little fat black poof.'

'Oh him! God no!'

Jane sat on her dainty golden chair and checked her teeth for lipstick while Suzy dabbed needlessly at her forehead with a miniature pink puff.

'The maître d' seemed very friendly,' said Jane.

'Used to know my father years ago but he was only lapping me up like that to annoy poor Ollie. What a twerp, though, honestly. And so rude! We shall have to do a bit better than that.'

Suzy filled the fading centre of her Butterfly Pink lips, tweaked a tissue from the lace box on the shelf and gave it a hard, passionless kiss.

'Ah well. Back to work.'

Work? Was it?

Ollie was suffering.

'So, Suzy. *Mam-zelle*. You seem very, very friendly with the head man here. This your usual table then? Are you on commission? They're all raking it in, Henry. That's how the system works, old boy. Isn't it, Suzy darling?'

'That's quite enough of that, Ollie old boy.'

'Well. Is she? Are you on commission, Suzy old girl?'

Suzy smiled as wide and as pretty as if Ollie were paying her a string of compliments. Henry looked on approvingly as she turned to face Ollie and said in her smartest, doggiest voice: 'Jerome used to work for Daddy.' *Deddy*. 'I've known him since I was a little girl.' *Gel*. She turned her head abruptly as if about to cry. Nice work. Margaret Leighton couldn't have done it better.

'Dance with me, Henry.'

Ollie hadn't realised. And kept on muttering about not having realised. Poor girl. Didn't realise. While Henry propelled Suzy round the dance floor in a sort of syncopated smooch. He could have Boston two-stepped very happily but the cha-cha was slightly beyond him.

Ollie knew he had to pounce. 'You're a very, very pretty girl, you know,' he cooed (just for a bloody change) and tried to grab Jane's hand. Jane kept a smile in place and looked around the room as if she were having the time of her life but she wasn't and there wasn't even a mirror to cheer her up.

A pint-sized redhead at the next table was being given the treatment by a slightly foreign-looking man in a tonic suit.

'You have beautiful hands, Monica.'

Which was a black lie. Monica was quite nice-looking in a Locarno sort of way but her hands were horrible little pink sausagey things. Nice curvy little figure, though – if it hadn't been squished into a tight Vilene puffball the colour of hospital teacups. Monica had obviously read somewhere that matching accessories were very smart so her beehive had a green bow on it plus green button earrings, green satin evening slippers and chipped nail varnish all in the same snotty rotten colour. She had pencilled her eyebrows all crooked which gave her a slightly roguish look. The spiv obviously thought so. He was holding one of those big, pink paws.

'They're lovely hands. You don't mind my saying that, do you, Monica?'

Of course she didn't but then poor, dozy little Monica didn't know what came next. He lowered his voice. Definitely foreign.

'And you've got a lovely figure.'

She wriggled and looked a bit coy.

'You shouldn't be shy about it, Monica. Having a beautiful body is nothing to be ashamed of. You don't mind me saying you've got a Lovely Figure, do you?'

Monica squirmed some more, loving it. All the hours in the mirror, all the busty gymslip years melting away in the heat of his compliments, but she was scared, too. Nobody had ever said things about her body before. 'Pretty dress' yes. 'Nice eyes' maybe, if she was lucky. But not her body.

'Because you have got a Lovely Figure, Monica.' He lowered his voice but Jane could still hear.

'You've got the Most Beautiful Breasts I've ever seen.'

Worked like a bloody charm. Even Jane was a bit excited but Monica went a very funny, dark pink colour that clashed horribly with the orange of her hair. Not just her face but her neck, throat and what could be seen of that beautiful cushiony cleavage. Monica was obviously horrified but you could see it was turning her on. It was all going according to plan. She might not come across that night but she'd get home, take off her green Vilene frock and suddenly everything would have changed. She'd look in the mirror and her body wouldn't be her own any more. She wouldn't be able to look at that fat, white bosom without thinking of him. He had already taken possession: moving in was just a matter of time.

Ollie was now asleep so Jane had to make do with the admiring eyes at nearby tables that kept straying from their own dates to check out the brunettes in the next booth. Which was all very nice but their admiration – no, *desire* was probably a better word – was all but cancelled out by the glum glances of the wives, girlfriends or paid help sat with them. It was one thing to make the effort – everyone made the effort but you were never really supposed to look like the picture on the packet. *Are you quite sure you want to be the best-dressed girl in the room? The men won't dare approach you and the other women will hate you.*

But there was one man staring more fixedly with a strange half smile on his face. He was stood at the bar and he was wearing a dark blue suit.

She could sit and be watched and hope he'd come over. Only he wouldn't. Not with bloody Ollie sat there snoring.

She got up and walked – the best, most beautiful catwalk – through the tables and up to the bar. Heavy velvet skirts tick-tocking over her slim little ankles, pretty French-pleated head held high. The barman (who was only twenty-one) practically fell over the counter leaning forward to catch her order. What could he get her? She smiled her sweetest smile.

'Do you know what I'd *really* like?'

It went all quiet. They knew what they'd like. And what they'd like her to like. Dirty buggers. Later that night in the bathroom mirror the barman – debonair, roguish, utterly confident – leaned further forward, raised one eyebrow (hours of practice) and replied, 'I think I know *exactly* what you'd like.'

But not now. Now he was too shy.

'Could. I. Have,' and she looked her man right in the eye as she said it, 'a Nice Cold Glass of Orange Squash?'

She climbed neatly on to one of the bar stools, crossed her legs (just so) and smiled shy and sidelong at the blue suit.

And he looked the same look. The same slow, sexy eyes mapping the length of her calves but everything was bigger, louder and better dressed, as if Streatham had just been a rehearsal for their big scene.

'Very pretty shoes. But can you dance in them?'

'You bet.'

It wasn't a jive this time; it was a rumba. And he could rumba. They didn't speak again until he had piloted her back to the bar, one hand on her waist.

'And?'

'And what?'

'What *is* a nice girl like you doing in a place like this?'

He looked around the room: the tarty girls and their 'businessmen' staggering off the dance floor in a cock-eyed conga; Ollie fast asleep; Henry warming his hand up Suzy's skirt.

Was he with anybody? She scanned the tables vaguely and spotted a large group of rather drunk but rather smart-looking people over in the corner. An unnaturally tall, long-legged showgirl in a lot of feathers was with them.

'I just came over to make a telephone call. I ought to introduce myself. My name's John Hullavington.'

'Great name. Your own?' What a good line that was.

'My very own. And you are?'

'Jane James. Really.' She nearly gave him the '*Do* call me Janey, everybody does' routine but she stopped herself in time. He wasn't everybody.

A blonde woman had broken away from the laughing group in the corner and was heading in their direction.

'Time for another dance, Miss James.'

Not a rumba this time. Much slower. The lights were lowered but Jane could see the woman hastily changing tack and making for the Ladies' instead, as if that was what she'd meant to do all the time. *It is not best behaviour to dash away and dance with some fascinating stranger who has caught your fancy.* Suzy was back on the dance floor with Henry and smiled approvingly, pointing to the table where Ollie was snoring in front of an empty champagne bottle. His fake teeth had slipped their moorings, making his face go a funny shape.

John's voice was warm and soft in her ear.

'I'm afraid your dancing partner isn't much use.'

'Oh. I wouldn't say that.'

Wide surprised eyes ringed with shiny pale blue. Like a dolly. As if they'd click shut if you pushed her over. She breathed in, pressing herself a shade closer and felt his arm snake tighter around her waist, his lips brushing against her neck. He smelled nice: expensive shaving soap and tobacco.

'Is this a slow foxtrot?'

'Certainly seems that way. Why?'

'Oh nothing.' She gave a careful little giggle. 'It's just that I can't do the slow foxtrot.'

'Could have fooled me.'

He held her still tighter and smoothly reversed them in the direction of the table where Henry and Suzy were back whispering sweet nothings to each other. Nuzzling and stuff like bunny rabbits. *Public intimacies between the sexes only render them absurd to other people.* Henry was much too old for that lark. He pulled away as they approached the table.

'There you are, Janey! I'm afraid old Ollie's a bit of a spent force this evening.'

Henry looked up at John, checking his barber and his tailor while he waited for an introduction.

'Henry, this is John Hullavington. John Hullavington: Henry Swan.'

'I'm afraid I should go back and join my party. I'll see you again, I hope? May I telephone you?'

Suzy gave him the number, the smart Langham exchange giving no inkling of the cracked old phone hanging on the wall in that cold, dirty corridor. John took a gold fountain pen from his inside pocket and wrote it down in a neat leather diary.

'Johnny, where *have* you been?'

The blonde had finally tracked him down. Citron yellow was definitely not her colour. She was furious and she was making a right mess of it. *Does he seem enraptured by another woman's company? Say nothing. Don't interrupt their tête-à-tête.* She should have stayed at the table and flirted like mad with one of the other men. Instead she was chasing him all over the club like she was his mother or something. There was only one more mistake to make and she went right ahead and made it.

'And who's your little friend? I didn't know they still did dancing partners here.'

Jane took yet another leaf from Suzy's book and decided to look hurt rather than put out. John smoothly introduced everybody.

'And I don't think you know Oliver Weaver? Ollie was at school with Charlie. How's Angela, Ollie?'

Ollie looked miserable and bewildered to be woken up by someone who knew the wife. The blonde dragged John away. Ollie began demanding the bill – asking nicely seemed beyond him. Jane and Suzy made a last visit to the powder room.

'That was fast work.' Suzy looked surprised, like Jane couldn't pull a fella without her help.

'I've met him before.'

'Rather a dish. I wonder if he'll ring? Not if the girlfriend has anything to do with it.'

At which point the blonde swung through the powder-room door with a friend. They could see her reflection in the mirror but she hadn't yet spotted them.

'Swine! Leaving me stranded with some feathered pervert while he was off dancing with that skinny little tart.'

'Oh don't be silly, Amanda. It was only a dance. You'd already said you didn't want to. And you are as good as engaged, aren't you?'

Maybe not. Not from the look on Amanda's face, anyway.

The skinny little tart and her friend got up and twirled critically in the mirror, checking for laddered stockings, stray curls. It was past midnight and the blonde – who was the wrong side of twenty-five – was looking a bit lived-in. It would have been fine if the evening had been going well but misery can do terrible things to the face: pouches of disappointment round the mouth, tramlines between the eyes. You might wake up one morning married to a face like that but not if you'd seen it coming.

Gushing goodbyes from Jerome at the door and then back into the car. Ollie got in the back with Jane this time. They were dropping him off in St James's first but he was determined to get full value for the five-minute drive down Regent Street. He had an arm round Jane's waist and a hand on her knee and his tongue in her ear, telling her what a very, very, *very* pretty girl she was. His hair had a stuffy, old-man smell, bay rum or something. His hand was fumbling its way up her nylons just as Henry stopped smoothly in front of Ollie's flat. *Tell him you had a lovely evening (don't thank him; he thanks you).* A dirty, wet goodbye kiss and it was over but she could still taste his spit on her lips.

When they got back to the flat Henry turned the corner into the mews beside the block and parked under the lamp post. Suzy took the bunch of keys from her evening bag while Henry nipped round to let Jane out.

'You run on up, Janey darling. Henry and I need to have a little chat.'

Jane turned to wave goodnight to them from the steps and Henry's hand was already under Suzy's navy-blue grosgrain like a rat up a drainpipe, inching above the stocking to where her knickers ought to have been.

The flat was freezing but it was far too cold to get into bed. She found a red rubber hot-water bottle hanging up on the back of the kitchen door and put the kettle on for it. She got as far as taking her frock off but had to huddle back into Glenda's fake fur while she crouched over the gas fire in the sitting room. She was just warming up again when the phone went. It was gone One.

'Hello?'

'Jane?' A deep, husky, slightly sleepy voice. 'Were you asleep?'

'No. I only just got back. I half got ready for bed but it's so *cold* I had to put my fur coat back on.'

Silence. She could just hear the noise of the club in the background. He must be calling from the booth in the lobby.

'Are you still there?'

'I'm sorry,' he sounded a trifle huskier, 'I just had a vision of you half undressed in your furs.' Another silence.

She looked across the corridor at the big gilded mirror: the strapless bra; the girdle and suspenders; the high satin shoes all framed by the silvery fur of the coat and lit by the street light outside. She thought of the fat girl and her wily little spiv.

She lowered her voice to a gravelly whisper.

'Did you?'

'Mmm.'

She caught her breath at the tone of his voice. Now she too would never be entirely alone in the mirror. She wedged the receiver into her neck and unhooked her bra, nipples brushing the chilly satin inside the coat. She could hear him breathing.

'I'll telephone tomorrow. Sweet dreams.'

'Yes.'

Chapter 11

> *Every girl, whatever her face, figure or finances, must put in the hours if she wants to keep and improve her looks.*

Suzy was already up and busy when Jane finally woke. Every heater in the place was switched on while she got to work on her weekly beauty routine: face masked in clay; legs and armpits plastered with smelly white cream; toes clamped apart with a little sponge thingy while the cherry-red nail varnish dried.

'Good morning, my darling. I can offer you black coffee, black tea or lobster bisque. Shall I run you a bath? The hair removing stuff's on the shelf in the kitchen.' (*Bristly calves are a cardinal sin.*)

Suzy was reading the *Sunday Times*.

'Blimey. Do you have a paper delivered?'

'Lord no. Annie fetches it for me along with the week's smalls. A girl's got to keep abreast otherwise you just sit there saying what a good band it is. Here. You can have half if you like.'

No scoutmasters here. It was all politics and foreign affairs. Algeria. Nigeria?

'It's what makes the difference between a squirrel jacket and a nice flat in Maida Vale' – or Curzon Street for that matter – 'the old "Your work must be fascinating" line can only get you so far. The wife talks about the children. The floosies tell him where they like to go dancing. You're the one who knows all about the book he's reading or what he should do on his business trip to Madrid. They love it. Two hours a week and they think you're

Marghanita Lasky. Henry takes the *Observer* so I get the other one.'

They had a busy morning making legs smooth, skin clear, nails shiny. And then another long, strange bath in the kitchen. Suzy had dashed down the freezing stairway to the lavatory when the phone began to ring. Jane wrapped herself in a grubby Japanese kimono that Glenda had left hanging on the back of the door and grabbed the receiver, remembering this time to put on a funny voice. She decided on Doreen's.

'Wot?'

The voice at the other end seemed taken aback.

'Oh. Hi. I'm sorry. I wanted to speak with Suzy. Suzy St John?'

'What you want and what you get are two different things, sunshine. I'm only the cleaner here. What floor's she on? She that big blonde number? Leopard coat? Bit boss-eyed?'

'No, no. Suzy St John. Nice-looking. Brunette. She's a model.'

'Well, they all say that, dear. You're not from round here, are you? You a Yank?'

'Nope. Canadian.'

The penny dropped. This must be the Dreaded Arnold.

'Walter Pidgeon was Canadian.'

'Excuse me?'

'Walter Pidgeon. Canadian. Married to Greer Garson.'

'I want to speak to Suzy Saint John.'

'Brunette? Skinny little thing? I know the one. No, the boss-eyed blonde's got her room now. She's gorn. Ong Kong. Went before Christmas.'

'Did she leave a forwarding add-ress?'

'I told you dear: Ong Kong.'

By now both of them were speaking slowly and loudly as if the other were very deaf and daft.

Suzy – still wearing just the bath towel – slipped back into the flat and gave Jane the thumbs-up sign.

'I can't be messed about writing down your messages all bleeding day. I've got my brass to do. Yes, on a Sunday. None of your business what days I work. Bloody cheek. You a vicar or summink?'

She replaced the receiver and joined Suzy in the kitchen where she was sitting up on the draining board rinsing the hair cream off her legs and armpits in the sink with an old pink face flannel. Jane thought for a minute that she'd actually done the washing up but Lorna wasn't going to get off that easily: the heap of cups and glasses and milk pans was now piled up on the floor in a big plastic bowl. Once Suzy had sponged off the last of the stuff she jumped down from the sink, sank into the bubble bath and began rubbing herself with a pumice stone – *Polish those elbows every week*.

'Mmmm. This could well be my last bath in the kitchen, Janey darling. Henry says he's found a Nice. Little. Flat.' She sponged her feet in time to this Happy. Little. Thought.

Jane kept her face in shape this time. She'd been thinking it over and had decided that a freezing cold fleapit behind Bourne and Hollingsworth shared with an Egyptologist's fancy woman was still better than life with Doreen. But Suzy was quick to remember last night's promise.

'You can come too if you like, Janey. You don't want to live in Norbury all your life. Henry says he'll run us over there on Monday lunchtime to have a look and see if I like it.' She was now soaping each leg with a great big yellow sponge she'd somehow managed to half-inch from a fancy chemist's in Piccadilly. The hairless leg was so smooth and shiny it looked like plastic. Like Barbie's bathtime. '*If* I like it he'll send one of his men round with a van in the afternoon to pick up our gear. We can leave all the hanging stuff on the rail. The rest is mostly shoes. You might as well have all Glenda's clobber. It'll all be out of date by the time she gets back from sunny Spain – if she ever does. There's some tea chests in Lorna's room. Now then. Do you fancy sharing my new flat with me?'

Be nice. Be very, very nice.

'I'd love to but I don't know if I could afford it . . .'

Suzy smiled a funny little smile.

'Don't worry, sweetie. That's all taken care of.'

Apparently the flat belonged to a business associate of Henry's who'd gone abroad for a year after his beautiful young wife was killed in a car crash. Only twenty-five. Two lovely little girls. Twins. Tragic. Hong Kong. And he didn't want it left unoccupied while he was away in case his sister-in-law moved in. Ghastly grasping woman. Ran one of those data processing places. Divorced.

'Why doesn't he rent it out?'

Suzy barely missed a beat.

'Oh, he reckons tenants are nothing but trouble. Cost you more in the long run. Dilapidations, all that. Rather lend it to friends. Anyway what do you say? I had such fun dressing you up yesterday and I'm sure the whole twin thing could work out. You'll have your own room. And your own bathroom.'

That clinched it. Doreen's bloodstained toothbrush. The death-wish boiler. The fuck-off-I-hate-you bath cubes. Or her own bathroom.

Suzy stood up in the bath and soaped the rest of herself. Nice figure. *It can't be denied that a superlative figure is top of the list for a beautiful woman.* Round tidy bosom, round tidy bum, nice neat waist in between. But it was no nicer than Jane's.

'What are your vital statistics?' wondered Jane.

'With or without?'

'With or without what?'

'Waspie, darling. You don't think anybody really has a 22-inch waist, do you?' *The foundation of all stylish dressing is a tiny waistline.*

'With, then.'

'34-22-35. And you?'

'The same. Only I haven't got a waspie.' Suzy stuck out her tongue. All right for Suzy with her Henries. A decent girdle cost fifty bob.

'Did Big Terry mean what he said about that photographer?'

'What? The twin thing? Could be a good gimmick. Have you ever actually done any modelling?'

'No. I did go to Trudi Morton once and they seemed quite interested but the woman just wanted to sell me a modelling course really and she kept asking me about my bust size.'

'Oh *her*.' Suzy pursed her lips and rubbed at her feet with the pumice stone.

'Did you ever do a course?'

'I did actually. Daddy won a fortune on a fifty-to-one outsider in the Two Thousand Guineas when I was sixteen and bought me six weeks with Mary Madison. I bunked off most of it but it knocked me into shape. And their agency isn't bad. Teaches you which jobs to say no to at least. But I got sick of being rung up and pushed around. They always warn you against going freelance – nothing in it for them of course – but if you've got a few regulars and you know a couple of photographers you can just about make it pay. I'm doing wedding dresses at Green's tomorrow. You can come along if you like. We'll say you're my dresser.' Thank you, Suzy. Thank you so much.

The phone rang and Doreen answered it again.

'Wot? Oo? Woshy look like?'

'Well,' he drawled, 'the last time I spoke to her she was half undressed in a grey fur coat.'

'Oh. It's you.'

'Yep. Did you sleep well?'

She returned to the new sexy voice she'd found the night before, letting Glenda's kimono fall open and watching her pouting lips in the mirror.

'Yes,' she whispered.

He cleared his throat.

'Do you like Italian food?'

Doreen didn't like Italian food. She'd not actually had any but there were some recipes in a *True Romance* magazine she'd seen down the doctor's, all mucked about and covered in sauce. She didn't like the idea of it although she did make an exception for tinned spaghetti because it made a nice change from baked beans. She didn't like Indian food either. Not only did she hate the smell – there was a curry house in the high street and she would make a point of crossing the road rather than walking past it – she didn't like rice. Not one bit. Uncle George and Jane had a little game in which the winner was the first person to get Doreen to say 'I don't like rice'. Jane would say something like:

'Joy says they're having risotto for lunch today.'

'Wossat?'

'Some Italian thing: bits of chicken cooked with mushrooms. And Rice.' It was murder keeping a straight face.

And, right on cue, Doreen would wrinkle her nose and shake her head and say the magic words. You got double points if she followed it up with 'never have liked rice'. Jane had been ahead for months until Uncle George invented a Chinese bloke at work who brought in his own lunch. Kenneth and June didn't even know they were playing – they never listened to Doreen anyway.

'Well. Do you?' persisted Johnny.

'Do I what?'

'Like Italian food?'

She couldn't very well say no.

'Mmm.'

'Well there's a nice little place down in Soho that's open for supper on Sundays. What do you say?'

Alarm bells rang loud in Jane's head. *When you meet someone nice it can be tempting to rush your fences. Resist.* Besides which, 'little place in Soho' sounded like the kind of dive Tony had in mind.

'This evening?'

'Not on your life!' A frantic whisper from the kitchen.

'I'm afraid I can't manage tonight.'

'How did I guess?' He sounded disappointed. Not just at not seeing her but as if he knew the rules too, and was sick of playing by them. 'What about tomorrow, then?'

Strictly speaking Monday was off-limits as well but she didn't want to risk waiting too long.

'Can we go dancing?' She tried to make her voice as velvety and seductive as his.

'Sure we can go dancing. I'll pick you up at eight. What's your address?'

She looked in panic at the bare floorboards of the hall, the stained and peeling wallpaper, the chipped yellowed paint. 'No, er, no. Don't do that. This will sound silly but we're moving tomorrow. It's Curzon Street somewhere but I don't know the exact address.'

'Curzon Street? Very smart.'

They agreed that he'd ring the flat on Monday evening after work and get the new address from Lorna. She wanted to stay talking but there was nothing else to say and she was starting to feel rather cold, standing there in her open kimono.

She was still leaning against the wall, half-naked, when Suzy emerged from the kitchen.

'Look at you! Was that lover-boy?'

'He's taking me out to dinner tomorrow night.'

Suzy always played by the rules. 'You should make them wait a bit longer than that, girl. Oh my God, you aren't going to let him pick you up here, are you?'

Suzy obviously didn't mind about how squalid the flat was so long as no one else saw it. She had already hatched plans to get the dress rail and packing cases down to the street so that Henry's man wouldn't need to see inside.

'Don't worry. He's going to call and get the new address. Failing that, I'm supposed to meet him at Isola Bella or somewhere.'

'Very nice. Do you like Italian?'

'I don't know. I know how you're supposed to eat spaghetti. Sort of. But I've never actually had any.' Oh God. The look on her face. Smug little bitch.

'Not to worry. We'll make some for you to practise with later on.' Suzy sat on the edge of the wonky sofa and began rubbing Nulon into her toes – *Minutes invested in foot care are minutes well spent*. 'Now then. Are you definitely moving to Curzon Street with me or not?'

'Definitely. Only goodness knows what my poor aunt will say.'

In fact she knew bloody well what Doreen would say. That Suzy was a jumped-up little tart setting herself up as mistress to some dirty old man cheating on his wife. Fortunately no one else could hear Doreen.

'Why don't you go and tell your aunt all about it over Sunday lunch and pick up whatever you need?'

Suzy probably imagined Sunday lunch as a roast. Bone china. Two kinds of potatoes. Gravy boat. Custard. Napkin rings. Not tinned red salmon and dried peas.

'Have you got a lot of clobber?'

'Not much worth bringing. A couple of quite nice skirts and twinsets and a few papers and things, I suppose.' Quite a lot of papers actually.

Chapter 12

*Anger, spite and bad nerves are the
sworn enemies of a pretty face.*

Next thing Jane knew she was at the bus stop at Oxford Circus
rigged out in a rather smart black and red reversible swing coat
– three-quarter-length sleeves, Persian lamb collar. Suzy had also
lent her a matching toque, long black kid gloves and a pair of
black patent-leather kinky boots. The effect was slightly spoiled
by the huge canvas holdall that Suzy used to cart her things to
modelling jobs. She'd just missed a bus but her wait was rewarded
with a few passing wolf whistles (*to suddenly find yourself whistle-
worthy is a wonderful moment*) and a lost American tourist who
was trying to find his way back to the Ritz and hadn't they met at
the New York Athletic Club and was she free for lunch?

The bus flew through the empty Sunday streets and within
the hour Jane was walking along Pamfield Avenue wondering
what she was going to say to Doreen. Mrs Grant from next door
was out walking her matted little dog (she called it a springer
spaniel but there was a lot more to it than that). Mrs Grant gave
Jane a very funny look. When she got to number sixty-three, she
realised why.

All her clothes, all her shoes, all her books, her poodle-
patterned rug and her foreign dolly collection were in a great
big heap in the front garden. Propped up against the house wall
(in case it rained) was a manila envelope untidily stuffed with
birth certificate, post office savings book, the dog-eared photos
of her mother and all her National Insurance gubbins. Inside it

lurked another, smaller envelope where she had hidden the cards for poor Mary Jane Deeks who hadn't lived to see her sixteenth birthday but got a National Insurance number anyway.

On top of the lot was Jane's red leatherette overnight case. Uncle George had bought this for her for Christmas. He knew she'd always wanted one. Doreen had gone completely spare. Overnight case! Overnight where? Stuck-up cow. Doreen hated the natty red suitcase with its pink moiré silk lining, its frilly inside pocket, its elasticated loops for dinky little bottles of shampoo and face cream. The whole world of friends and parties and spare bedrooms and weekends away and travelling alarm clocks and baby-doll pyjamas conjured up by that ducky little bag made sad, fat, old Doreen quiver with envy and rage.

Jane rapped the knocker good and loud – Doreen's moods didn't matter any more. June opened the door the four inches allowed by the security chain. Doreen had got George to put this on after a man selling vacuum cleaners had managed to get his foot in the door and given her the full sales pitch and his entire war record before she could get rid of him.

June had a very serious face on but she was obviously thrilled to bits at all the drama.

'Auntie says you're not to be let in.'

'I don't want to come in.' She said it loud enough to be heard in the kitchen. She jerked her head at the heap of her possessions. 'What's all this in aid of?'

'You weren't at Joy's house last night at all. Joy phoned here this morning wanting you to go round. Auntie says you're a Dirty Little Stop-out and I'm to have your room.'

'I wouldn't hold your breath. She's not your mother, remember. She'll give the big room to Ken or Georgette, you wait and see.' The upstairs curtains had all been taken down and you could hear the scrape of beds and wardrobes and the sound of Doreen shouting instructions as she carried out one of her big furniture shuffles. She didn't do any of the lifting herself (not with her

Trouble) but poor Uncle George and Kenneth would be made to 'see what it looks like over by the window', toddling wardrobes backwards and forwards while Doreen stood with her head on one side before deciding that she preferred it the way it was and tutting about dust as if one of them had put it there.

'Oh well. Want to give me a hand with this lot?'

'Don't you care? Aren't you *ashamed?*' June had been a patrol leader in the Guides which had done her no good at all.

'I stayed the night with this really nice girl I met. She's got a flat up in the West End and she's asked me to share with her. I've only come back for a few bits and pieces. She's got loads and loads of clothes and we're exactly the same size.'

Jane thought happily of that wonderful rail of frocks, and Glenda's shoes. Twenty-two pairs. She'd counted.

'Sounds like white slavery to me,' said June, cluelessly.

'Don't be *schew-pid*. Come on. Give me a hand.'

June slipped out into the garden while Jane fished through the heap for her cashmere sweaters and her nice tweed skirts and the summer frock with the blue poppies – although they did say next summer was going to be more gingham and polka dots. They all fitted neatly into the holdall. When she opened the overnight bag it gave off a lovely bedroomy smell of freesia-scented talcum powder (her Christmas present from June). She stuffed the big brown envelope into it then clicked it shut. She left everything else lying on the concrete. She hesitated for a moment over her precious books but she almost knew them by heart and anyway she didn't want Suzy bloody sneering at them.

'You can have the rest.'

June's eyes lit up: summer frocks, cheap shoes, a navy suit from Etam. Jane hadn't the heart to point out that none of it would fit until she lost a stone. Maybe she would now she'd got Gaylord Hauser's *Guide to Intelligent Reducing*. Doreen would love all the leftovers. She gave June the phone number of the flat. They'd be gone from there by Wednesday but maybe Lorna would pass on a message. She was at the gate when Doreen appeared on the doorstep. Jane did the best Paris turn she could manage and posed on the path, feet just so, gloved hand flared out from the body, chin prettily tilted. Very Bronwen Pugh.

'Hello, Auntie. I'm just off,' for all the world as if her entire wardrobe wasn't littered round the hydrangea bush.

'Don't you "Hello Auntie" me, you slag. Coming back here, done up like a dog's dinner.' She jerked her head disgustedly at Jane's beautiful red coat. '' 'E buy you that lot, did 'e?'

Jane switched back to her ultra-ritzy voice to wind Doreen up nice and tight.

'No, Auntie. My new friend Suzy lent them to me. I'm going to be sharing a flat with her from now on.'

'A likely story. Coming home Friday gone eight o'clock smelling like a four-ale bar. "Late customer" my eye. You must think I'm daft. Well, I won't stand for it.'

Net curtains were being twitched ecstatically on both sides of the street. You could hear the deaf old bitch opposite opening her casement window to hear better. Doreen didn't usually like people knowing her business but it was still quite nice to have an audience once in a while. She raised her voice.

'I've tried to bring you up right but I've got my own children to think of.'

Bang on cue Georgette began screaming. It wasn't real crying, just the wah-wah noise she made when no one was taking any notice of her.

'I can't have that poor mite growing up with a slut like you for a sister – *half* sister. Gawd knows what your poor mother would say.'

Doreen even had the cheek to look up at this point. As if her dead sister were peering out of the front bedroom window enjoying the show like one of the neighbours.

'My poor mother will know that I was staying with Suzy. Bye-bye, June. Ring me if you need me. Give my love to Ken and Uncle George.' Sod Georgette.

The two bags were very heavy but Jane managed to give the neighbours a nice little show as she walked off down the avenue, head high, while Doreen was screeching after her that she wouldn't be coming back. Bloody right she wouldn't.

She stopped for a rest once she was safely round the corner. Carrying a heavy bag in high-heeled fashion boots was no joke.

'Want a hand with that?'

Uncle George had abandoned the furniture-shifting and come to say goodbye properly, dashing out in his shirtsleeves with no collar on.

'I really was staying at this girl's flat, you know. I only said I was staying with Joy because if I said "Suzy" she'd want to know all the ins and outs. And she's a model. Auntie hates models.'

'Jumped-up clothes horses,' quoted Uncle George, smiling.

'And No Better Than They Should Be. But Suzy's really nice and she's asked if I want to share her flat.'

'Where is it?'

'Up round Oxford Street but she's moving to a new one tomorrow. Mayfair.'

Uncle George had always lived and worked south of the river. He hardly ever went into London but he knew (or thought he knew) how much rent you'd pay where. If Jane had said Pentonville Road or Northumberland Avenue he'd have been fine but this sudden advance to Mayfair worried him.

'Must earn a fair bit, then. For a model.'

Uncle George put his arm around her shoulder.

'You sure you know what you're doing? I know you want your independence but wouldn't you be better off sharing with a few of the girls from the arcade? You only met this Suzy yesterday. Why does she want you to share with her all of a sudden? You got a rent book?'

'Not exactly.'

'It doesn't sound right.'

Oh why couldn't he shut up? He was spoiling it. Doreen carping wouldn't matter. With Doreen it would just be envy. Jane was already young and pretty with smart clothes and an overnight case. But a nice friend? And a nice flat? Aunt Doreen didn't have any friends – nice or otherwise.

When Doreen was young she used to go about with her younger sister. Her social life dried up very suddenly when Jane's mother got married but it picked up again when the war started. Doreen quite enjoyed the war. She met Uncle George when she was working in the Naafi out at Ascot and for some reason he had asked her to marry him. Everyone was at it. One hundred and twenty thousand of them got divorced right after the war but not Doreen. Till death us do part, as she was bitterly fond of saying.

Doreen and her sister had grown up in Stepney (or Essex, as Doreen now preferred to call it). When Jane's mother first got married she and her shy-looking, black and white husband had moved in with his mother in Norbury. She wasn't an easy woman to live with but they didn't have to stand it for very long. She died one night during the Blitz (her heart, not the Germans). They found £500 in white fivers and a photograph of her late husband's brother sewn into her corsets.

Doreen had just got herself transferred to another job pouring tea at Croydon Airport and took the large back bedroom in the house in Norbury to give poor Gloria a hand with little Jane. Jane's father wasn't too thrilled but he was only on leave once in a blue moon and it was company for Gloria. When Doreen got married the following year George moved in too. The two couples jogged along together for two tetchy years before the Jameses died and Doreen moved her things into the front bedroom. By rights the house in Pamfield Avenue belonged to Jane and June but Doreen never told them that. That was the real reason why Mr and Mrs Deeks never got round to adopting their orphaned nieces. There might be questions, nosey parkers, forms to fill in.

It was also why Doreen kept her distance with the neighbours who'd all have remembered old Mrs James. She didn't want to be humped up with them anyway. Snobby lot. Washing milk bottles and polishing doorsteps. It was all just Swank.

Sixteen years since moving there she now knew all the neighbours' names and all their business but they weren't friends with her. Friends would have meant invited in for tea, shopping expeditions to Croydon, picnics with the children on the rec, trips to the pictures even. Doreen always said she didn't want to be bothered with all that – not that anyone ever asked her.

Doreen was much happier talking to complete strangers. She spoke to anyone and everyone, usually in queues for things: in the post office; in the self-service; at the bus stop. But the doctor's was her favourite. You had more time to get a monologue going. Dr McCartney's National Health patients weren't entitled to a proper appointment like the private ones. Instead they had to sit round the edge of the uncarpeted waiting room on Tuesdays and Thursdays, bumping their germs on to the next chair every time another person got their turn in the consulting room. Doreen would usually start with the weather (too hot; too cold; too bleeding wet) and then shift her complaint to London Transport, the Co-op; or Dr McCartney. Her victim would then chime in with the responses: 'Oh dear' or 'That's nice' (usually 'Oh dear'). If it was a woman – which it almost always was – she might move on to the birth of her children or even her hysterectomy but never, strangely, the two dead baby girls. Jane once got stuck next to some old dear in the doctor's (gall bladder and funny turns) – who'd obviously had the full Doreen treatment.

'Your aunt's had a very hard life.'

She knew all about Kenneth's adenoids, Uncle George's false teeth, June's athlete's foot but when Jane wondered aloud about what it must be like to have a baby and yet not keep it the woman looked mystified. It obviously wasn't in the authorised version.

Nor was Jane's scholarship. Or her poetry-reading certificates. Jealous, that's why.

Uncle George wasn't jealous. Uncle George knew about having friends. So why was he spoiling it about Suzy and the flat? What difference if it was Park Lane or Park Royal?

'It's all completely above board, honestly it is.' Was it? 'You'd really like Suzy. She's smashing. I'll give you a tinkle once we're straight and you can see for yourself.'

Mercifully there was a bus coming. The conductor, dazzled that such a taxi-looking woman should be waiting for a bus in Norbury, took the holdall from Uncle George and stowed it under the stairs. Like a porter. Jane waved goodbye – 'Goodbye, George' rather than 'Uncle George'. Not in that shirt.

She sat on the long seat by the entrance and put her overnight bag at her side. It exactly matched the red coat as if the whole outfit had come pinned to a card – like dolls' clothes.

She played up the part of a Persian lamb lady who wasn't quite sure how buses worked.

'Do you go anywhere near Oxford Circus?'

'Stop right there.'

'Super. How much is that?'

She counted the change out of her purse and her kidskin fingers held on to the ticket as if it were all a big novelty. She looked around the lower deck of the bus as it whizzed through Brixton and peered out at Big Ben, smiling excitedly at the three other passengers as if she were on a great big merry-go-round.

It was already getting dark and she was dreading the long, wobbly walk from the bus stop at the other end but what Doreen would have called a Well-Spoken Young Man stopped in Portland Place on his way to work at the BBC and offered to carry her bag and was she busy that evening? She wasn't sure. As far as she could tell there was only lobster bisque and stale Ryvitas in the cupboard.

She couldn't very well let him carry the bags up the stairs – though he did ask. She imagined his face at the sight of the flat. This nice clean Oxbridge boy with his brainy tweeds and college scarf.

Jane explained about the elderly aunt she was lodging with using a wealth of Suzy-style detail: arthritic; war widow; very old-fashioned. But she did let him have the telephone number. He might not be Mirador material but he'd be all right to practise on.

Chapter 13

The all-male gathering can be a hearty occasion. The female equivalent – a poached egg on toast listening to the wireless with a friend – is simply an evening wasted.

Suzy, now smoothed, plucked, varnished and moisturised, was tricked out in a rather natty weekend get-up: dogtooth-checked slacks and a black cashmere polo neck. She looked very pretty but much younger without her face on. She was lying on the three-legged sofa after a long day of self-improvement, reading a copy of *Queen* and smoking her way through a packet of Woodbines – she saved the good fags for going out.

'That was quick. Did she cut up rough?'

'No. Not at all. She helped me get all my things together.'

Suzy arched her body into a long, pin-up stretch.

'God, I'm starving! I've had nothing but black coffee and cheese footballs all day.'

'I know how you feel. I decided against staying for lunch. Auntie was just having something on a tray.' She pictured Doreen with a bit of smoked haddock and a glass of hock. 'I wish I'd said yes to the dinner date now.'

'Not on your life, darling. Kiss of death.'

Suzy had run out of coins for the meter and the flat was freezing again. Jane clunked her last two shillings into the slot and gingerly lit the gas before slipping reluctantly out of the red coat and hanging it up on the rail that Suzy had wheeled into the passage. The shoes had all been pegged into pairs and bundled into one of the three tea chests. The other two were full of cashmeres, underwear, handbags and hats. The whole arsenal of Suzy's charm. They had made the place look a tip but without all those glamorous things lying about, the flat was as dirty and sordid as Doreen's back kitchen.

'Well it's much too cold to stay indoors.' Suzy went through to the bedroom and started work on her face, blotting it out with a grubby little bottle of make-up base, then drawing the whole lot back on again. She scrabbled in an old tobacco tin for a matching pair of false eyelashes, pulled off the snotty strings of old gum, squeezed a skinny worm of glue on to each one from a tiny tube, and patted the lashes into place, beefed up with two coats of automatic mascara.

'Your turn.'

Jane slid into her place on the piano stool and Suzy repeated the whole process.

'Where are we off to then?'

'Well we can't stay here eating Twiglets. I was thinking we could treat ourselves to a sherry and nuts at Claridge's and see what develops.'

She helped Jane put the finishing touches to her face and gingerly ran the comb over last night's hair-do – when Big Terry pleated your hair, it stayed pleated.

Jane had her eye on a gorgeous fuchsia-pink corded velvet cocktail dress but Suzy knew better.

'Not on your own in Claridge's, darling. They'll take you for a tart and chuck you out. We'll have to pretend to be meeting someone to be let in the bar at all.'

Apparently unaccompanied Sunday night drinking in a West End hotel – always supposing they let you in, unchaperoned – called for smart tweeds. Not too mumsy but nothing to frighten the horses.

Jane was about to slip into her Hardy Amies when the phone rang.

'Oo? Oh you mean Mrs White's niece. Oo wants her?'

The posh voice stammered feebly.

'Er. It's Michael. Michael Woodrose.'

Jane covered the receiver with her hand.

'It's the man I met at the bus stop. He was rather sweet. Works at the BBC. He's about to finish his shift. Wants to know if I fancy some supper.' Supper sounded cheaper than dinner.

'Get him to take us both out for a Chinese,' stage-whispered Suzy. Claridge's was certainly smarter but might yield nothing on a Sunday night in January.

'Well. I'm meant to be going out for supper with my friend Suzy. Would you mind if I brought her along?'

Snookered. He couldn't very well say no it was nice to hear the disappointment in his voice. They arranged to meet at Ley-On in Wardour Street at eight.

'Can you work chopsticks?' Jane shook her head. 'Well there's time for the crash course before we head off. I think there are a few cornflakes left.'

Jane dashed into the icy kitchen, tipped some cornflakes into a curved saucepan lid – the single remaining clean thing in the cupboard – and found a pair of chopsticks in the dresser drawer (one said Ley-On, the other Lotus Garden). The next half hour was spent tweezing the stale yellow flakes out of their bowl and into the ashtray.

'It'll be easier tonight. The sauce glues the stuff together. You can always attack it with a fork if you get desperate – loads of people do – but it's much more impressive this way. They like it when you know all the tricks.'

They. The men who bought dinner.

'Do you ever go Dutch?'

'Go Dutch! Wash your mouth out! Look, darling. They've got a pretty girl on their arm and a kiss and a cuddle on the way home. Dinner's the least you should expect. Dutch! You are funny. So. What's he like, this conquest of yours?'

'Young. Private school.'

'Public school,' corrected Suzy. Snobby cow.

'Quite nice-looking. Tweedy.'

'Sounds all right. Sounds *virginal*. But it might be fun. Where does he live?'

'Not far. Round the back of the BBC somewhere, I think.'

The planned Claridge's get-up was switched for tight, low-cut black sweaters (Glenda had three of these) and full felt skirts. They didn't leave the flat till gone eight. The streets were deserted and apart from the odd thirty-watt twinkle from St Anthony's Chambers, there was no light from any of the surrounding buildings. Down in Oxford Street the fancy window dressing sulked unseen in the lightless displays. The taxi was surprised to find a fare at all – particularly one that only wanted to go four hundred yards but Suzy didn't really believe in walking. What was the point? You just arrived with sore feet and a red nose. The cab let them know you weren't a cheap date and with any luck Janey's tweedy little friend would pay for it anyway.

He hadn't much choice.

Chapter 14

> *The whole date through she will want to be treated like Someone – ideally Lady Someone. That means red carpet under every footstep, waiters on best behaviour, everything she wants before she realises she wants it because you, Dream Man, will anticipate her every whim.*

Michael Woodrose was wearing out the pavement outside Ley-On when they arrived. He looked really cheesed off at being expected to fork out for the taxi.

'Oh that *is* kind of you,' gushed Jane.

'I was afraid you weren't coming.' Idiot. Since when did a date arrive right on the dot?

He was almost handsome in a baby-faced sort of way, in his I-went-to-a-good-school uniform of tweed jacket, checked shirt and knitted red tie.

He had been slightly dreading the 'friend'. In his (limited) experience decent-looking girls usually had a fat, spotty companion with a Sloppy Joe pullover and a hairy mole. Suzy was a rather wonderful surprise. They both were. He led the way into the cavernous restaurant in a happy wet dream. Waiters, who normally snubbed him, seemed to jump to attention at the sight of Jane and Suzy and treated him with new respect – and envy. Michael Woodrose sat opposite the pair of them, gazing from one to the other in happy disbelief. The waiter buzzed round him annoyingly.

'Do you both like Chinese food? Or would you prefer something from the English menu?'

This was, in fact, a trick question. Michael was a terrible snob and always sneered delightedly at anyone who ordered plain roast chicken in an exotic restaurant, or ate their spaghetti with a knife and fork, or drank red wine with fish. It hadn't dawned on him that there was a parallel universe of prejudices in which he, with his tweeds and well-drilled chopsticks, would offend on numerous counts: drinking halves of bitter; wearing ties with pullovers; tipping exactly ten per cent; bathing only once a week; poncing about in a college scarf.

Suzy was enjoying herself.

'Whatever you say, Tiger.'

The waiter's face twitched very, very slightly while he wondered what this seven-stone weakling had to offer these two. *Tiger?* Did he take them both at once? In the waiter's hot and sour little mind a mental picture sprang up of some delicious English sandwich. He could barely concentrate on the order.

Michael Woodrose had been looking forward to ordering. A year in the pronunciation department had given him the basics of Cantonese inflection which he very much liked showing off. Even the normally poker-faced Chinese waiters found it hard not to laugh when he said 'chow mein'. But today's waiter wasn't amused.

'You give numbers. Numbers more quick.'

'Oh. I see,' sulked Michael, 'Well in that case we'd like three 12s, a 17, a 23, a 28, a 36, one 41 and three 62s.'

'Bingo!' exclaimed Jane.

Michael Woodrose thought that this was really a bit common but then maybe not. The other one was laughing out loud and she wasn't common at all. Very few fillings. By now he just wanted the waiter to go away so that he could concentrate on this amazing double vision of loveliness. Because they really were lovely. More paint than his mother would have liked but he didn't mind that. If anything, he was flattered that they'd made the effort. Big eyes – two brown, two blue – soft pink lips and surprisingly large breasts. Padded? He hoped not.

Michael thought about breasts quite a lot. Breasts. The very word made him grateful for the generous cut of his flannels. He had a little collection of artistic photographs back at the flat. And some not so artistic that he'd bought from a Maltese chap in Old Compton Street. He hadn't much experience of the real thing. A schoolfriend's fourteen-year-old sister – an early developer – had allowed thirty-second gropes (timed mercilessly with the second hand of her gold-plated Timex) in exchange for sherbet lemons and there had been grudging fumbles under chunky jerseys while he was at Oxford but he was – as Suzy had suspected – a virgin. He had no plans to remain one. Indeed, only last week he had been lured to an upstairs room in Wardour Street by the promise of a 'busty young model' only to scuttle back down on finding a desiccated old tart picking her teeth on a dirty candlewick bedspread. And now here he was with *two* busty young models. And the irony of course was that he only needed one. But which? He watched them both, pinching fastidiously at their chop suey.

They were really very alike. Suzy seemed the livelier of the two. She was asking him something about D. H. Lawrence – there had been an article in one of the Sundays and she had absorbed it very cleverly. Give her a few of the learned weeklies and you could probably introduce her to colleagues. He imagined their faces. Brian, this is Suzy. And those soft red lips would smile – a slightly pitying smile at Brian with his stained tie and his dandruff and his flat-chested girlfriend (a primary-school teacher from High Wycombe). And Suzy would read and digest *Encounter* and *Nation* and then quietly dazzle with a few smart remarks about the modern novel – not too smart, obviously – *Don't waste time trying to be 'smart' with a man.*

But of course the other one was rather lovely, too (if less chatty) and she did seem to have a narrower back. He imagined slipping that low-cut jumper off her shoulders and scooping one of those ripe young breasts from its black lace brassière (he had glimpsed the strap when she reached for a spring roll). He shifted into a more comfortable position.

'Or do you?' Suzy was saying.

'Or do I what? I'm sorry. I was miles away.'

Suzy flashed him an unguarded glance from under those fluffy nylon lashes as if she knew exactly where his dirty little mind had travelled to.

'Prefer blondes?'

What was the woman talking about?

'Er. No. No-no-no. Far, far from it.'

He toasted them ineptly with his half of lager. Suzy sipped at her pineapple juice, eyelashes working overtime. Then she tossed her head back and laughed, showing those pretty white teeth. It was the pose from the matchbook: the pose of a woman having the time of her life. Jane stored the move away for future reference and opted to lean forward and work the conspiratory giggles.

Jane didn't really like rice, she discovered. Not without jam on it, anyway. The food was all chopped up – God knew what meat was in it – and you ate it out of little blue and white sugar bowls. Michael appeared to be putting some kind of brown sauce on his but it tasted nothing like the normal kind. Jane was managing the chopsticks rather well – better than Michael actually – but the unfamiliar grip was giving her a pain in her hand.

The restaurant was quite full – not many places opened on a Sunday – and there were quite a lot of Chinese people which Michael seemed to think was a good sign although they'd probably eat any old rubbish. There was an English couple at the next table arguing half-heartedly about where to put the garden shed. She was all for putting it down at the end next to the dustbins with a bit of trellis in front. He wanted it bang next to the house (in case of bad weather). That was what marriage did to people. He was wrestling with a big plate of slippery fat noodles and she was eating roast chicken and chips and holding her knife like a pen.

Shed Woman was wearing home-made tan crêpe with powder-blue piping and she kept checking the banquette beside her to make sure her bag was safe. Nasty plastic thing. Navy blue. Didn't go with the dress at all. She looked sidelong and sulky at Jane's larky little get-up. She probably had a 22-inch waist when she got married.

Jane carried on pecking at the meat – chicken? She hoped so. And giggled obligingly at Michael who was boring on about some book he'd been reading. *Never let him know you're bored!* He might be all right for humping suitcases but he was a bit of a wash-out conversationally. It was all very highbrow. Disarmament. Cyprus. But there was nothing intellectual about the way he stared at her bust. Suzy was marvellous, playing with him, pretending to know all about it – or maybe she did know all about it? Maybe it was in the *Sunday Times*. Seemed a bit daft, really, just sitting there quoting the newspapers at each other.

Would they like to go to a jazz club later? And wasn't Kenneth Tynan right about jazz being a post-mortem on a dissected melody? Tosser. Did she look like a girl who read Kenneth fucking Tynan? Of course she bloody didn't. She looked like a girl who read *True Romance* and *Romeo*. So what was all that nonsense about? He was either taking the mick – which, given those hungry green eyes glued to the tilt of her bust, seemed unlikely – or he thought she'd be impressed.

Film their table and frame by frame Jane and Suzy would seem to be having the time of their lives, like an ad for king-size cigarettes. Envious glances flashed across the room: some, like the waiter, trying to work out how this chinless wonder had managed to swing such a five-star double date, others just wondering why their evening wasn't turning out that well.

An old bloke at the corner table by the window was staring at them while his chopsticked hand ferried rice from his bowl to his moustache. Jane batted her eyelashes some more. The nylon filaments were strange and scratchy against her eyelids.

The old bloke by the window was actually Michael Woodrose's boss from the department. He could only see the back of Woodrose's tweed jacket but he could see both girls: young, laughing, confiding, teasing, hanging on Woodrose's every word. He'd never thought of Woodrose as a ladykiller. False hope dawned. Maybe they were his sisters? No, he remembered now. Woodrose had brought his sister into the office once. Joyce? Jenny? Geraldine? Jill. That was it: wan little blonde in horn-rims and very pronounced views on pronunciation. Only she pronounced it *pronounciation*. Amazing how many people did that.

What could Woodrose possibly be saying that entertained them so thoroughly? The last 'conversation' his boss had had with him was a Woodrose monologue on the theatre of the absurd. Woodrose had just discovered Beckett at the Royal Court and would bore anyone who would listen with the ins and outs of Beckett and Ionesco. Parker, the other junior assistant, told him exactly where he could stick it but the department secretary had let herself get cornered for a good ten minutes while Woodrose showed off his new knowledge – most of it stolen from an article in some egg-headed weekly. She wasn't rescued until the *Brain of Britain* producer had rung to check the pronunciation of Ottoline Morrell. Philistine. Michael's boss sneaked another look at the table. Woodrose could hardly be regaling these lovely young things with N.F. Simpson's greatest hits. They didn't look like the women who went to the Royal Court. Far too clean for a start.

*   *   *

Finally, after what seemed like days of self-glorifying claptrap, the waiter brought the bill and Michael spent an embarrassing few minutes checking the maths. Jane reckoned that if you weren't one of those people who could add up columns of figures in their head – like Uncle George – you should just pay whatever it said. They'd probably done most of the cheating when they priced the bloody menu in the first place – it was only a few scraps and some rice, after all, not a proper dinner. Woodrose had obviously undertipped the waiter and they had to wait for their coats which he then fumbled them into before they walked out into the night. Where next?

'Are you going to take us dancing, Mr Woodrose?'

He winced like a salted slug.

Michael Woodrose couldn't dance. His mother had insisted on lessons after watching him sneering on the sidelines of a birthday party when he was thirteen. Spotty, boring but peculiarly arrogant, the teenage Michael's only interests were wanking and the wireless.

He was not a hit with the (mostly female) dancing class. They complained about his sweaty hands, his big feet, the way he stared dumbly at their cardiganed chests. Mummy relented and he was too vain and proud to try again. Which meant that dances – the one time you were actually licensed to grope girls – were terrible ordeals spent loafing on the touchline with half a pint of bitter trying to talk smart while better men foxtrotted their way over the stocking tops.

'I don't dance.' He used to practise saying it in the mirror: world-weary, a little contemptuous, a tiny bit reproachful – how could they talk of dancing with so much sadness and uncertainty in the world? It never had cut much ice and Jane and Suzy were no different. Jane knew he'd say no to dancing. He just wasn't the type.

He took a deep breath. Would they like to come back to his flat for a nightcap?

'Your flat?' Suzy was surprised – and impressed. He looked more like the type that lived at home.

'It belongs to my uncle but he's down in Sussex most of the time.'

Michael's 'uncle in Sussex' was a bit like Jane's 'aunt in Surrey'. Uncle Jack ran a chain of gents' outfitters in the Bexhill area but there was no need to dwell on that. Gents took a lot of fitting out in the Bexhill area and Uncle Jack had spent much of the proceeds on a West End bolt hole where he could entertain willing young boys without endangering trade. He popped up about once a fortnight and Michael would doss down on a friend's sofa or go home to his mother's in Sevenoaks until the coast was clear.

'I've got some whisky . . . and I think there's some crème de menthe' (Uncle Jack's younger friends liked a drop of crème de menthe).

Jane didn't especially want to go back to their freezing cold flat but she wasn't too sure about the nightcap at his place either. What for?

'There's a taxi,' said Suzy. It wasn't a statement; it was an order.

'I've got the car,' trumped Michael, happily. The girls purred with surprise. He didn't look much like a driver – but then it didn't look much of a car. Uncle Jack's finances had been stretched buying the flat, let alone the runabout to go with it, so he'd settled for a smart new Ford. He'd wanted red but red was Export Only for some peculiar reason – why? It was only paint, for God's sake – so he settled for black with snazzy red seats.

'Ooh!' squeaked Suzy. 'I've driven one of these. My uncle used to have one.' Uncle. Like hell.

Woodrose became very panicky and started muttering about third party and no syncromesh.

'What makes you think I can't double declutch? Cheek. Daddy taught me. I can double declutch in my sleep – often do as a matter of fact.'

He was really panicking now but Suzy was already behind the wheel – first time she'd opened a car door for herself since she left school.

'Have you passed your test?'

'Oh don't be such an old woman, Mikey.'

Had she passed her test? Unlikely. She might be all right with double declutching but she used far too much choke and her steering was terrifying. She blithely shot a red light crossing Oxford Street. Suzy carried on regardless, squealing with excitement, fag stuck jauntily between her smiling red lips. Her skirt had ridden high above her knees but Michael Woodrose was past caring. There was a horrible knot of fear in his stomach, a nasty, queasy feeling that dredged up blushing memories of long-forgotten boyhood crimes. Uncle Jack's Ford Consul might not be much of a car but every Sunday he was in London he would be out with a chamois leather polishing the chrome trim, waxing the bodywork. One of his young friends had been sick in it once – having discovered (a bit late in the day) that red biddy and blue curaçao didn't really mix. Uncle Jack had blown a fuse, obsessively rinsing and wiping the floor and clearing out all the crevices in the map pocket with an old toothbrush. God knew what he'd do if anyone scratched the paintwork.

'This is it, on the corner.'

Suzy braked very abruptly, and stalled to a stop outside the mansion block, thoroughly exhilarated by her little spin.

'That was *fab*, darling, I must get a car. How much are cars, darling?'

You could practically hear the tumblers working in that little tart's brain of hers. Would the generous Mr Swan be good for a car as well as a flat?

'I do wish we had a car. Maybe we should see about getting one. Can you drive, Janey?'

She thought of Uncle George teaching her to drive round the block in his old Austin.

'Yes, actually.'

Well, if you called that driving she could bloody drive.

Michael Woodrose was back to normal now, able to appreciate Suzy's stocking tops. Had she worn panties this evening? Jane wondered. Probably. It was a cheap Chinese, not a Mayfair flat after all.

Uncle Jack's flat wasn't too bad so long as Uncle Jack wasn't actually in it. The old boy gave the place a rather snacky smell of pipe tobacco and hair oil and suits that were pressed but never cleaned but he hadn't been up to town for nearly three weeks (up to his eyes in the January stock-take) and the whiff was starting to fade.

The phone was ringing as they came in.

'No, Mr Woodrose is away. No. No. I'm his nephew. No. No, honestly. I really *am* his nephew.'

The girls sat at each end of the chesterfield while Michael poured two very large crème de menthes and a small whisky. He remembered now that you were supposed to get them to talk about themselves. They liked that, apparently.

'So, er, what sort of modelling do you do?'

'Lingerie mostly,' lied Suzy.

This was just to get him at it, of course. She was breathing oddly so that her bust rose and fell.

'We do quite a lot of double shots. One of us in the long line, the other in the strapless. We're both sample size, you see. Both E cups.'

Michael had gone the colour of his tie.

'And I do quite a bit of photographic work for lipsticks. Just my lips. Showing all the different colours.'

Jane couldn't see her face down at the far end of the sofa but she could hear her backcombing her voice into the full Joan Greenwood, could practically hear her lips pouting for his kiss. He made a disgusting noise doing it. Like someone eating.

'Don't you think you ought to kiss poor Janey as well? Fair's fair.'

Oh God. Still bright red and starting to sweat unpleasantly he turned to Jane and began kissing her. It was horrible. He hadn't a clue what he was doing and his tongue kept flicking around the inside of her lips as if he'd lost something. He tasted of beer and whisky and that Chinese brown sauce but there was something else: the fresh, Polo-mint tang of Suzy's liqueur mixed with the oily fragrance of her lipstick. That was quite nice. Jane hadn't kissed that many boys – a few fumbles at the Locarno was about it. She'd had more practice with the back of her own hand. Suzy was probably a really good kisser so, although Jane didn't fancy this berk in the slightest, she still wanted him to think she was sexy. Just as sexy as Suzy and so she kissed back, arching herself against him slightly, hoping to goodness he'd keep his hands to himself.

He was planning on one more kiss each – to get them both going – and then he would mould his hand around the outline of one of those firm young E cups. Then who knows what might happen? Was the bed made?

'It's been a super evening.' Liar. Suzy had stood up and was checking her hair in the mirror over the fireplace. Thank God for that. He'd had his hot wet hand on Jane's waist and you could practically smell his next move.

'Yes, it was really delicious.' Jane stood up too, leaving poor Michael Woodrose sat forlornly on the sofa wishing he'd made a grab earlier. Once you got them really worked up, they lost their inhibitions. He should have bought them wine at the restaurant. Fifteen bob a bottle was exorbitant but it would have been worth it. As it was, he'd have to work it off with his little photograph collection. Not the artistic ones this evening, he felt.

He hoped they'd just leave but Suzy stood there in her coat, expectantly. Surely they didn't think he was going to drive them home? Of course they bloody did. It was only down the road, for

God's sake, and there were two of them. Selfish bitches. He'd have lost the urge by the time he got back. Glumly, he put on his coat.

'It's *so* kind of you to give us a lift.'

Michael Woodrose was hoping for a quick grope across the long front seat but Suzy put the tin hat on that by sliding into the back with Jane.

'Home, James. And put the heater on, can't you? It's freezing in here.'

Only there wasn't a heater. Uncle Jack had struggled to find the six hundred and sixty quid to buy the car in the first place, let alone unnecessary luxuries like radios and leather seats and heaters.

Suzy had decided against goodbye kisses. What kind of cheapskate ran a car with no heater in it?

'Cheerio, darling. Dinner was scrummy.' And she and Jane slipped from the car without even waiting for him to whizz round and open the door for them – not that he showed much sign of wanting to do this – and they were on the doorstep and in before he had a chance to ask for another date.

Chapter 15

> *Every woman who isn't downright*
> *deformed can approximate the*
> *harmony that will pass for beauty.*

The lights were on when they got upstairs. Lorna, still in her coat, was slumped in front of the gas fire smoking Senior Service through a silly jewelled holder Suzy had left by the phone and sipping unhappily at a toothglass of neat gin. There was a new half bottle of Gilbey's and a fresh pile of shillings on the mantelpiece. Brighton had not been a success.

Lorna was really quite pretty (for a redhead) but she obviously wasn't the glamour type: patch-pocketed tweed skirt; Viyella blouse; hairslide. Suzy had once persuaded her to let her do her make-up. Big Terry had put all that ginger hair into a wormy fat mound on top of her head and Glenda had lent her a frock – green strapless taffeta. She didn't look half bad but Lorna thought she looked like a tart and said so and the Egyptologist was so unnerved by this sudden nasty rash of glamour that he couldn't get it up until she'd washed her face and stripped down to her knickers (navy-blue school leftovers).

That was months ago and the professor had obviously not been having too much trouble in that direction because Lorna was now three weeks late and had spent the weekend in the hotel room either crying her eyes out or being enthusiastically comforted by lover boy, who had decided to take full advantage of the fact that there would be no need to withdraw.

Lorna had always known he would never divorce Aileen – charming woman, apparently, head of modern languages at a girls' grammar school in St Albans – but she didn't ever want to have it proved conclusively. He hadn't even mentioned the possibility of divorce, just fretted uselessly about how One went about arranging, ahem, Such Things and wondering if any of his colleagues had any idea what One did in these situations – and whether he could trust them to keep the whole Sordid Business to themselves.

'It might affect his chances of promotion, apparently. Selfish pig. It didn't occur to him that I might actually want to keep the rotten thing.'

The careful curve of Suzy's eyebrows jumped nearly to her hairline.

'Of course it didn't, you dozy cow. What would you want with a baby, for Christ's sake? They'd only make you have it adopted anyway. Imagine your mother with a bastard grandchild.'

This hit home. Suzy had only met Lorna's mother once. She'd worn flat shoes specially. They hadn't dared show her Suzy's flat: they'd shown her round the one downstairs that belonged to a sweet old queen who worked in a wallpaper showroom in the next street. It was very nicely decorated – him being in the trade – but Mrs Lorna was still appalled by the idea of a lavatory on the half landing. Couldn't understand why the darling daughter couldn't travel in from Haywards Heath every day. Plenty of people did. Gaynor Charlesworth took the train to the P & O office every morning. What would people think?

People would probably think that poor Lorna was better off out of it: finally free of Mummy and her doilies and her musical doorbells and her koi carp and her vols au vents and her hostess aprons and the ludicrous bright brown nylon wig she wore to the shops on Wednesdays and Thursdays while she was holding on for Friday's shampoo and set.

There was a Mr Lorna, back in Haywards Heath, but he hadn't featured in the whole no-daughter-of-mine nonsense when Lorna had first moved into the flat and Suzy had never met him. Mr Lorna worked late whenever he possibly could and spent summer evenings and weekends in the greenhouse, faffing about cross-pollinating fuchsias and potting up dahlias or mixing composts in the nice warm shed he had built (at the very far end of the garden behind some trellis, as far away from Mrs Lorna as possible). There was a primus stove, an old armchair and, slid down between its sagging seat cushions, a small collection of rather dirty, dirty magazines. Not *Playboy* or anything like that. They were too clean. Too wholesome. Like a prettier, nuder version of the girl he'd married. No. Something grottier, and slightly hairier was more his cup of tea. Ginger if at all possible. It was finding one such grubby little photo in her father's stash of reading matter that had made up Lorna's mind to leave home.

She had stopped crying now but she hadn't cheered up. Suzy poured her glass of gin down the sink, rinsed out a cup and made her some black tea. Lorna thanked her, ruefully wiping a half kiss of old lipstick off the rim of the teacup with her thumb.

'Have you still not washed up?'

'Not on your nellie. That's your department. You can hardly get into the kitchen for mouldy plates. What must poor Janey think?'

Lorna smiled wanly at Jane.

'Sorry about this. Are you moving in?'

Suzy looked slightly uncomfortable.

'Well, yes. Moving *out* is nearer the mark, Lorna-my-darling, as you can probably tell from all the tea chests. The ever-obliging Mr Swan has a friend with a flat lying empty in Curzon Street who's looking for two house-trained females to mind it for him and so Janey and I are moving in. Probably tomorrow. Janey's boyfriend was at school with Henry's kid brother, you see. Don't worry about the rent. I'm paid through to Easter and you're bound to find someone by then.'

The lies rattled past Lorna who sat, nursing her cold, bitter tea, glummer still at the thought of being left alone in the flat.

Suzy read her mind and immediately tried to sell her the idea of flat-sharing with some of the girls from the department. Surely they'd be queuing up? Only round the corner. Dirt cheap. Whether they would or not, Lorna was more worried about the next few weeks.

'Will he leave the wife?' Suzy only really asked out of politeness.

'No. Didn't even come up.' Lorna's tears streamed soundlessly down her face and into her cup.

Suzy might have made tea but there was no sympathy. Married men didn't leave their wives and even if they did leave their wives (which they didn't) they didn't leave them for pregnant girlfriends with stubbly armpits. No chance of granny minding baby back in Haywards bloody Heath. No sense going through all that ugliness and agony just to save some other bitch the trouble. Which left Dr Tom.

Dr Tom couldn't be telephoned. You had to put an ad in the evening paper and then he rang you. Suzy chatted on matter-of-factly about how long it all took and how Lorna could probably come and stay at the new flat for a couple of days – there was a tiny maid's room up in the roof of the block, Henry said. And while Suzy was speaking Lorna's face dried and hardened and she drained her cup and went to her bedroom without saying goodnight.

'Mmm,' wondered Suzy, 'I get the feeling Lorna's going to make her own arrangements. Silly cow. Do you *like* babies, Janey?'

Jane summoned up a picture of wailing, wet Georgette, bib crusty with crumbled rusks, face sticky with rosehip syrup, angry pink bum stuck in an envelope of smelly grey towelling.

When Georgette wasn't in her high chair she was in her pram, a creaking pre-war wickerwork number, and left in the garden 'to exercise her lungs' or left outside the Spar for a bit more such exercise. Doreen preferred the Co-op really but the Spar gave Green Shield Stamps and Doreen was saving up for one of the clocks in the catalogue.

Doreen had raised Kenneth on strict Truby King lines: four-hourly feeds; no sweets; regular habits and now look: a spotty berk who collected bus numbers. Doreen had thrown her Truby King book away, thinking she'd done with all that, and so Georgette had no regular habits at all – unless you counted crying and shitting.

The Croydon area health visitor was very keen on routine. So much so that she always made her calls on the second Thursday of the month at eleven in the morning, enabling Doreen to regularly meet her at the front door in her hat and coat on her way out for some 'pure fresh air' for baby's little walk (actually Doreen's little walk to post Doreen's little pools coupon). The woman – interfering stuck-up bitch – would then have to struggle to do the weighing in the front passage and mutter something about 'baby's routine' and she'd be back on her bike.

Did Jane like babies? No she bloody didn't. Yet Carol and Eileen could hardly wait. Carol had actually tried knitting a bonnet and matching bootees. Ideal if it turned out to have a club foot . . .

'My mother was only nineteen when she had me.'

'Same here, darling, but that doesn't make it right.' Suzy's mother was dead, so she said. There was a picture of her (was it her?) on the grotty makeshift dressing table wearing Molyneux and gazing poshly into space. 'Poor old Lorna.'

Suzy seemed to have washed Lorna from her mind: she'd offered to help the only way she knew how but if Lorna wanted to ruin her career, her figure and her life with a screaming brat, that was her funeral.

'Up early tomorrow, darling. I'm showing evening and bridal at Green's Gowns. Nine sharp. Henry said he'd meet us at

Fortnum's at half one and take us to look at my nice little flat. I'll need the blue holdall for work but there should be room for your stuff in one of the tea chests.'

She frowned critically at the smoke-stained wallpaper, at the cobwebby cornice and the threadbare orange and brown chenille curtains as if noticing them for the first time.

'This time tomorrow, Janey darling! Aren't you excited?'

She looked at Jane's face but it had been switched off. Jane quickly pulled herself together.

'This is so kind of you.' Would that do? Probably. Suzy was picturing her new life.

'This time tomorrow, darling. Central heating; wall-to-wall carpet; fitted wardrobes and big, fat king-sized bed. Each.'

She'd only been between the starchy new king-size sheets a couple of minutes when the telephone rang.

'Were you in bed?'

'Mmm.'

'Asleep?'

'I can't seem to get to sleep.'

'Me neither.'

She tried to imagine him, stretched out on one of those big dimply leather settee things, a balloon of brandy in his other hand. She pictured his lips whispering into the receiver.

'I've got the car again tomorrow.' Not his car then. 'There's a nice place on the river.'

'Dancing?'

'Dancing.'

'Sounds super.' Super.

'Sweet dreams.'

Chapter 16

> *Most men are on the lookout for a*
> *bargain and like to see a sizeable return*
> *in gratitude for a very small outlay.*

It was a dogtooth check sort of day. The weather had turned milder and the pair of them hit the sunny street at a quarter to nine: eyelashed; powdered and tricked out in sixty guineas' worth of novelty tweed suiting. The hair was still holding up reasonably well after a quick tickle with the comb and a burst of lacquer. Suzy had the crocodile bag neatly tucked into the crook of her arm.

The pair of them catwalked round the corner to Green Gowns, a thriving wedding and after-six business in Great Portland Street. Unusually for a rag-trade showroom, there was a large window display: a huge fashion drawing of a skinny, supercilious brunette in a sheath of nasturtium silk and the actual dress itself, thrown elegantly across a gilded show chair with a sign saying 'one of last season's creations' (you didn't want rivals nicking any of your new ideas). Mr Green always reckoned that buyers were just like anybody else: they might have an appointment elsewhere but you never knew who might be walking past or what might catch their eye.

The showroom was on the ground floor. The office was on the first and the upper storeys were packed with machinists French-seaming their way through mile after mile of organza, dupion, paper taffeta, duchesse satin, silk damask. Not to mention the Tricel, Vilene, Rayon and Banlon required by the budget lines and Junior Dream collection. The basement stockroom was forested with great bolts of material and huge dress boxes ready to receive the finished gowns that travelled down in a creaking old goods lift.

Suzy gave Jane a final once-over as they rang the bell and smiled smugly at the pretty picture she had made.

'You'll do, darling.' Thanks a bunch. 'Walk your best walk and he'll snap you up.'

Jane sashayed into the showroom which was still extra chilly after a whole weekend without heating. It smelled expensively of hothouse lilies and floor wax. Jane's tidy suede toes crossed the floor, then did a half turn towards the waiting Mr Green. He smelled nice and expensive too. He wore a single-breasted blue Savile Row suit and Turnbull and Asser shirt and tie. His cufflinks were plain yellow gold knots. Every detail beyond reproach. Like a spy. His (actually rather sexy) brown eyes followed Jane closely.

'This is my cousin Janey. She's going to give me a hand getting dressed, if that's all right. Janey James: Lawrence Green.'

He took her hand and came straight to the point. Suzy wouldn't have brought her in unless there was a reason.

'Ever done any modelling, Miss James?'

'Do call me Janey, everybody does. I've only done a little modelling, I'm afraid.' She smiled shyly and slyly at him from under her heavy, brown-black automatic eyelashes. 'Why do you ask?' As if they didn't both know.

'Lots of gowns to show this morning, Miss James, lots of gowns. Tell you what, the first client won't be here for half an hour. Why don't you slip one on for me right now and show me what you can do. You know where to go, Suzy.'

Their heels pick-pocked their way across the shiny parquet, behind a fancy screen and through a polished mahogany door.

You could see why they kept the screen in front.

The models' dressing room was a chilly little cubby-hole with manky black and white lino and a single sickly striplight on the peeling ceiling. The morning's models were ranked on a dress rail next to a full-length looking glass and there was a yellow Formica table with a dressing-table mirror, a desk lamp and a Watney's ashtray still overflowing with lipsticked fag ends from last week's shows. There was a used corn plaster stuck on the mirror.

Suzy was already slipping her suit on to a spare hanger, flicking along the rail with the other hand.

'That ought to do it.'

Riviera Secret was strapless sapphire blue with a duchesse satin bodice and a tiered lace skirt. It had built-in support and Jane was just stripped down to stockings and panty girdle when Mr Green's handsome dark head popped round the door. Jane's hands flew to her breasts. So did his eyes.

'All right, ladies? My first buyer will be here in ten minutes. Get your drawers on.' He flashed a smile. He had beautiful, very real-looking teeth. They might even be real. There was one missing round the side. And a snazzy gold one at the back. You didn't see that with dentures.

Jane swanned out from behind the gilt screen. Mr Green had now been joined by a thin but handsome woman with honey-brown tweeds, marmalade hair and tiny lizard shoes the colour of Marmite. This was Mrs Green and nothing was ever really going to happen without her say-so. Goldie Green would commère the show but she was never introduced as the wife and there wasn't a spark of life between them. In office hours Lawrence had eyes only for his buyer.

Jane crossed the floor then risked a full basic turn. There was nothing basic about it. *Pivot on the balls of both feet. Go back on your right foot, which must be at right-angles to the left. Pause. Then step off again with the left foot.* Just as she completed the manoeuvre she saw that Suzy had entered the room having somehow managed to zip herself into the identical dress in white satin. She was wearing the white pumps from her kit bag. They were slightly grubby but then so was the frock after umpteen

...gs. They passed each other then both did a full turn and ...ed the Greens. Mrs G walked up to Jane and checked the fit of the bodice.

'Not bad. Not bad at all. Quite a nice effect, the two of them. What do you say, Larry? Nice effect?'

She drew on her cigarette, deepening the hollows beneath her high, bony cheeks. She lowered her powder-blue lids slightly, glancing sidelong at Larry, waiting for his agreement.

'Very nice effect, Goldie, should be very good for sales. They'll find it hard to choose between them: take both colours.'

He nipped back into the changing room and re-jigged the running order, ringing the stockroom to send down a few more duplicates: lupin and rose; black and white; silver and gold; marigold and violet (African violet was going to be very big next season).

Mr Green turned to Jane. 'Very nice. Very *promising*.' (Promising was cheaper than nice.) 'Thirty bob for the morning all right for you?' This was way below the going rate but she needed the experience.

'Aren't you going to throw in a frock, Larry?' Mrs Green was back in the workroom so Suzy could work the lashes. 'You must have lots of stuff hanging about from last season. What about that sale or return deal you did with Barkers? They can't have shifted all of it. Not the small sizes. Be a darling. Janey's got a really hot date tomorrow.'

She posed demurely on a little gilt chair, hands crossed at the wrist to deepen the round, creamy cleavage visible over the white satin rim of the bodice. Like a very naughty bridesmaid. Lawrence Green straightened his Windsor knot and gave them another flash of that smart gold tooth.

'We'll see how it goes this morning. I've got one buyer coming down from Manchester; Firbridges Young and Gay department and the head of model gowns for Debenham and Freebody — first time we've had her here. One of her suppliers has let her down and she needs some spring models in a hurry. Wedding gowns are big business at the moment. Nobody wants a Windsor grey costume in a register office when they can screw daddy for white faille and six bridesmaids.' Jane thought of Eileen and her four fat cousins in home-made peach pongee.

The first buyer arrived on the stroke of half nine. A huge, heavily corseted Manchester woman who had picked out a showy fat personality to match her size. She was on the lookout for 'soomthing a bit different' which was why she always came up to London to service her 'special' customers: toffee-nosed, butterscotch-blonde matrons from Wilmslow.

In fact, as Lawrence Green well knew, 'soomthing a bit different' actually meant something very plain indeed. The gown manufacturers of the North West were still hopelessly addicted to bugle-beading.

Mrs Stockley loved coming to Green's. All the gown buyers did. Goldie Green would stay out of the way while her husband worked them over: hand-kissing; flirting; smiling that handsome smile; oscillating around them like an attentive boyfriend. Almost all the buyers were single – most big stores (and most husbands) frowned on female staff keeping their jobs after marriage – and almost all of them were susceptible to a little professional flattery. Place a big enough order and you might even get lunch at one of Mr Green's regular haunts: the Langham Hotel or maybe even L'Etoile. Like Henry Swan, he knew the value of a familiar face (and a big fat tip). Half the fun of coming to London was to be wined and dined by a witty, handsome, hand-stitched creature like Lawrence Green. And he listened. All her problem customers, their fads, their tantrums. Her staff. And the orders were always turned around nice and fast.

When he could, Lawrence liked to schedule a good fifteen-minute firebreak between appointments so that his buyers didn't see each other coming and going. He'd have had separate entrances if he could. Everything was always Exclusive but that could mean a lot and he didn't want two rival stores seeing each other buying. The important thing was to sprinkle the collection across as wide an area as possible so that none of the model gowns brushed against each other at the same dinner dance – the punters would be mortified and the shops would get it in the neck. The budget customers had to take their chances.

In the tiny changing room Suzy was zipping Jane into a green creation in ottoman satin – 'In a Jade Garden' – while Jane hastily stuffed some paper handkerchiefs into the dyed-to-match shoes.

'Try to keep your left side to the wall. There's a coffee stain down the skirt.'

The dress was fat and heavy with fabric, giving the ballerina-length skirts a slow, graceful sway. She swung out from behind the screen and Mrs Green began her running commentary to an audience of one ('Janey's gown has standaway fluting in the Balenciaga manner'). Jane had watched such shows dozens of times, played models in the mirror till her feet burned. She paused by the screen as if scanning the room for her date, raised her chin and smiled as if she had spotted him on the far side of the room, then loped purposefully towards him, swinging her hips very slightly to exaggerate the lilt of the skirt. A hasty full turn (to keep the coffee stain on the move) and then a classic pose while Goldie drew the buyer's attention to the built-in boning – 'for a smoother line'; the pistachio net petticoats – 'ideal for dancing'; the clever new Seenozip and the fact that the same style was available in tangerine, raspberry ice and Capri blue. Other colours by arrangement. Jane's next basic turn twirled her behind the screen.

The buyer was settling back for the usual grouch about whether 'those nipped-in numbers were right for her Larger Ladies'. Lawrence Green flashed his teeth politely but said nothing. Half his output was outsize but nobody wanted Larger Ladies doing Paris turns in the showroom. He had once tried using a Young Matron type (three inches bigger all round) to show the models for his winter collection but the dresses didn't look half so well and he abandoned the experiment after the first morning when a head buyer from Dickins and Jones – a flat-chested, stony-faced, pear-shaped pudding of a woman with the legs of a hockey international and a fluffy little moustache – had complained that this year's collection seemed a bit on the frumpy side. The poor model – Shirley, her name was, lovely-looking girl. Wore the merchandise like a queen. Natural blonde. Baby-blue eyes and very modern ideas – ran about the dressing room practically starkers. Goldie Green wasn't sorry to see the back of her, to tell you the truth. Anyway, poor Shirley was sent packing after six gowns leaving Goldie scouring the building for size tens and Lawrence on the phone to the agency trying to find somebody – anybody – to work the rest of the day. The agency got very hoity-toity and said they had no one available. For one terrible moment Lawrence Green thought that he was going to have to show two dozen model gowns 'in the hand' until he suddenly remembered Suzy.

He'd met her at a rag-trade party the previous week. A fellow gown merchant had had a big fortieth birthday affair at his house in St John's Wood. Champagne, caviare, chopped liver and a wild party game in which Lawrence and five other dress designers were given ten yards of 'art' silk, a box of pins and a half-naked model to dress. After a certain amount of groping and tucking there was a fashion parade which the wives judged and Lawrence and Suzy had won first prize (a box of Havana cigars) by a landslide.

Suzy had made it round to the showroom in half an hour and had twirled through his winter collection so fast that no one saw the pins and bulldog clips holding the size fourteen frocks in place. Lawrence sold every stitch.

Today's buyer was just settling into her usual whinge when Suzy appeared in a turquoise velvet sheath with matching satin train. The woman was quite startled to see what looked like the same brunette appear from behind the screen. They hardly gave her pause for breath: burnt-orange bayadère stripe, citron lace, cerise ribbed silk. *Jane is wearing 'Midnight Moment', in Prussian-blue figured satin with black evening coat lined with the matching blue fabric. The ensemble is completed with a matching organza stole.* Jane let the stole droop to her waist as she twisted and gazed over her shoulder at the imaginary man just behind Lawrence Green's buyer. It was Johnny Hullavington, she decided, wearing that nice blue suit. She imagined his slow smile listening to the prattle of 'my larger ladies' and the 'select foonctions' they attended. Ballerina length might be all very well Down South but they wouldn't let you through the door without a long frock in Wilmslow, apparently.

The final part of the show was bridal wear. They did this as a pair. 'Suzy and Jane wear "Rosy Whisper" and "Lemon Dream", bridesmaids' dresses of paper taffeta with tulip skirts.' Suzy and Jane tore back into the changing room – by now strewn with warm silk – and hurriedly wriggled into their gowns for the double wedding finale. The showroom, which had been chilly at nine o'clock, was ringed by fat old radiators and the room's only window was painted shut. By half eleven it was like an oven. *There are, don't forget, approximately three million sweat glands in the human body.*

Jane had never tried on a wedding dress before. Carol had already got hers ready for the Big Bloody Day and a gang of them had gone round to drool over it. Norma was allowed to slip it on, but not Jane – afraid she'd look better in it probably. Eileen's was going to be a cheap flocked Tricel number but it would still set her dad back fifteen quid: *Man likes woman to look exciting, luxurious, adorable … So man made Tricel.* Carol's was much more swanky but it was an absolute swine. After trying on every wedding dress in Croydon, she'd finally plumped for a peculiar-looking crinoline affair in French brocade patterned with silver frosted roses cut into a huge shawl collar, the wide revers forming a sort of double-breasted effect on the front of the bodice. Carol, who was only five feet two when she took off the shoes (covered in matching French brocade), had read something about adding height with a coronet so she'd picked out a silver satin pill box with a full short veil of pure white softlon silk gossamer – she'd have done better with an old net curtain, quite honestly. Dress, veil and shoes cost fifty-five guineas – more than Jane earned in three months – let alone the going-away outfit – no final decision as yet, but there was talk of shell-pink Tricosa.

Today's wedding dress was 'purest white satin'. Whiteish anyway. It was nearing the end of its showing life and the underarms were so stiff with stale sweat that they left scratches on Jane's skin. Still looked gorgeous, though, even in the fluorescent half-light of the changing room. The shiny silk cast a soft white glow on her face and neck. Jane shifted her weight from one foot to the other, setting the big hooped petticoat in motion. She practised a demure smile, imagined stepping out of a mossy old church, bells ringing, a Savile Row morning suit by her side, then the girlish fantasy creaked to a halt at the cold, wet thought of Doreen. Doreen in her lemon two-piece carping about the expense of the Do or how they had to have one tier in plain Victoria sponge because the currants Got Under 'is Plate. No. Forget the white satin. It would have to be a dove-grey shantung at Caxton Hall after all. Or not bother.

Jane and Suzy sailed out from opposite ends of the screen.

'Suzy wears "Creamy Secret", a vision in hand-clipped witchcraft lace. The soufflé-soft full skirt is gently lifted at the waist in front' – we all knew why *that* style was so popular – 'sweeping back to trail softly.' Lawrence Green threw an expert handful of multi-coloured paper confetti while Goldie pointed out that the pure silk dyed beautifully to make a lovely evening dress for the budget-conscious bride.

The buyer clapped awkwardly while the two models retreated to the changing room for a cup of instant coffee and a fag. Goldie darted in to check the running order on the sagging dress rail. It was time to be Dolly Teens which meant skipping round the showroom in cheap nylon party frocks and matching hair bows which they were somehow supposed to look cute in. Jane glared glumly at her reflection in 'Bubblegum Baby', a pink and black nylon organza arrangement. The cheap fabric stank of someone else's sweat. The heavy gathers across the bosom were designed to flatter the teenage figure but they made Jane look like Gina Lollobrigida on heat. By now Suzy had finished her coffee and wriggled into a disgusting yellow-spotted outrage, 'Polkadot Parade'. Goldie stuck her ginger head round the door.

'Ready when you are, ladies.'

The Junior Miss buyer turned out to be a rather embarrassed-looking young man whose hopes of inheriting the family firm (which he had every intention of selling to Hugh Fraser first chance he got) depended on his learning the business from the bottom up. He'd done stints in the post room and stockroom, he'd spent every Saturday morning on the shop floor and made a thorough nuisance of himself in dress fabrics. He had shadowed the model gown buyer all last season and now he was being let loose on the newly-launched Young and Gay department (answering the phones was no joke).

This was his twenty-third autumn fashion show and he never wanted to see another frilly nylon party dress as long as he lived. Lawrence Green watched young Firbridge's face light up as his Bond Street models tripped out in their high-street clothes. The dress-show 'lead with the thighs' lark didn't go with Vilene can-can petticoats. Jane and Suzy forgot all about Bronwen Pugh for a minute, walking out arm in arm, giggling slightly as they took turns to do a jiver's twirl. The cheap single underskirts flew up as they span round and Jane could feel eyes burning into her knickers.

'Young Mr Firbridge' had bought hardly anything at the twenty-two other shows and had come to the conclusion that one budget gown was very, very much like another and that the sensible thing was to go for a bulk discount with Lawrence Green and make a bid for a couple of phone numbers while he was at it. He didn't know much but he did keep a very keen eye on the kind of thing that ended up gathering dust on the sale rails. None of Lawrence Green's oily patter about what Paris had to say about butterscotch and marigold and lime green cut any ice whatsoever. While poor Lawrence thought anxiously of those big bolts of chartreuse Banlon languishing in his basement stockroom, young Mr Firbridge briskly did a nice little deal on a full range of blue, black, black and white, red, pink and violet party frocks. He finally agreed to take three of a size in butterscotch and lime but only on a strictly sale-or-return basis. It was only when the stock started to come in, weeks later, that he realised how skimpy and cheap the frocks looked when they didn't have Jane and Suzy inside them.

Mr Green had half an hour before his final appointment – the speciality model gown buyer from Debenham and Freebody – and while Goldie was upstairs checking on the girls in the workroom he joined his models for a swift panatella. The air in the changing room was already thick with smoke and face powder.

'It's going very well, very well. You're a natural, Miss James. You and Suzy together makes a lot of sense. Very nice effect. Keeps the show moving along nicely. Piques the client's interest, if you know what I mean, having twins.'

'We're not twins, Larry.' Suzy sounded cross as she teased carefully across her hair with a dirty steel styling comb.

'I know you're not but you should play it up just the same. Nice little gimmick.' He allowed himself to forget about business for a moment and looked them both over. 'Very, very hard to choose between you. I'd like to have both.'

He didn't mean showroom modelling but Jane was sure it was just the cigar talking. Nice Jewish businessmen with their handsome wives and beautiful children – they were bound to be beautiful children – didn't mess around. Jane flirted happily, sure that she was quite safe. Suzy slipped off to the loo – not the one the clients used but a smelly little cave behind the basement stockroom. Jane wriggled out of the tangerine nylon tulle she was wearing, took off her bra and slid into model gown number one, carefully settling herself into the chilly silk whaleboned bodice while Lawrence Green's dirty brown eyes watched her reflection in the cracked cheval glass.

She wasn't quite as safe as she'd thought. He had calculated the time it would take his wife to get up to the fourth floor, have a ruck about something, then trip back down in her slingbacks, and he reckoned that left just enough leeway for a bit of expert fitting. He rested his cigar on the stub-stuffed ashtray and with a smooth glide (he was a lovely mover) was behind Jane, his freshly shaved lips sank on to her neck and his manicured brown hands slipped inside the back of her dress. She nearly screamed with shock. He must do this all the bloody time.

'So, Janey, have you picked out what dress you're taking?' As he spoke his lips stitched their way across her shoulder and up the side of her neck while his fingertips fiddled about inside her bodice.

'Please –' she began.

'It's my pleasure. So which is it to be?'

Jane squirmed awkwardly which he seemed to take for excitement. It was her own fault, walking round the room half-dressed, getting him at it. She arched her head away from his kisses and ran her eye along the rail of grubby model gowns.

'Can't I have a clean one?'

His hands were less gentle now and he raised his head to check the mirror: the dark handsome man seducing the luscious young brunette in blue velvet trimmed with white(ish) mink ('Starlit Surrender'). He stored the image away so that he could look at it later in his mind's eye in his super-king-size bergère-style bed in Maida Vale when he was gratifying Mrs G with an unusually vigorous seeing-to. *Lots of women, especially wives, are extremely aroused by a rough sexual approach.*

He stepped back and retrieved his cigar.

'A clean one?' He turned back the neck on an eau de nil duchesse satin and pulled a face. 'I don't see why not. I'll see what I can dig out.'

Jane was still panting slightly when Suzy got back from the lav.

'Did you get your frock?' The look on her face. No wonder she'd been gone so long.

'I think so.'

'Larry's a bit of a gent, all things considered.'

Gent? That was gents, was it?

Larry slipped back into the room with an old dress box with drawings of Harrods all over it. Strips of the patterned cardboard were missing where countless chunks of Sellotape had been ripped away. He winked at Jane.

'You'll knock him dead.' It was hard to breathe in the tight blue velvet as he looked her up and down.

Goldie was suddenly back in the room. Anxious. And picky. The speciality model gowns had a very nice mark-up but then they were a big investment to start with. Since Green's – like everyone else in the London rag trade – had been caught napping by the New Look back in '47, Lawrence and Goldie took no chances. They either bought Paris designs or stole them (having paid their 'caution' to see the collections). The results – the 'Monsieur Lawrence' Collection – were put together in the workroom by the senior cutters and machinists and usually found their way to the very smartest madam shops and department stores but it never said Green's on the label. It was a miracle Debenham and Freebody had got wind at all. Good suppliers were a closely guarded secret. That was where Lawrence's canny little window display came in. The queen bee of Wigmore Street had spotted it on her way to buy from a rival supplier and finally twigged where all these elegant little numbers were coming from.

The model gown buyer at Debenham and Freebody, after two decades of buying – daywear, junior fashions, after six, evening, model gowns and finally speciality model gowns (own secretary; office with a window; Paris four times a year) – was finding it harder and harder to work up any enthusiasm for this season's colours, or whether Paris said duchesse satin or beading or hand-cut lace or panne velvet or organza.

But she liked the twins gimmick. So much so that she gave both girls her card. One of the house models in Wigmore Street was leaving to get married – silly little fool. She hadn't really wanted to give up her job – ten pounds a week and a nice staff discount – but the fiancé insisted that they could both manage on an under-manager's salary. Not in Ferragamo slingbacks they couldn't.

She liked a few of the gowns and placed quite a big order after a long chat with Lawrence insisting on some exclusive colours and fabrics. One of her regular suppliers had gone broke and she needed them delivered by mid March (which was asking a lot) and she wanted them 'exclusive to London W1' but Larry wouldn't play. What would Dickins and Jones say?

Jane had been enjoying herself when the morning began. She'd got the turns down to a fine art (parquet was much smoother than lino) and she'd worked out a nice repertoire of looks: Surprised, Shy, Playful and Seductive (the imaginary Johnny Hullavington played a big part in Seductive). But after the umpteenth twirl she was getting hot, sweaty and tired. She had rough red friction patches on her ribs from rubbing up against sweaty whalebones, her back ached and there was a blister starting on each heel from walking in the cheap dyed-to-match satin stilettos, all of which were at least two sizes too big. Suzy gave her some Elastoplast from her kit bag but it had rubbed away and kept sticking to her nylons and twisting the seams.

Suzy and Jane hung up the last of their dirty hot frocks, smoothed their hair and eased back into their suits. The Debenham and Freebody lady was still finalising petticoat fabrics with Goldie when the girls left. Thirty bob had sounded reasonable three hours ago but now she'd actually done the job she didn't quite see why Suzy should get double. Still, there was the frock in the box. She had been afraid Larry would palm her off with some misfit in chartreuse Charmaine but he turned out to be a bit of a gent after all: cherry-red velvet copied from an original Givenchy toile. The bows were a bit last season but they were only tacked on.

Larry saw them to the door, feeling the quality of Jane's cashmere and wool skirting as they went.

'That was a nice morning's work, Miss James. I hope we'll see you again for the new collection in September, if not before. You take my advice, Suzy my love, and work up the heavenly twins angle. You'll make a fortune.'

One last pinch and they were back out in Great Portland Street. Suzy hailed yet another taxi, raising her arm in a cheery, imperious wave – like Wenda Rogerson doing spring fashions as if somewhere round the corner lurked Norman Parkinson with his fancy Japanese camera, ready to snap her mid-swank.

Suzy told the taxi to leave the meter running while they staggered up the stairs of the flat with the bag and the Harrods box. Annie stuck her head out as they passed, then dived back inside to produce a brown paper carrier bag filled with fluffy white nylon underwear. Suzy rummaged in the crocodile bag for the promised half-crown.

'Annie.'

'Wossat, Suzy my darlin'?'

'How would you fancy a nice little cleaning job? I can't promise anything but Janey and I are probably going to be moving to a new place and I think we might need a tiny bit of dusting doing.'

Annie, who survived on National Assistance (having never paid a penny in Stamps), was yes darlin' ooh not half darlin' very very keen on a nice little cleaning job. Small-time prostitution didn't offer much in the way of a pension. Annie could usually cadge a glass of stout from one of the old faces in the Fitzroy – at least it was warm in there – but you couldn't live on stout.

Suzy promised to ring Lorna with the details.

Back in the flat they dumped the bags in one of the tea chests and did a few running repairs to their faces – a quick stroke with the pan-stick and a bit of powder and Bewitching Coral. Suzy dived downstairs to the loo just as the phone rang in the hall. Doreen answered.

'Janey oo? No Janeys living 'ere. You must have the wrong number. What do you mean "brown hair, nice figure"; this isn't a knocking shop, you know. It's a private house. Niece? I'll niece you.'

So much for Michael Woodrose and his busty young models. Jane was just replacing the receiver as Suzy trolled back through the front door, freshly dabbed with Joy.

'Poor Lorna. She'll have to man the switchboard for a few weeks when we move.' This seemed the least of poor Lorna's worries.

A normal person might have fretted about old employers and old boyfriends not having their new number but Suzy seemed quite pleased to be shot of them. She had the numbers of the ones she liked: the employers who paid reasonably well and were generous with their remaindered stock; the dates who bought nice little presents and didn't make a nuisance of themselves. And as for the mistakes – the big spenders who suddenly wanted to be paid back; the lovesick widowers and randy deadbeats from the BBC pronunciation department – move house and you could wipe your wires clean and start over.

The taxi driver had been starting to wonder. They had fire escapes, them old buildings. Cheeky tarts. But it was going to be all right after all. The two cheeky tarts had just slammed the street door behind them. Smashing-looking birds, both of them. Lovely pins. And not short of a few quid. Fortnum's for lunch. All right for some.

Chapter 17

> *Always live as centrally as you possibly can.*

Suzy had been getting happier and prettier and lovelier from the moment they climbed back into the taxi. She told Jane a funny joke – good and loud so that the driver would laugh too. Then she gushed delightedly about Janey's nice red-velvet present and what a great model she'd make. Then she tipped the driver two bob and waved gaily at Henry who was already installed at a window table.

Her good mood hit Fortnum's like a stink bomb. Even the crabby old stick of a waitress cracked her face into a smile at sir and his two pretty daughters. The house model, pacing the restaurant every lunchtime like the Flying Dutchman in daywear, made a point of stopping at their table. They ordered lobster burgers (more bloody Chablis) but were careful not to have more than a bite of the bun. Jane tried to imagine what Doreen would have ordered. At those prices? Not likely.

The Fountain Restaurant was full of ladies dabbing with napkins, tongues checking dentures for bits of trapped Elegant Rarebit or traces of lipstick while anaemic unpainted eyes scanned the room awarding black marks: Milk-In-First; knife held like a spoon; taking a knife to a bread roll; sips of tea taken while food remained in the mouth. No food crimes were being committed at Jane and Suzy's table but they watched them anyway. Huntsman suit, handmade shoes, cashmere socks. Was he Daddy or Sugar Daddy? Very hard to tell. Suzy's manner always suggested a bit of both.

'Can we go and see the flat after lunch?' Can we, Daddy? Can we?

Suzy hardly ever asked Henry about his life away from her. 'Did you have a nice weekend?' would have been stupid. He probably didn't – why else keep Suzy? – and if by any chance he did have a nice bloody weekend, if, by some incredible chance, his dearly beloved wife opened her skinny grey legs for the first time in twenty years, it would have been the last thing Suzy wanted to hear. Besides, she wasn't that interested in what he got up to when she wasn't there.

As a tiny child Suzy had believed that other people only existed while she was in the room – which explained why they were always so bucked up when she arrived. She'd never quite shaken this feeling and anyway it was true. Rubbish evenings came to life when Suzy told a joke or suggested champagne or, later, more softly, said that no one had ever cared about her this way since Daddy died. No wonder people were pleased to see her.

Henry handed them nicely into a taxi which whizzed along Piccadilly then up into Mayfair. They stopped outside a big once-white stone block of flats round the back of the Dorchester Hotel somewhere. Henry introduced the girls to the porter as his nieces who had just moved up to London from the country and said he hoped Jim – it was Jim, wasn't it? – would look after them. Yes sir he would sir thank you very much sir. Nieces his arse but enough five-quid tips and sir could have all the nieces he liked. Five quid down the drain, of course, if Suzy didn't like the nice little flat.

She liked it.

The front door of number fifty-two opened into quite a big square hall with a crystal chandelier in the middle and shelves all round it with books and fancy china – not the kind with 'Foreign' stamped on the bottom. There was a door in the near corner leading to a guest cloakroom which had a toilet (lavatory, *lavatory*) and washbasin and a big linen cupboard full of fluffy matching towels and starchy sheets and room enough at the bottom for a huge Mayfair Laundry box.

The double doors on the left led into a twenty-foot sitting room, two more doors to the bedrooms and a swing door to the kitchen. The kitchen (which didn't have a bath in it) had walls of white cupboards and a door leading on to the fire escape (which might come in handy in a bedroom farce-y sort of way) but who cared about the kitchen? People who lived in Massingham House only went there on the maid's day off.

There was no washing machine. Even Doreen thought washing machines were common. Mrs Grant next door had one. Dirty great mangle on top of it and a garden full of drying sheets and shirts. The woman on the other side wheeled hers down to the laundrette in her wicker trolley then pegged it out when she got back. But Doreen had a magic cardboard suitcase from the electric laundry company that turned dirty clothes into clean. It wasn't cheap but Doreen had Better Things to do with her time than wash bloody sheets. What Things?

Suzy's bedroom was pink and white and gold. The whole of one wall was fitted wardrobes with enormous great mirror doors showing a second king-size bed, a second fancy white and gold dressing table, another chandelier, another mile of fat, furry white carpet, another Suzy.

Suzy watched herself do a basic turn into Henry's waiting arms – no joke in high heels on shag pile – while Jane went off to explore her own room which was the same only blue: hyacinth blue. Jane's king-size bed covered in silky satin; Jane's dressing table; Jane's hand-blocked blue and gold wallpaper. You opened the curtains by pulling a brass pineapple on a string. The view wasn't up to much – just the windows and fire escapes of the other half of the block – but the raw-silk floor-length drapes shimmered so beautifully in the light that you didn't want to see out anyway.

Through the white door and into Jane's very own private bathroom which was blue to match the bedroom, even the bath was blue and it had gold-coloured taps – hot and cold, but no sign of a water heater – and a boiling hot chromium-plated rail covered in half a dozen soft, fat bath towels in exactly the right shade. The whole of the right-hand wall above the bath was one big mirror and the mirror over the washbasin had tiny lightbulbs all round it. Jane checked her reflection for damage, only there wasn't any. Only a pretty young face rising from the neatly tailored shoulders of a cashmere suit. Very pretty. Pretty enough for a flat of its own.

Jane sat down at the dressing table and began opening each of the little drawers. They smelled of Quelques Fleurs and hair removing cream. The imaginary Mrs Collins had left quite a lot of stuff behind in the top drawer: a powder compact: a lot of hairpins and some nice twist-up lipsticks: Pango Peach; Cuban Rose. The drawer underneath was full to the brim with about two hundred bookmatches, shiny blue ones with Mayfair 3515 embossed on them in gold lettering. Jane had read about these in the *News of the World*. Call girls had them. They'd have been handy for lighting the gas – only there wasn't any gas.

Suzy was still thanking Henry so Jane had a nose round the sitting room: no plastic fruit; no atomic magazine rack; no cheap prints (*Reproductions of 'Sunflowers' or the Annigoni royal portraits or Rédoute roses have no place in the Good Taste Home*); no sideboard and not a pouffe in sight.

Henry and Suzy had slipped out of the bedroom. He'd had as much gratitude as he was getting for a weekday afternoon.

'Now then, you two. Have you got everything packed? If you give me the keys I can send my man round right away if you like. No need for you to go back to that place ever again.'

He squeezed Suzy's sticky little hand. Suzy had been having another think about schlapping back to St Anthony's Chambers and smuggling the gear down to street level so that Henry's driver wouldn't see the state of the flat and she had decided it was more trouble than it was worth. Who cared what some driver thought? She'd already told Henry it was a slum but that it was all she could afford (after Daddy died) and how she felt sorry for her poor pregnant flatmate and Henry had been very, very understanding. The bigger the contrast, the more generous and magnificent the Mayfair flat seemed, the bigger and better Henry would feel.

'Bill will bring all your bits and pieces over in an hour or two. I'll pick you up at seven thirty. I thought you and I could have a bite to eat somewhere and then go on to the River Club. What are you up to this evening, Janey?' He had a very polite voice, he was a very polite man but it wasn't an invitation.

'Janey's got a date.' Definitely not an invitation.

'I'm sure she has.' Henry ran his eyes over Jane in her expensive suit. Any floozie could wear a smart evening dress but dollies in daywear were in another league. 'So, Janey. Do you like the flat?'

'I don't like the flat at all, Mr Swan. I *love* it.' Service with a lick. Did he believe her? He didn't look as if he believed her somehow. His smile seemed to dry on his face, shrinking slightly at the edges, but he kissed her hand anyway.

Once Henry was in the lift, Suzy kicked off her shoes and threw herself on the big white sofa. This was definitely the life. She reached across to the side table for the phone – white with gold trim – and dialled Big Terry. Then she rang Lorna at work to give her the new number and see how the professor was shaping up.

Lorna obviously couldn't talk – in a roomful of graceless eggheads from Romano-British antiquities the typist could go whole days without speaking to a living soul – but she obviously had something to say. There was also the danger that the switchboard was earwigging.

'About the newspaper cutting we discussed?'

'Oh yes. Are you going to put the ad in?'

'I think that would be best.' Lorna's voice was tight, resentful even.

'Would you like me to do it?'

'If that would be convenient?'

'I'll do it right now. Now can you do me a little favour, darling. We're living at Fifty-two Massingham House and our new phone number is Mayfair 3515. I don't want you to pass it on to any of the pests, obviously, but could you be an angel and pop in and see Annie on your way upstairs and get her to give me a ring? Oh yes and can you give the address to Janey's Johnny when he rings?'

As soon as she'd hung up she found a bit of paper in the desk drawer, tore the letterhead off the top and wrote out half a dozen words in neat block capitals. She then buzzed down to the porter to send up the messenger boy – like she'd been doing it all her life. Would he be a darling – given half a chance he would. He was only sixteen and his eyes were on stalks at the sight of two pretty popsies and all that shag pile – and take this to the classified ad department of the *Evening News* in Fleet Street? Thirty bob should cover it. He could keep the change. And the following evening, in a pub round the back of Gower Street, young Dr Tom would check the personal columns, make the call and save another young life – that was how he liked to look at it, anyway.

Jane wandered back into her beautiful blue bedroom. The smart fitted wardrobes were filled with empty coat hangers covered in padded satin. Some of them had scented net sachets still dangling from them. She hung her suit on one of the hangers and laid her black cashmere crew neck on one of the empty shelves.

She decided to have a bath while they waited for Henry's Bill to arrive with their things. The bathroom cupboards were full of goodies. The one under the washbasin was mostly medicinal: Andrews liver salts; aspirin; a funny rubber tube with a squashy bag on the end and three packs of French letters. There was another stash of things behind the bathroom mirror: soap, body lotion and bath essence and two pots of Helena Rubinstein

Beauty Overnight cream. Jane decided on Stephanotis – Lily of the Valley was a bit mumsy. She was so used to the slow, pissy stream of Doreen's dodgy Ascot heater that she nearly let the bath run over.

Suzy had found a pair of see-thru pink nylon baby dolls in one of her wardrobes and was skipping around the flat opening cupboards and drawers to see what else the imaginary Mrs Collins had left behind. She found a cupboard full of art silk kimonos, several pairs of poplin pyjamas, a dozen pairs of Irish linen sheets and a parcel containing two navy-blue maid's uniforms.

'Size ten. Oh wait till I show Annie.'

Her tour of the flat had finally reached the blue bathroom where Jane was up to her neck in scented bubbles. 'Are you washing your hair? You might as well. I've got Big Terry coming round at six.' *Some girls find that a bi-monthly shampoo is ample. Others find that their hair becomes oily and unmanageable within ten days or even a week.* Suzy looked herself over in Jane's bathroom mirror – as if she were registering her face with every glass in the place – then checked the baby dolls in the big reflection behind the bath.

'This big mirror's a bit kinky. I haven't got one of these in mine.'

At about half four the porter, still running very smoothly on his nice crisp fiver, called up to say that Mr Swan's driver had arrived and the girls hurriedly slipped on kimonos and unpacked the tea chests as fast as they were brought up, filling the empty cupboard shelves. The dress rail wouldn't fit in the goods lift so Henry's Bill and his boy, a well-built lad of nineteen, had to bring the frocks up in silky, scented armfuls and hang them straight into Suzy's wardrobe. Jane's cupboard had far less in it but Larry Green's cherry-velvet down payment and her two Hardy Amies numbers looked well and Glenda's shoes filled the racks that ran along the floor. There was even a red satin pair to match the frock.

Henry's driver didn't know what to make of it all: the clothes, the slum, the smart flat: didn't make sense. But Suzy was one step ahead of him, unravelling a whole string of chatty little lies just so that some van driver wouldn't think badly of her.

'Thank you so much. They seem to have taken care of everything. I was a bit worried. Where did you have to pick it all up from in the end?'

So that was it. Not her flat at all. Of course it wasn't.

'Some dirty little place north of Oxford Street, miss. Filthy it was. Stank of damp.'

Suzy pretended to inspect the hem of a lavender lace evening gown.

'Oh well, no harm done. I expect they were only there over the weekend. My old lease in Bryanston Square ended at New Year so we've been staying down in the country while my maid found somewhere to store all our things.'

She romanced on for a bit then gave Bill a pound and Bill's boy ten bob. Bill's boy could hardly wait to get home and unpack the memory of Jane and her loosely wrapped kimono leaning over a tea chest.

The phone rang.

'Mayfair 3515.' You could hear the excitement in her voice. Like a little girl showing off. 'Oh hello, Annie darling. That was quick. Lorna must have clocked off early. Yes we're both very well. Now then. How do you fancy that little cleaning job we talked about? Good. Well why don't you hop on a bus and get down to Massingham House. It's right behind the Dorchester. I *know*, darling. Posh or what? Anyway hurry on over and then you can see how you feel about it. There's a service entrance round the side. Number Fifty-two.' Service entrance. Swank.

In the time it took her to pull on her bootees and her old tweed coat and hop on to a number 73 Annie had arrived at the flat.

'Nice and warm in here. Fitted carpet. Silk, them curtains. Pure silk.'

She had wriggled into her smart navy-blue uniform before you could say three bob an hour, then she walked through the flat stroking everything.

'You look the business, Annie my love. Like a maid in a play. You couldn't be an angel and make sense of those shelves for me, could you?'

Annie amused herself by going through all the cupboards, folding Suzy's sweaters into little private rainbows and stacking them neatly in the shiny blond wood pigeonholes. Then she got to work on Suzy's frocks, grading them from the grandest ball gowns down to the mildest After Six. She'd already rinsed out their discarded stockings and hung them on the rail when the doorbell rang.

'Mr Thomson, madam,' said Annie, good as gold, then went back to building naughty little nests of bras and girdles in the white and gold chest of drawers.

Terry was not as impressed as Suzy hoped he would be.

'I've been up this gaff before, you know. Two toilets: one pink; one blue – that right? Yeah. Definitely been here before. Two blonde birds used to live here. Soft perm. Roots done once a fortnight. Very groovy pad. Nice little business by the look of it. Much more your style. Better than that shit hole in Oxford Street.'

Annie, who had been rootling through the kitchen cupboards, suddenly appeared carrying a jug of dry martinis and three glasses. Turned out she'd been a cocktail waitress at the Embassy Club in about 1927.

'I can't afford for you to be here all the time, Annie darling. I was only thinking of a few hours' cleaning – you know what a slut I am.'

'You pay me what you was going to pay me and I'll keep me own time, Suzy darling. I'd only be stuck in that freezing rotten flat listening to the wireless. I might just as well be here in the warm looking after all your little bits. I'll bring a pint of silver top when I come in of a morning. Make you a nice cup of tea.'

Once Terry had done their hair Suzy insisted on moving one of the bedroom easy chairs into the kitchen so that Annie could sit and listen to the radio in comfort. Then she began to get ready for a grateful evening with Henry Swan.

She'd chosen a dress of strapless crimson lace that came with its own built-in waspie, another present from the gentlemanly Mr Green. You could tell by the cut (another straight steal from Givenchy).

The phone rang. It was Lorna to say that she had given the new address and phone number to Johnny Whatsisname and to confirm that he would be picking Jane up at eight. Lorna was already sounding cheesed off with the answering-service lark.

'That Canadian pest rang for Suzy again. I told him to fuck off.' Which seemed quite a good idea, really. Why faff about with the South African accents when you could just tell it to them straight? Probably because Suzy never really liked to let go of a nice little meal ticket for those hungry Sunday nights.

Henry had already arrived by the time Jane had finished creaming the hair from her legs and armpits, buffing her fingernails, shaping her lips, plucking and pencilling her brows, lining her eyes, curling her lashes, rouging her cheeks, scenting her neck, powdering her nose and polishing her bloody elbows – *Are you armadillo-elbowed?* She carefully clipped her stockings to her suspender belt then pulled on a tiny pair of black lace panties that she'd found in one of the drawers. Brand new. Still had the label on.

The phone rang again. Some man wanting Jeanette or, failing that, was Bettina available? That was Mayfair 3515, wasn't it? He said the number as if he were reading it – off a book of matches maybe. Jane took a tip from Lorna's book and then hung up the cream and gold receiver before he could think of a reply.

She was nearly ready but the densely boned bodice of the cherry velvet was definitely a two-man zipper. She held the back together and went to find Suzy who was sitting on Henry's knee in one of the big white armchairs telling him a dirty joke about the three daughters of a bishop. Jane stuck her head round the door.

'Sorry to bother you, Suzy, but do you think you could zip me up?'

Henry followed Suzy into the hall and watched the dress close over the soft white skin. Suzy stepped back and he stood behind her, watching Jane's reflection in one of the big gold mirrors. His hand suddenly slid down the front of Suzy's frock but his eyes were on Jane as he did it. Suzy giggled at the picture they made: the dark-suited man and his two scarlet women, like a Sexton Blake cover. Jane flushed and turned away. What was he after? The bell rang and the other two retreated back to their armchair as Jane opened the door to Johnny Hullavington.

'Good evening.' Clever, the way he managed to make it sound surprised and delighted. He didn't have to tell her how nice she looked: just the tone of his voice was a compliment. He leaned forward to kiss her cheek hello but she turned her face towards him, put her arms around his neck and surprised him with a big fat kiss on the lips. She could hardly breathe in that tight, red dress. 'Good *evening*.'

Jane slipped back into her room to get her bag and Glenda's Furleen and to step out of the black lace panties. He'd never know – but she would.

Once downstairs he opened the car door for her and waited while she tucked the fat skirts of her frock out of harm's way. It was a very smart car with its own radio and a wooden panel covered in knobs and buttons. She had to remind herself not to gawp at all the fittings, to look as if handsome thirtysomething gents took her dancing every night of the week. She ought to say something. The books said to make small talk – *bore him and he will soon look elsewhere* – but it was easier said than done. The good-listener bit would have been a breeze but he wasn't actually saying anything. What would he like her to say? Funny stories? She didn't think he'd go for the elephant's foreskin story somehow. Suddenly it came to her.

'*Do try to make entertaining conversation. Men like a girl who can keep them amused and will dump a girl who doesn't.*'

He seemed startled, but intrigued.

'There's a whole book full of it: *Best Behaviour*, it's called. There was a copy on one of the bookshelves in the flat. *Never commit the cardinal sin of boring your man. Learn to charm him.* Do you think a person can actually learn charm? Like French or basket-weaving?'

They had stopped at the traffic lights at the bottom of Curzon Street.

'No. I think you're absolutely right. There are some things that can't be taught. What an astonishing girl you are.'

He reached across and squeezed her hand.

There was a group of girls waiting for a 137 on Park Lane and they looked up as the car passed and Jane could almost hear the envious little thoughts being broadcast from that chilly wet bus stop as a better-looking, better-dressed, better-spoken girl glided by. Acting the part, she turned to smile at Johnny and almost squirmed with pride at the sight of his handsome profile caught in a passing headlight. Like a drawing of a boyfriend.

Part Two

Chapter 18

> *In surrendering herself outside marriage,*
> *a woman sacrifices* inner *status.*

Madge had pitched up at Carpenter's just in time for the next round: a bottle of light ale; a brandy and soda; gin and French for Sylvia; gin and tonic for Janey; a double Scotch and water for Reggie (as long as someone else was paying) and three double gins with orange for Madge who'd missed nearly an hour's drinking time and wanted to catch up. Ted the barman lined them up tidily in front of her then neatly clammed a fresh ashtray over the full one.

Madge had spent the best part of the missing hour fighting for mirror space in the ladies' powder room of the Café Royal, making good with Pan-stick and eye pencil after a day's work in a fur showroom off Bond Street somewhere where she was part saleslady, part house model. She was tall and very skinny (thanks to a special diet of Camp coffee, Granny Smiths and gin) and well-groomed enough to show off the skins. Although she hadn't ever been particularly pretty, she looked so much classier, so much *happier* once she was safely wrapped up in a full-length ranch mink with dolman sleeve and half belt that she turned out to be surprisingly good for business.

Madge had grown up just outside Aldershot and her first pair of high heels – stolen from her big sister when she was sixteen – had carried her up the hill to her first army dance, her first glass of gin and the first in a long line of stupid, randy men who didn't care if she lived or died provided she came across. At least Reggie paid the electricity bill for the grotty 'open plan' bedsit in Clapham that she shared with her Mario Lanza records and a pair of blue Persian cats (Bezique and Canasta). Reggie even paid the vet's bill once. Suzy said that Madge ought to come to some sort of arrangement with that vet. Cut out the middle man.

The thick peachy paint on Madge's cheeks cracked slightly as she smiled her thanks for the drinks. Alpaca Pete gallantly slid off his stool and she hoicked herself up on to it, wincing as the top of her high-waist girdle rolled over and wedged itself into her ribs.

Pete was in the middle of a very rude joke.

'So. The eager young bridegroom says, "Don't worry, my angel. Hubby doesn't mind if you make naughty noises in your knickers." Well, anyway, next morning after a night of mad, passionate love – close your ears, Janey my darling – his lovely young bride tiptoes across the honeymoon suite to the bathroom and she goes and farts again: "That's right! Stink the fucking place out!"'

Madge, already knocked for six by the three double gins, practically fell off her stool laughing. *You should find his funny stories extremely amusing.* Only it wasn't amusing. Jane wasn't laughing although she would have photographed that way: head thrown back, Suzy-style, to show those lovely white teeth. What was funny about it? Poor cow, stuck for life with a pig like that. Doreen always said a man wouldn't respect you if you let him take 'liberties'. All the books said the same. Doreen never went into details about these stolen liberties but the pickled-onion look on her face suggested terrible ordeals from the inside pages of the *News of the World*: *hands over stocking tops; interfered with; consenting party; intent to ravish; intimacy took place; the flogging you so richly deserve.*

Jane's stocking tops had been strictly off limits (for Johnny anyway). Johnny might be a textbook boyfriend but men were men all the world over. Jane had an idea he had a woman in Streatham he went to (which would explain him killing time in the Locarno that night). He knew South London surprisingly well for someone who lived in Gloucester Road. What was the exchange rate south of the river? Fur? And if so, which sort? Squirrel if you were lucky.

Johnny had been taking Jane out two nights a week but his presents were all strictly by the book: a bottle of scent, the odd silk scarf. No big stuff. No *payments* – there'd been nothing to pay *for*. Jane had drawn a prim line at doorstep kisses. *When Mr Right does make an appearance he won't be pleased to learn that one slice of the cake has already been enjoyed.*

Jane had actually passed the cake plate round quite a few times since she'd left Norbury but only when there was a very good reason – a decent bit of fur or a really well-paid modelling job. People said you could tell 'that sort of girl' just by looking at her, but could you really? Jane sipped her gin and straightened her smile in the mirror behind the bar. The same face. The same smile.

Johnny clearly had no idea of her own double life and – after a few false starts – didn't seem to mind the ice-maiden treatment. That was probably why he was still chasing her three months after that first fantastic date in Lawrence Green's red-velvet dress, dancing rumbas till two in the morning. He'd bought her sweet champagne and when the diddicoy kid came round with the single red roses he gave a fiver for the whole basket. Waste of money really: they'd only die off. You could have bought the whole three dozen for fifteen bob in Berwick Street. Or two pairs of stockings. Or six lipsticks.

Jane had hated the sex lark at first. She couldn't say she'd been disappointed exactly because she hadn't really expected much. Suzy acted as if she quite liked it but then Suzy acted as if she quite liked caviare and Jane knew for a fact she didn't – she used to throw up in the Ladies' afterwards. Even if you did turn out to like it, sex was still a men's thing. *A woman's ability to reach orgasm enables her to share her husband's pleasure but a sexual climax is no more essential for starting a family than a mink coat or a lipstick.*

There was certainly no climax the first time but there was a mink, thanks to some friend of dear old Henry's – like Ollie only a bigger tipper – who paid for his Norbury virgin with a nice little trip down Bond Street. Mean bastard in other ways, though. Took her to a hotel for the night another time (rotten old Regent Palace, no private bathroom) and then left for a business meeting after breakfast in bed and a bit more how's-your-father, never thinking how was she supposed to get home in strapless navy taffeta and a mink jacket. She had to get the chambermaid to zip her back into the dress and there wasn't enough money for a taxi in her beaded evening bag which meant an excruciating ride down Piccadilly on a number 9 bus, her gown and petticoats sticking out under a cheap raincoat borrowed from the same chambermaid, her mink stuffed into a laundry bag. She'd slipped back into the flats through the side entrance rather than let the porter see her in that state. She felt like a tart. She looked like a tart . . .

The sapphire bracelet brought back happier memories: an Italian business associate of Henry's who took her to the White Elephant club and told her in a sexy Rossano Brazzi sort of voice over a dozen oysters that she had beautiful eyes, a beautiful neck, beautiful ankles, beautiful shoulders. You name it. It was hard to know what to say in reply, really. She decided to play safe and drop lashes, raise lashes, lean forward (giving him an even better view down the front of her frock) and work the old 'Are you trying to seduce me?' line. He lapped it up. He wasn't trying to seduce her, he was *going* to seduce her. And then he began to whisper a few of his plans for the rest of the evening. She couldn't understand a word but just the tone of his voice made a peachy blush spread steadily across her chest. He could hardly wait to get cracking.

Jane was exactly his type. Not a virgin (virgins made him feel bad) but Unawakened. He enjoyed himself. She didn't have a lot of conversation but she was clean, she was the youngest, prettiest, best-dressed woman in any restaurant, she knew which knife and fork to use and she went like a rabbit (after a little instruction). A hundred and fifty pounds (including purchase tax) had seemed cheap at the price.

Apart from doing a stock-check on her charms, he didn't really say much himself. She tried asking him about business – *Many men like to talk about their business affairs and you must be sure to find it all very interesting* – but he just smiled and pointed out another place of interest: her hands; her knees; her ears. His English vocabulary was fairly extensive (on parts of the body, anyway). Jane had learned how to stretch a yawn into a smile (she'd watched Suzy doing it). Sergio even taught her a bit of Italian, mostly just things he wanted her to say to him – *'Piu forte! E cosi grosso!'* – things like that. He didn't tell her what any of it meant but she had a bloody good idea. She did manage to get a few useful phrases out of it: colours; fabrics; what is your wife's size (a large sixteen by the sound of it). Bracelet length was *'I manici lunghi fino al braccialetto'*. She actually got mixed up one night after a long evening of oysters and champagne and began moaning *'fino al braccialetto'* at the height of passion. She thought he'd never stop laughing. That was how she got the sapphires.

None of Henry's other friends had Sergio's technique, but at least Jane knew what was expected of her now and could make all the right noises. Enough to earn a nice little suede jacket, a quadruple string of Japanese cultured pearls, a smart dress watch and her very own Hermes alligator bag (they definitely did take the price ticket out). There hadn't been any nasty accidents – so far. A doctor friend of Henry's (Henry had a lot of friends) had a sideline in rubber goods and had been happy to supply 'Mrs

James' with a disgusting little brown thing that seemed to do the trick. Failing that, there would always be the *Evening News*.

Poor Lorna was still living on her own in St Anthony's Chambers. Suzy's Henry, like Glenda's spiv, had paid three months' rent up front so Lorna hadn't yet bothered finding a flatmate. Jane had bumped into her in Great Portland Street on her way to a modelling job (Finefit slacks). Lorna said she'd strong-armed the landlord into repapering the hall, sitting room and kitchen (by promising not to breathe a word about the two scrubbers in the basement). He'd even offered to do the bedrooms but the only bedroom paper he had gave Lorna a headache just to look at it. She'd borrowed a Hoover from the old poof downstairs who'd said he might be able to dig her out a few odd rolls from the stockroom at work if she didn't mind slight seconds so all in all things were looking up, she reckoned. She didn't say anything about the baby but she had a new skirt – natty plaid number with a waspie waist – so presumably all that had sorted itself out. She'd given the professor the scrub and got herself transferred to Books and Manuscripts where one of the librarians had been very understanding. Boring. Balding. But very understanding.

Lorna said that the bloke from the BBC still rang now and then, looking for Suzy or Jane (he didn't seem to mind which). Lorna had tried telling him to fuck off – having had such lasting success with the Dreaded Arnold – but Michael Woodrose seemed to quite like being sworn at by women with posh voices (his mother back in Sevenoaks had a lot to answer for). He had been ringing about once a fortnight for a fresh slice of tongue pie.

Suzy had got a new job demonstrating some stupid brooch-clip thingy that let you wear a silk scarf in all sorts of peculiar ways, ringing the bloody changes on a tired old coat and skirt. She had a stand in DH Evans draped with silk squares (only they weren't silk, obviously) and as soon as anyone came within charming distance she'd begin the spiel. Men bought them for their wives but they bought Suzy presents too. Chocolates mostly.

She hadn't been working lately, though. There had been another small ad in the *Evening News* a fortnight ago and Suzy had been resting in bed ever since, kept going by regular deliveries of hothouse grapes from Fortnum's and cups of Bovril from Annie who had moved into the attics of Massingham House where the maids and valets lived.

'Them gentlemen's gentlemen is all gentlemen's gentlemen, if you know what I mean, dear.'

Annie's gummy old face folded up with happy disgust. She was quite taken with the maid's quarters otherwise. There was barely room to get out of the bed divan but it was all centrally heated and she spent most of her time down in the flat anyway, either washing their lovely little bits or polishing the mirrors or playing with the Hoover – 'it's got attachments. Does curtains and everything' – otherwise once her two dolly birds were off out she could just put her feet up in the easy chair in her cosy kitchen, eating handmade chocolates and listening to *Mrs Dale's Diary* on the wireless. Mrs Dale wasn't Annie's cup of tea at all.

'Stuck-up bitch. Doctors' wives are the worst. Like her shit don't stink. She's probably having it with that Caradoc bloke. They don't let you hear what really goes on in them places.'

The only man Annie had ever really had any time for was killed in France somewhere the war before last. Died instantly they said. Never knew what hit him – unless he did know . . .

Henry had been visiting Suzy every day with silk dresses, lizard shoes, straw hats, suede gloves, a gold wristwatch (*It wasn't feminine to know the time – until she had a Rolex*) and finally, jammy jammy tart, he'd promised her the deeds to the Nice Little Flat. Henry had never had it so good. He had just persuaded the London County Council to let him pull down what the Germans had left of New Oxford Street and he could afford to say sorry any way he liked.

Suzy had spent most of Thursday at a beauty parlour in Bond Street being massaged with placenta oil (which was a bit peculiar in the circumstances) before taking a cab the three hundred yards up the road to visit Big Terry at the shiny new black and white salon and turn his fully-booked afternoon into a nightmare of be-with-you-in-a-moment-madams. Then she got another taxi over to Carpenter's and swanned into the bar looking like a million dollars (so Pete always insisted on saying).

'Mmm. Monopoly money, darling,' oozed Suzy.

Suzy kissed a few cheeks and popped herself up on a stool, crossing her legs with a soft whizz as nine bob's worth of five-strand 15-denier s-t-r-e-t-c-h nylon rubbed itself together. Her crocodile bag was tucked over the sleeve of her suit jacket and under her arm was the very latest *Vogue*.

'Big Terry let me have his. He's got a hairdo in it.' She flicked through the pages quite casually before holding out the open magazine to Alpaca Pete.

'See anyone you recognise?'

And there they were, Jane and Suzy in a full-colour, half-page ad for Frockways' Double Dates.

Three months ago Lawrence Green had recommended them to a man called Feldman who ran a huge budget-fashions business in Eastcastle Street. He had a whole new line and the sample run had been such a hit that he'd decided to advertise. There was a big craze for anything reversible and Solly Feldman's Double Dates were a stroke of genius.

'What is it?' Poor Reggie was going cross-eyed looking at the same girl in two frocks.

'Basically, darling, it's a frock with great big lacy holes in the skirt, double-sided petticoat underneath. One side matches skirt: invisible. Other side red or gold lamé or sky-blue pink: bingo. Ready to party the instant you clock off work.'

Reggie glanced obligingly at the picture. 'Cunning. Very cunning.'

Double Dates. The perfect day-to-evening ensemble for the budget-conscious career girl who's really going places! Just switch the petticoats and reverse the matching coatee and your Frockways Double Date is all ready for a night on the town. Twice the appeal from only £9 15s the set. Extra contrasting petties available from 59s 11d. Coatees from £4 10s. Sizes 8–16.

There was a picture of Jane stuck in the background behind the typewriter looking demure in a navy dress and jacket while Suzy wore the same thing only with the red bits showing and a flower in her hair looking deliriously gay in the arms of some deb's delight in a dinner jacket. The deb's delight (who lived with an antique-dealing friend in Lower Sloane Street) got paid half as much again (being a man, of sorts) but no one remembered him. It was the two girls – 'the virgin and the gypsy' Pete called them – bastard – that caught the eye. Mr Feldman had already bought some junior page ads in the *Daily Sketch* but *Vogue* was much more exciting.

Frockways couldn't run them up fast enough and Solly Feldman was already looking at swatches so that he could rush out a Summer Secrets range. They were doing the shoot on Monday.

The photographer's studios were in a dirty back alley off the King's Road somewhere. The desk and typewriter had been borrowed from the secretarial bureau downstairs and the bare boards of the freezing cold room were covered with coloured paper stapled to the floor by his assistant. For the next shoot Jane was going to be sat at the bloody typewriter again in Capri-blue shantung back to back with Suzy, a vision in blue and white on a garden chair having her glass refilled by the deb's delight in blazer and yachting cap.

Suzy had got tired of showing off and had begun to tell them her latest funny story.

'So she says to her fiancé: "Uncouth? Your mother thinks I'm uncouth? Did you tell her about Daddy's place in Gloucestershire? About the flat in Park Lane? Does she know I went to Roedean?" and the boyfriend nods every time. "So what's this 'uncouth' crap about?" '

Madge laughed so hard the top button on her skirt flew off.

Jane suddenly felt a hand on her upper arm.

'It's Jane, isn't it? Long time no see.'

She turned to see a tall, quite nice-looking blond bloke. She did the shy, puzzled look she used for bridal wear and played for time while he carried on talking. She watched his eyes flicking over her. Noticing. Noticing the smart make-up, the model-girl hair, the perfect manicure, the flirty eyelids of a pretty girl who knows to the nearest orchid exactly how pretty she is.

'I hardly recognised you, to be honest, but I remembered the outfit. You look smashing!'

So did Tony. Everything that had made her squirm had gone. It seemed that he'd moved from Hardy Amies to be head of bought ledger or something at Sharp and Butler further up Savile Row. Old Mr Sharp wouldn't let anyone be seen on the premises in a fifty-shilling suit so for the first twelve months your wages were docked until you'd paid cost price for a bespoke Sharp and Butler single-breasted special. The haircut was thanks to a word from young Mr Butler who had also taken Tony to an unofficial sale at the shirtmakers Sharp and Butler used for the dummy in their window. It only remained for the elderly typist to leave a deodorant on his desk one lunchtime (the accounts department had had an emergency whipround) and the result was a new, improved Tony, fit to be introduced to the gang.

'This is Tony Cole, an old friend of mine.' He couldn't remember that many names at once but immediately offered to buy a round so they liked him anyway.

Jane could see the cash register in Suzy's eyes clocking up the eleven-ounce made-to-measure blue worsted, the Jermyn

Street shirt and tie. Not bad at all. Like Prince Philip without the uniform.

'Janey and I have been showing off.' She let him look at the Frockways ad.

'It doesn't do either of you justice.' He smiled at Suzy but it was Jane he really wanted to talk to. He lowered his voice while the others carried on yacking.

'You disappeared off the face of the earth. None of the girls at Drayke's knew where you'd gone. Just pulled faces and said you'd had two weeks in lieu and that was that.'

'Old Drayke never let anyone work notice. Reckoned they just caused trouble and nicked all the stock – or let their friends nick all the stock. I'm only sorry I didn't get a chance to thank you for the dress and coat. That was so thoughtful of you.'

'Miss Winter insisted. Like it was made for you, she said. So. You still living in Norbury?'

A spasm crossed her face as if someone had trodden on a corn and he tumbled at once that Norbury was a no-no. She papered smoothly over his mistake.

'No. Auntie's still down at the cottage in Norbley,' she fantasised, suzily. The picture still tickled her. Doreen was on a sunny seat in the orchard this time, shelling peas for lunch. 'I did want to stay with her but the journey was taking far too long so I've moved up to town with Suzy.'

'Whereabouts?'

Hooray. Hooray. She had been lying in her beautiful blue and gold bath, dreaming about bumping into old friends and boyfriends – she was usually wearing the violet dress and coatee, funnily enough – and telling them where she lived and what she did. But she was beginning to give up hope. When did Norma and that crowd ever come to Piccadilly?

'Suzy's got a place in Massingham House – just behind the Dorchester.'

It was his face's turn to do a little dance this time.

'Strewth. That must cost a packet.'

She had been going to rattle off the widower-in-Hong Kong story. She'd told it often and she told it well but she didn't think Tony would believe it somehow. His sharp rag-trade eyes had already totted up Suzy's Harry Popper suit; the Bond Street coiffure; the shiny black crocodile bag. Clothes no honest woman could afford to buy. Even the top photographic models didn't earn much more than a tenner a day. His face sort of winced then he turned back to Jane.

'So. Will you finally let me buy you dinner?'

'You don't give up, do you?' Tilt head three-quarter left profile to three-quarter right profile, lowering and raising lashes. 'I can't tonight.' Never tonight – she'd grown as strict as Suzy about that and besides she had a dinner date and tomorrow was supposed to be a double date: her and Johnny; Suzy and Henry. She didn't fancy it much. She might let Tony take her out for supper on Sunday. It always seemed a pity to spend so many hours getting sanded down and varnished and then not get any appreciation. Tony was bound to be very appreciative. It all depended where he wanted to go.

'I might be free on Sunday.'

'How about the Guinea? Only round the corner from you. They do a pretty good steak.' Very nice too.

'That would be lovely. I should be ready by eight.' He lit her cigarette and she gave him the full works, sucking hungrily on the filter as she looked up into his face with those big, blank brown eyes. It was too easy really.

'Party time, darling,' whispered Suzy, who had just checked her smart new wristwatch. She slithered neatly off her stool – *Don't ruin the whole effect by pulling down your girdle* – stubbed out her cigarette and kissed Pete's cheek goodbye. It was a long time since Pete's hand had strayed above the fifteen denier but Suzy was very good at staying pals. You never knew when you might need that glass of stout.

'You ladies back here tomorrow lunchtime?'

'Very possibly, darling, but right now we've got to love you and leave you.'

'Can I give you a lift?' Tony again. His car, quite a smart-looking Zephyr Consul, was parked on the corner outside. First the suit and now this.

'Not bloody likely,' laughed Suzy, who'd been taken to *My Fair Lady* three times. 'I've got the taxi waiting, darling.' *Darling*. He wasn't her bloody darling.

Chapter 19

> *A man should date a girl purely for the
> privilege of her company, not to buy her
> intimacy. Her pleasure in his hospitality
> and her warm thanks for a lovely
> evening should be reward enough.*

It was just seven when they got upstairs. Suzy, having spent the whole day being beautified, just peeled off her suit and her girdle and lay down on the pink satin eiderdown for a little beauty sleep. Jane undressed and slipped into the bath Annie had run.

She had a date with the under-manager of the posh grocer's in Piccadilly – two more smoked-salmon sandwiches and he was eating out of her hand. She wasn't convinced the first time he asked her. He could only be on about a tenner a week but it turned out he was learning the family business and it was going to be dinner at Prunier's and then dancing. She wouldn't get much more than a box of chocolates out of it although the sick flatmate might pull in a hamper. He'd already sent an orchid – plain white, thank goodness. Those big, bruise-coloured ones never went with anything. She decided to stick it in her hair. Very mumsy, corsages.

What to wear? He didn't look like the red velvet type. Too showy. She called through to Suzy who had had her nap and was now wriggling into a rhapsody in pink organza. She was seeing Henry at least two nights a week now and she liked to build in plenty of variety. She was going through a fluffy, *jeune fille* phase lately.

'Is the forget-me-not faille clean?'

'Give or take. Annie's been over it with the Dabitoff, haven't you, darling?'

Jane, all dried and lotioned, was dribbling the glass stopper of the Jolie Madame bottle behind her ears and down her front. *Make the most of your chosen scent. Let the world know that someone lovely has drifted by.* She had been using Miss Dior but a girl who worked on the scent counter in Selfridges told her that Ruth Ellis always used to wear it which made her feel a bit funny so she gave the bottle to Annie and then took Sergio shopping.

The blue faille was very, very tight. What Yanks called a Willpower Dress because it helped you say 'no' to food – say 'yes' and you either threw up or blew off. It looked fabulous, though, once Annie had trussed her into it. The bodice looked quite demure from the front but from above her tits looked like two fat dollops of ice cream. That should keep the waiters on their toes.

Quick check of her three reflections in the dressing-table mirror. Hair fat and glossy; skin powdered and peachy; lips young and pink as berries and eyes . . . eyes like little brown bits of wood. Even Jane could see that. Dead eyes. *All the eye make-up in the box will not make your glance appealing if your eye is merely on the main chance.*

The phone on her dressing table rang. Henry had arrived early and Annie was busy shoe-horning Suzy into the organza (she'd lost a few pounds over the last fortnight but a size eight was a size eight) so Jane went into Maid Mode with a nasty Norbury voice.

'Yais? Mayfair 3515.'

Completely threw June. Umming and ah-ing at this unexpected hurdle.

'Is Miss Deeks there please? Miss James, I mean.'

'Hi shall enquire.'

Jane put the finishing touches to her lips.

'Hello?'

'Jane? It's me. June. I thought I'd better ring. It's Auntie. Something's happened.'

Jane studied her reaction in the three angles of the white and gold dressing-table mirror and let the drama flood across her skin. She pictured Doreen under a bus, Doreen in an oxygen tent, Doreen broken and bleeding at the bottom of the gorilla's cage.

'Aunt Doreen? Oh my God! What's happened? What's the matter?'

The Fantasy Coral lips trembling, the stiff dolly's eyelashes clicking shut and then opening again on shiny new eyes. Not blue ones – why were dolls' eyes always blue? – but hot and wet like melted chocolate. That was better.

'She's had a really Nasty Turn.'

What the bleeding hell was that supposed to mean? Definitely one of Doreen's that was. Nasty Turn. What? Heart attack? Epileptic fit? Stroke? Brain haemorrhage? Stomach on the chest?

'Is she in hospital?' Jane got a little catch into her voice. She leaned forward so that she could see her breasts (all six of them) inflating into view with each breath, brushing the fluffy blue bow affair at the front of the frock.

Doreen was at home (so the turn was only so nasty in other words). They'd put her in Jane's old room.

'She's asking for you.'

This was hard to believe.

'Is it serious?'

'Doctor doesn't know.' A breath in June's voice and suddenly, clear as bloody day, Jane could picture her sister stood in the draughty passage by the hall stand, checking her own reflection in the big old speckled mirror. Drama queen, honestly.

'Uncle George didn't want me to worry you.'

'I'll come over tomorrow about twelve. That be all right?'

She pictured herself at the side of her old bed, on the dressing-table stool looking smart, cooing sweetly. Cooling flannel? Spooning soup? No thank you. More June's style.

She could, in theory, have taken a bus from Park Lane (number 137, change at Streatham Hill) but sod that.

Suzy was curled up on Henry's lap in the sitting room being comforted (again). Bit late to start crying about it now.

'Was that the lovely Sergio on the telephone?'

Suzy had stretched her leg out over the arm of the chair, letting her new pink suede Ferragamo shoe – one of the week's nice little presents – dangle daintily from her stockinged toe.

'No,' compress lips grimly. 'No. It was my aunt's housekeeper. She's very ill apparently.'

Hospital? No. Home? Yes. Asking for her. Got to get down to Norbury. 'Down to Norbury.' Made it sound a major expedition especially to those two. Henry just sat in the backs of cars reading the share prices until Bill switched off the engine and the southern borders of Suzy's known universe only stretched as far as Sloane Square.

'You poor darling! Is there a train or something?'

Henry wanted the conversation to stop so he could get his hands back down the front of Suzy's pink organza dress. He looked like a man being attacked by a giant stick of candyfloss.

'Don't be silly. Bill can take her in the car. I'll give him a call and tell him to be here for – eleven all right for you? We don't need the car till tomorrow evening, do we?' 'We'. Not 'I'. 'We'.

This was very, very kind of Henry. Jane didn't know how she could thank him enough (trembling slightly as she said it in case the randy old bugger thought of a bloody way). But he wasn't even looking at Jane and her grateful tears would have been completely wasted if the doorbell hadn't rung. She opened the door with bright, gooey eyes and her handsome, posh grocer was ready and waiting to whisk her down to Daddy's Daimler which was vrooming respectfully on the forecourt below.

'I shan't be two seconds.' It was imagining her suede stiletto snaking out of the passenger door that gave Jane the brainwave.

She dived back into her room. How long would she actually be spending with Doreen? Half an hour? An hour at most. At that rate Henry's Bill could practically leave the engine running on the Bentley. Oh goody. The Bentley. She picked up the receiver and, using the end of her eye pencil to protect her manicure, dialled Joy in South Norwood.

It was more like Panic in South Norwood, actually. Where had she been, what her aunt had said about her, all that rubbish – until Jane cut her short and suggested they meet for a drink tomorrow lunchtime in the local hotel. You could hear the big gulp of oxygen Joy needed to take this one in her stride, not sound nonplussed and nineteen. She agreed to get the gang together and meet in the lounge bar of the Nelson (it was just a glorified pub really but Joy had never dared set foot in the place) at one o'clock.

Young Master James was straightening his bow tie in the hall mirror.

'Jolly nice flat.'

As they whizzed down in the lift she explained about the aunt in Surrey and the friend of a friend in Hong Kong. Not too much detail, though. That was where Suzy fell down. Nobody wanted details.

She'd just finished brushing her teeth in the powder room – you couldn't eat pâté and toast and wear a Willpower Dress, the bloody thing had a 21-inch waist – when the door swung open to reveal Johnny Hullavington's shop-soiled blonde 'fiancée', Amanda, keen for a spot of gossip and nose-powdering between the *boeuf en croute* and the *bombe surprise*. Jane immediately ducked her head as if fiddling with the heel of her stocking. Amanda was with the long-suffering friend.

'He seems to be being perfectly pleasant,' said the friend, trying to swallow the yawn in her voice.

'Yes, well that's all very well but he still won't talk *dates*. Mummy won't shut up about it.' Amanda was fed up with the whole thing. She'd even let him take her to bed a couple of times but there didn't seem much point. He hadn't been particularly appreciative and the whole thing only lasted for about thirty-five rather nasty seconds. Hardly worth taking your stockings off.

'Yes, but did he ever actually propose? Not even afterwards?'

Afterwards? Oh dear, oh dear. Poor Amanda.

'Oh do shut up, Celia.'

No date had been set for the wedding in other words. Serve her right. Silly cow.

Amanda and Celia both disappeared into cubicles to struggle with their girdles (*Holds its shape – and your figure – with a gentle determination*) while Jane escaped back downstairs. So. Johnny was in the restaurant somewhere.

Jane loped smoothly back to her table, giving the room the bland all-seeing stare of the catwalk model, while the room pretended not to look at the cartoon curves of her figure in its blue silk sheath. She could hardly breathe in the bloody thing but it was definitely worth it. They'd probably still have stared at her three months ago but only to wonder what she was doing there. Jane had a nightmare once where she walked the length of the room at L'Etoile and no one turned to look. It was only when she got to the Ladies' and looked in the mirror and saw the old Jane – long brown hair, chartreuse velvet – that she realised why. It must happen – or not happen – to older women on a nightly basis but it must have been terrible the first time. She shivered prettily.

'Are you cold?' A chance to take her hand in his.

'Someone walked over my grave.'

She had spotted Johnny at his corner table. She had been sitting with her back to him but he'd seen her now and seen the handsome young man she was with. Thank God it was only the grocer: Sergio or one of Henry's generous old pals and he might have smelled a rat.

She began to work on her escort, like a photographer after a particular look, making his face register amusement, desire, tenderness. Her smiling eyes were on his face but her mind was five yards back, imagining how the scene was playing behind her at that corner table.

Johnny hadn't wanted to be there at all. He'd only agreed to come when Amanda said that Celia and Hamish would be making up a foursome but Celia was obviously in on it and kept leaving them alone so that Amanda could have another go at charming him into submission. That was the plan, anyway. Amanda was no fool. Amanda's mummy was certainly no fool: three husbands and counting. She'd told her she shouldn't nag, shouldn't act desperate. Amanda managed to keep smiling, keep the conversation light (Mummy's advice), but she couldn't get that hungry, scared look out of her eyes. She just didn't have the training.

Johnny's eyes kept straying to the back of Jane's head: the silky white shoulders and the angle of her slim young neck as she chatted sweetly with her date, some gormless deb's delight. He was laughing at something Jane had said – one of Suzy's jokes possibly. All very polite and civilised but his hand shook as he lit her cigarette. Johnny closed his eyes and imagined those prettily painted lips blowing out the first breath of tobacco, as if her mouth were on fire.

Seconds later she was stubbing it out and turning her attention to her entrecôte. Johnny imagined her eating her steak (*saignant*): a little meat; a little moutarde; a little pomme sautée. Tiny bites that let her flirt and chew at the same time and that didn't wreck the shape of her mouth. A technique she'd perfected years ago by eating Canadian cheddar on toast in front of the dressing-table mirror.

The non-fiancée had a depressingly hearty appetite and took such big mouthfuls that if you made the mistake of talking to her mid munch her jaws had to work overtime in order to clear the decks for a reply. There had been a slimy sliver of meat at the corner of her mouth all the way through the main course.

It could have been quite earthy, quite Sophia Loren, but not the way Amanda did it. Her eyes hardly left her plate as she stoked her five-star dinner into her three-star body.

Amanda was still pouring her hard little heart out in the powder room and Johnny decided to stagger across to Jane's table. She could sense his approach from the look in her date's eyes: uncertain and a bit put out. He didn't want some debonair thirty-year-old to come muscling in on his luscious brunette.

Johnny wasn't on his best form. His table had already got through eight champagne cocktails and three bottles of Nuits St Georges. He'd drunk most of it himself. He bowed in a sniffy way to Jane's escort then stared rather woozily down the front of her frock.

'Sweet little Alice-blue gown.' Definitely sozzled.

Jane selected a face for poor young James's benefit: bemused; amused; tiny bit irritated.

'What's an *ice* girl like you doing in a place like this?' Christ. It was funny the first time but this was getting beyond a joke.

'Do you know something?'

She twitched a tiny smile, raised a bored eyebrow.

'I love to watch you eat, Janey-my-darling.'

What was that supposed to mean? It was hard physical work not to let her face look cheesed off: pert; tolerant; politely intrigued.

'I love to watch you eat because you do it so, so *perfectly*.'

Mercifully, manky old Amanda had finished her weekly whine and was stalking crossly back through the restaurant in last year's nasturtium lace. She'd caught her heel round the back of the petticoat and the hem was coming down. *Many a miss has lost a man because her slip had slipped, so beware.*

Johnny skulked back to his corner without waiting for introductions and Jane refocused her attention on the game in hand.

'Who was that?'

'I think his name's John something. He's a friend of my flatmate's. Frightful lush.' *Frightful*.

But loverboy didn't want to talk about Johnny; he wanted to talk about him. Every now and then he'd realise that he'd pulled the conversation too far over his side like so much eiderdown and push a little her way. Did she know Paris? No she bloody didn't know Paris. Swank.

'I'd love to show you Paris.'

If he hadn't been so wet behind the ears that might have been an invitation but it was just another way of letting her know that he *did* know Paris.

'*Parlez-vous français?*'

Where that conversation was supposed to go if you didn't actually parley-voo was anyone's guess but he'd struck lucky this time.

'*Un peu.*'

Turned out he was a lot less shy in French.

'*Vous êtes la plus belle fille içi. La plus belle fille du Londres. Très chic, très soignée, très sensuelle. Avec les tétons merveilleux.*' (The waiter perked up at this point.) He rather liked having her smile politely while he talked dirty. Risky, but rather exciting. He'd read a list of useful froggy chat-up lines in a men's magazine once and this was the first time they'd come into their own. He had some even fruitier ones in reserve but decided to save those for the drive home. She might let him take her up in that lift. He rather liked lifts. The funny murky light – and the mirrors.

The Willpower Dress had called a halt to Jane's entrecôte (eighteen shillings: only the lobster cost more) so it was back to the Ladies' to freshen up.

Johnny was there waiting on the stairs when she came out. Pissed but dishy. His tie was slightly loose and he looked like a very naughty fifth-former.

'So who's the boy wonder?'

No answer to that, really. She leaned against the wall of the stairwell and just looked right back at him. Let him figure out what she was thinking. She was tired of trying to work it out.

'You look lovely in that dress.' Tell her something she didn't know. 'Younger somehow.' Was that good? 'Like the night we first met. Why wouldn't you see me tonight?'

'I had a date. I'm nineteen. I have dates. We're not engaged, you know.'

'Why aren't we?'

Here we bloody go again.

'Don't start all that. We'll talk tomorrow.'

Then a nice half turn and back down the stairs to young James.

She decided against crêpes Suzette. She was getting sick of brushing her teeth – besides, just-a-coffee-for-me was always terribly sophisticated.

She let him kiss her in the Daimler, although not as much as the chauffeur would have liked. She let him kiss her again, harder and closer, in the tiny two-man lift. He even pressed the red 'stop' button between floors which was cheeky. Doreen never kissed anybody and she wouldn't even let George kiss June and Jane for some dirty-minded reason or other. Jane had had a lot of ground to make up. She'd had more kisses in the last three months than she'd had in her whole life and being kissed goodnight was just about her favourite thing. Got you from nought to sixty in five seconds: hot, wet, excited. Only kissing was never really enough for them. It was all downhill after that.

James dug out a bit more smutty French as his hand slid up from her waist and his lips started to follow the actually rather well-worn path down to her cleavage. She pulled back sharply, keeping a weather eye on her reflection: pink; wide-eyed; slightly shocked.

'Please. Don't. You mustn't.' That old rubbish. *No man can seriously be angry, whatever he may say, if a girl shows that she has decent standards of behaviour.* He was very, very apologetic. A two-dozen long-stemmed apology at the very least. Roses, honestly. You couldn't eat them, wear them or sell them. Waste of bloody time.

'Please say you'll forgive me. It's just that you're so ... so.' More of the old *je ne sais quoi*. Why couldn't he say these things in English? 'May I see you again?'

'I don't know. I don't know what to say.'

She couldn't very well say that an evening playing dream girl, pretending to like black coffee and running backwards and forwards to the loo to be sick wasn't her idea of a good time. That he was too young and soft to understand about things like proper presents and she wasn't about to start giving it away. Not at this stage of the game.

Chapter 20

> *The smart girl should be as deft
> at whipping up a soufflé as she is
> at pondering existentialism.*

It was lovely back inside the flat. Annie had left the lights on and it was all warm and creamy and polished. There was a box of chocolates and a huge bowl of hothouse peaches – three bob each – on the coffee table.

Suzy wouldn't be back yet so Jane released herself from her armour-plated, Alice-blue gown and slipped into something more comfortable – not exactly difficult. She wrapped herself in a kimono, poured herself a glass of Grand Marnier and arranged herself carefully on the long white sofa, adjusting the silk robe to show off a hint of cleavage for her imaginary audience, then lay there, pecking at the three chocolates she'd decided to allow herself (she had to eat something) and watching telly. Just as the national anthem was starting up she heard the lift gate opening and hurried away to her own room. She didn't want to get roped into one of Henry's three-handers. Mind you, she had a funny idea he wouldn't be going in for all that lark again. Besides, she needed her beauty sleep for Norbury.

She couldn't get to sleep straight away. Johnny was getting to be a right nuisance. It wasn't just dates any more. He'd been proposing on and off for the last six weeks.

About a month after their first date he'd borrowed a car and taken her down to Putney to meet Mummy. It was a nice enough house with all the right accessories – French windows, wisteria, *Country Life* and Earl Grey bloody tea – but Marjorie Hullavington wasn't half as posh as she liked to make out. Mr Hullavington Senior had been killed (instantly) during the Blitz. This made keeping up appearances a great deal easier. No one could sneer at his tailor or cringe at his vowels any more. Marjorie certainly did her best to look the part – thirty-year-old Creed suit; lisle stockings the colour of ointment and a thrifty dab of orange tangee lipstick. But the house didn't smell right. Posh houses (like Nice Little Flats in Mayfair) smelled of brandy and beeswax, of cut flowers and Diorissimo. Dogs (at a pinch). Marjorie Hullavington's front hall smelled like the inside of a biscuit tin. Not a posh smell. And that triple string of pearls was definitely fake. They exactly matched her dentures, which seemed a lot of trouble to go to.

Jane hadn't taken any chances: Hardy Amies, brown shoes, a russet felt toque and a tan bag borrowed from Suzy – she didn't think her own shiny new pet alligator would play well with the kind of woman who could make a bottle of sherry stretch to twenty tiny glasses and who served macaroni cheese for Sunday lunch. Who thought that one up? It looked like toasted vomit.

'What does your father do, Jenny?' Did she get the name wrong on purpose or was she going gaga?

The wonderful, wonderful thing about Jane's shy, squinting dad was that, like Mr Hullavington, he was very, very dead and so had a wide choice of careers open to him. Jane usually chose the law. Respectable and no one would expect her to know the first thing about it.

'And where were you at school?'

God, the woman was nosey but Jane could safely stick to the facts on that one. An Anglican convent in Surrey might not be Roedean or Cheltenham but it was quite posh enough for most purposes. There were only a handful of girls' schools that anybody had ever heard of anyway so provided you said 'St Ursula's' with enough confidence you were certain to get away with it.

'John tells me you're a *mannequin*, Gillian.'

She might just as easily have said 'John tells me you'll perform fellatio for a nice mink scarf' from the tone of her voice.

'I was living with my aunt in Surrey' (Doreen was on a swing seat with a straw hat on this time, doing a bit of needlepoint) 'after Daddy died'. If you didn't mention Mummy at all they tended to assume she died-when-you-were-born and asked no further questions. 'But when my aunt died my cousins were forced to sell the house and I had to think about making my own living. Modelling was the only thing I was fit for really.' A little shrug. Poor me. Poor brave little me.

'And where do you live now, er, Janet?'

She could answer that one in her sleep: friend Suzy; widower in Hong Kong. Like falling off a log.

The final test was to bowl Jane a googly about current events. Which was a bit like Philip Drayke asking her whether she spoke Italian – the last thing Mrs Hullavington actually wanted was a daughter-in-law who could bore for Britain about the international situation but it gave her a cast-iron excuse for giving her the thumb's-down: 'I *know* you, John. I know you could never *really* be happy with a wife who couldn't hold her own at dinner parties.'

Jane had only skim-read the *Sunday Times* that morning but luckily John's mother (who was a *Telegraph* reader – *The man's newspaper intelligent women read*) preferred talking about the Queen's latest baby to the nuclear threat so it was a piece of cake. Johnny sat watching the pair of them, practically burping with pride, before announcing that it was really time to be making a move.

Jane slipped away to give her nose a thorough powdering while Johnny got the green light from Mummy. Marjorie thought John had made a Very Wise Choice: young, pretty, sweet-tempered, *mouldable*. He could certainly do a lot worse. Amanda was a lot worse, Mummy thought Amanda was Fast (if she only knew) and, almost more to the point, she loathed Amanda's ritzy bloody mother who saw right through the façade and tended to patronise 'poor Marjorie and her doilies'. The only good in-law was a dead in-law, Marjorie had decided.

The pilgrimage to Putney was followed by a dinner party in Roehampton or somewhere (it was dark, there was definitely a bridge involved). Getting dressed had been a nightmare.

'It'll be black tie but Nick and Daphne are very relaxed,' said Johnny, who thought he was being helpful.

Jane knew the type. They used to come into Drayke's. 'Very relaxed' just meant that the women's clothes would be two seasons old and the men would be wearing their fathers' dinner jackets and never dry clean them. Practically everything in the entire flat was too flash – Annie's uniform included.

Suzy told her to stop worrying.

'The women will all be fat and thirty and passée so they're bound to hate you anyway. Just wear something Johnny likes.' She settled on a rather pretty old crimson chiffon number of Glenda's with a folded satin waist and spent twelve and six at a hairdresser's in Berkeley Square being groomed to a standstill (Terry had gone to Brighton to do the hair for a swimwear catalogue. The poor cows were going to freeze to death).

It was a big, ugly red-brick house. There was a pram in the hall and a nasty familiar smell of burned toast and baby lotion. Jane was herded into a group of half a dozen women by Daphne. She'd flicked through a handful of Suzy's magazines the day before but nothing prepared her for the rubbish she was supposed to talk about. Recipes (Keesh? What the fuck was that?); marrow moussaka; natural childbirth; breastfeeding; child psychology. Most of them were doing a course in something. Daphne left her up to her armpits in spermicidal jelly and then tore back to the kitchen to stir something. Whatever it was, she didn't stir it enough.

Daphne claimed to have spent most of the day locked up in the kitchen with Elizabeth David but the food was still absolutely disgusting. After two months of West End dinner dates it wasn't just smoked salmon and sole grillée any more. Jane had pretty much eaten the lot: snails; frog's legs; brains; calves' liver. It might not always stay eaten but she'd got to quite like most of it. Daphne was giving them cheese soufflé and 'her' coq au vin: 'hers' in the sense that nobody else's was made with half a bottle of sweet cider and burned to a crisp.

The wine was rotten too (Nick had been at school with someone in the wine trade). This was a pity because the glasses were really lovely. There used to be a shop near the Arcade that sold crystal like that. It made a lovely noise if you dipped your finger in the wine and skimmed it round the rim.

'Lovely, aren't they? Waterford, I think.' Some bloke. She couldn't remember all their names: Gerald? Jeremy? He had unbelievably bad teeth whoever he was and rather dirty yellow fingernails.

'I'm no expert but they look more like Baccarat to me.'

He thought not. He started pinging annoyingly at the rim with his fingernail before finally deferring to Our Host in a loud, prove-me-right-will-you sort of way. What an idiot, honestly, as if anybody cared. Only they did care and they were all terribly surprised and impressed that she knew and he didn't and all looked at her differently even though she was the same.

The funny thing about all but one of the couples was that you didn't seem to get two good ones in any one pair. If you quite liked the wife, the husband was sure to be a complete git. Jane had been having an almost pleasant chat with a woman called Linda – about the Ideal bloody Home Exhibition but she meant well. As she was speaking to Jane, Linda waved across the room at the last couple to arrive but her face was being monitored by her husband who was standing on the other side of the bay window: 'Don't smile in that insincere way, darling.' Her face looked like someone had pulled the plug on it: all the life, all the confidence draining away.

Lavinia and Wossname were the exception. They were a perfectly matched pair. Lavinia, seeking vengeance for her husband's cock-up about the glasses, waited until there was a lull in the conversation before asking Jane, good and loud, what she thought about Penguin publishing *Lady Chatterley* in the summer. It was like falling off a log. None of them had actually read it anyway but Henry had smuggled a copy back from Paris and made her and Suzy read the rude bits out loud. There was an expectant silence around the table.

'Lawrence isn't really me, I'm afraid. He's so sentimental and all that terrible sex just makes me laugh. It's such *English sex.*'

That stumped them. They'd only ever had English sex and while there was always the outside chance that they'd already read that month's *Encounter* she couldn't see it somehow. They'd done all their serious reading at Somerville or somewhere. It was just keesh and Kingsley Amis from now on.

Some old trout called Felicity in what looked like a short-sleeved stair carpet had another go a bit later on, as if she were dragging the conversation down to Jane's level.

'So what should we all be wearing next season, Janey?' As if that shabby fat cow would be in the market for a flocked organza overskirt or a gingham bikini. Never mind, Jane knew a good answer to this one.

'I haven't the faintest idea, I'm afraid. I just put on whatever's on the rail and try not to fall over. I put on a garment bag by mistake once.'

Mirthless laughter. Approving glances.

The men were much, much more straightforward.

Lavinia's husband cornered her in the hall on the way back down the stairs from the loo. He stank of cheap brandy and his face was flushed and sticky-looking. She was a very pretty little thing, apparently, so pretty that he felt he must take her hand and press it against the lump in his gravy-stained trousers. She slapped his face so hard that he lurched sideways into Johnny who had just come out of the dining room. Whatsisname looked very, very surprised and horribly, horribly excited.

'Take me away from here. Now.' Why should she sit down and pretend nothing had happened? Why spare poor Lavinia's feelings? Fuck Lavinia. Luckily for Johnny, it was time to go in any case.

All in all it had been an impressive performance: pretty, clever and virginal. Amanda wasn't any of those. Never had been. Poor Amanda. Amanda was thirty next summer. She had lowered her sights a good long way since she first came out. Not that she could swank about being presented at court any more, not since the new Queen put a stop to it. It showed your age. But Johnny would definitely do. The Gloucester Road flat wasn't too bad and they could sell that ghastly Putney villa as soon as the old bag died and buy somewhere decent. The friends would have to go, obviously. Those suburban bluestockings and their ghastly grammar-school husbands. Johnny had been to the right school, knew the right tailor, drank in the right bars, even if his mother was a bit common. She couldn't live for ever.

Nick (well pissed) had taken Johnny on one side already to say how very, very, very pleased he and Daphne were. It was time he got married. They were running out of single women to make up the numbers. They'd neither of them liked Amanda who couldn't follow their conversation (mind you, they did tend to talk about Civil Rights and disarmament on purpose) and who sneered at them for not living in Kensington.

Amanda's name was Methune, which was God's gift of a name for a snob like her because nobody was entirely sure how to pronounce it. You began the game with a ten-point start. Only poor dozy Amanda never saw that the handicap might not always work in her favour, that her name might simply never be called.

Johnny was dead chuffed at how well Janey had gone down with the old pals but then again he wasn't absolutely sure how he felt about having a wife that other men would really want to fuck. Nobody else would ever fancy Amanda – but then neither did he. Poor Amanda, who thought that 'letting him' would make her more desirable rather than less. As if anyone would want to screw that for the rest of their lives.

Jane was a very different kettle of fish. You could tell by the way she danced, by the way she kissed him goodnight. And yet he hadn't managed much more than a kiss so far. She had a fabulous figure. He imagined her at the head of the table in the dining room in Putney – Mummy had always promised she'd move into the flat in Gloucester Road if and when he got married. He imagined standing behind her chair and pulling down the zip on that saucy red dress of hers.

Johnny proposed to Jane that evening after an unusually steamy goodnight kiss. Her breasts were actually much larger than he'd thought. Mmm. He drove away from Massingham House loosening his bow tie slightly with his right hand as he headed down toward Knightsbridge. Amanda had pretty much kept her knickers on once she'd realised they weren't worth a sapphire and diamond cluster. In the end he decided to pop down and see the lovely Barbara for a little light relief. Good old Barbara. He turned left into Sloane Street and surged on towards Chelsea Bridge and the South Circular.

He had been quite surprised when Jane hadn't accepted him. She wasn't supposed to say No. Was there someone else? She said not. Would she think it over? If he insisted but couldn't they go on as they were? All very frustrating but she was sure to come round eventually now that she'd met his mother and his friends. Playing clothes horses with that foxy little trollop was no life for a nice girl like her. And that whole Mayfair flat business was very suspect. Johnny didn't believe a word of Suzy's Hong Kong story. The flat was obviously being bankrolled by the sugar daddy and they just had poor Jane in there to make it look respectable.

He'd danced with Suzy once. They'd bumped into her and Henry at the Stork Room one evening and although neither couple wanted to share a table, they'd swapped partners for a swift rumba, just out of politeness.

'God help poor Janey,' laughed Suzy, as she sashayed into his arms. 'Henry came very late to the rumba.'

The dance floor was fairly crowded so it was hard to be completely sure but it seemed that whenever they passed behind a pillar Suzy pressed herself closer. It seemed churlish not to respond. He held her a little tighter and, once he was quite sure he wasn't mistaken, began rubbing himself against her hip bone. She did a little work with the eyelashes at that one but she didn't pull away. And then the music stopped and she trotted back to Henry and Johnny could see them at their table for two, nuzzling soppily. How old was Henry? Fifty, maybe? Could he get it up that easily?

Janey had beaten him back to their table.

'How was your rumba?' He was afraid she'd read his thoughts.

'Very nice. Tiny bit rheumatic,' and her face smiled sheepishly at him while she mentally ran through the wardrobe for the following night in search of something Sergio hadn't seen. The new jade-green chiffon and paper taffeta creation that Lawrence Green had given her might be nice. It had cost slightly more than the usual quick feel (the workroom were up to their eyes in velvet speciality models for Debenham and Freebody and Goldie had had to nip down to John Lewis for some bias binding) but it had definitely been worth it.

Jane smiled absently at Johnny and sipped at her Grand Marnier while imagining herself stretched out on the bed in Sergio's suite at the Connaught (you really could walk home from there) screaming 'bracelet length!' at the moment of climax:

it still made him laugh and, besides, she quite wanted another bracelet. Blue didn't go with everything.

Johnny gazed at the suddenly very sexy look in her half-closed eyes and immediately proposed again.

He'd proposed pretty much every date since. She never actually said no outright – a girl had to eat – but she was getting sick of being asked, of his assuming that she would say yes eventually. He'd probably be at it again tomorrow after the double date if he got the chance – he went down on one knee sometimes (usually when he was tight). Did she want to be married to him? She certainly didn't want to *get* married. She thought again of Doreen in the yellow jerseylaine coatee.

Suzy asked her if he'd proposed and seemed quite surprised – fucking cheek – when Jane said yes as a matter of fact he had. Cow. She was even more surprised that Jane had turned him down.

'You must be out of your tiny mind.'

'I reckoned he was probably joking.'

'Men never joke about a thing like that. You should have bitten his hand off.'

'I don't need to be married. I'm making nearly fifteen guineas a week what with the Debenham and Freebody job and all the showroom work. And the Double Dates should get us more bookings.'

'Might do. Might not. A gimmick like that might work too well. A woman actually stopped me in Fortnum's this morning. If we become the face of Frockways, nobody else will touch us. Besides, none of this is for ever, darling. Do you really want to be doing Paris turns and being nice to Sergios in ten years' time? More to the point, will anyone even want you to? This is a young woman's game. Even Iris used to be a model, you know, darling – house model at Wondercoat, in all the magazines, ten guineas a week *then* – now look at her:

three quid a week alimony from Mr Iris and the odd handout from Dougie if she comes across. Or you end up like Madge, selling your body to the Reggies of this world just to keep the vet from the door.'

And there was Johnny offering to rescue her from ending up like Iris and Madge. Some rescue. He only made about three grand a year at his job in the City. You couldn't live happily ever after on that kind of money. You could live on macaroni cheese and hand-knitted woollies and last season's sweat-stained satin evening gowns ever after but what was happy about that?

He didn't really love her. How could he? He loved the hourglass figure, the model gowns, the perfect make-up all right, but one whiff of the marrow moussaka and he'd be back sniffing round Amanda – or his Streatham fancy-piece.

And he had the cheek to ask what she was doing in a place like this. A place like what? And she looked around her at the chandelier and the china ornaments and the gilded mirrors and the beautiful white sofas and wondered what kind of place he had in mind. Four bedrooms in Barnes or Kingston or Wimbledon or Esher or somewhere? With nice neighbours. And mingy little 'young marrieds' drinks parties – *Allow two to three drinks per person or three bottles for ten people.* And poxy 'mmm-did-you-make-these-yourself?' coffee mornings and snobby rotten dinner parties of lousy French food wearing a cheap black frock (home-made, even. People did) being groped over the drying-up by other people's husbands whose wives, you bet your sweet life, did not understand them at all. Where the nearest any of the women got to a job was manning the bloody cake stall at the school fête.

So long as everything was cooked and washed and starched and ironed and polished and waxed and vacuumed and baked and bottled and sewn and roasted and wiped and brushed and swept and perfumed and combed and disinfected she'd never have to earn another penny, pay another bill, open another door, wear another waspie, mow another lawn, open another bottle, empty another dustbin, read another book, pluck another eyebrow, wax another leg, paint another wall, slap another cheek, suck another cock. And she'd rather fucking die.

Chapter 21

> *To begin the story of Norbury we must*
> *go back in time to 50 million years*
> *ago to the time known as the Eocene*
> *period when this area of south-eastern*
> *England was covered by sea.**

Annie shuffled in at half nine with a cup of tea, the *Daily Express* and two dozen red roses – 'Please forgive me for being such a brute'. Handwritten in a man's writing. He must have been up at the crack of dawn seeing to that.

'Suzy and Love's Young Dream are having a lie-in.'

That was one way of putting it. Suzy and her Mr Swan were at it like knives in the big pink-quilted bed next door. You could hear the velvet headboard banging against the wall. There was a mark on the wallpaper already.

'You'd think he could leave the poor little cow alone.'

Annie muttered her way back to the kitchen and Jane shut the door behind her and climbed into her waiting bath. She made up and dressed as carefully as she would for a date. More carefully. Not just to wind up Doreen. Not just to cheer up Uncle George. This was going to be the full passing-out parade.

The whole flat already reeked of flowers so she decided to take the roses down to Norbury. They clashed rather boldly with the violet dress and coat – *Run the risk of bad taste rather than dress like a mouse.* The whole effect was very Bronwen Pugh Goes Hospital

* *Norbury: The Story of a London Suburb,* J. G. Hunter and B. A. Mullen, 1977

Visiting. It was a bit chilly to go without a coat but she would be in the car most of the time and, besides, she'd decided to ritz it to them good and proper with the mink scarf and matching flowerpot hat that Sergio had given her for her birthday. She had just got the scarf to sit straight when the porter buzzed up with the magic words: 'Your driver is here, Miss James.'

Henry's Bill had a wedding to go to, so the Bentley was being driven by Henry's Bill's Bob. He was holding the door open but she had to walk round the car to get to it. He wanted her where he could see her in the rear-view mirror.

The car creamed away into Knightsbridge where ladies of a certain age – messers, by the look of them – were out killing time, dressed up to the nines, trying things on and stealing squirts of scent until the stores shut at one and they skulked back home to a tin of soup in their sunless flats in Lowndes Square.

You never saw a pram in Sloane Street. Sloane Street babies were walked by nannies in parks and squares, not by mummies in high streets. Over Chelsea Bridge into the red-brick terraces of Battersea and Clapham and it was a different story. Clapham pavements were chock-a-block with huge old baby carriages and funny, low-slung pushchairs all parked outside shops with hand-knitted bundles of shit and sick strapped inside them, screaming with outrage while stupid old women with no nappies to wash stopped and coochied and nosily matched size for age. Older children, too large to strap in and wheel about, had to be dragged in and out of shops being refused things by women with faded headscarves and cross faces. Young women, really, but aged at a stroke by the magic ring that had taken away their dressing tables and left big, fat prams in their place.

Jane smugly snuggled her nose against her mink scarf sniffing the sweet expensive smells that clung to the fur: Jolie Madame; Chanel No 5 and a ghostly whiff of Miss Dior. As they cruised past Streatham Common, Jane snapped open her alligator bag – would any of the Deekses even know it was real? Would they even dream how much it cost? – took out her compact and checked her face. She could see the shy, randy little eyes of Henry's Bill's Bob watching in the rear-view mirror from under the patent-leather peak of his cap. He was actually very nice-looking in a skinny sort of way. High, slightly girlish cheekbones and a really lovely mouth. Her lipstick was perfectly all right but she put some on anyway, rubbing the waxy red stick across her mouth and yumming her lips together to spread the colour evenly across her smile. She saw him lick his own lips in sympathy.

'It's Bob, isn't it?'

He nodded. A horny little lump in his throat made speech impossible.

'You don't have a tissue or something, do you?' What a sexy little word that was: *tissue*.

He fumbled in the pocket of his cheap blue suit and passed her his clean white handkerchief – show, not blow.

'I can't possibly use this.'

'No. It's all right. It doesn't matter. It'll wash.'

Only it wouldn't wash. Henry's Bill's Bob lived at home in Ilford with his old mum who wouldn't have approved of lipstick on his laundry. He watched Jane's lips make their Plum Crazy monogram on the corner and thought of other uses for her second-hand kiss.

They finally hit Norbury.

'It's the next on the left, then second right.'

Moments later, the long, shiny, coffee-coloured car purred to a halt outside number sixty-three. Parking was not a problem in Pamfield Avenue. Uncle George used to park his old banger outside but then it packed up and he couldn't afford to get another one. Doreen always said the Big End went but that wasn't actually the trouble. She just liked saying it.

Only two vehicles ever parked in the street now. One belonged to Mr Nottage at number fourteen. Mr Nottage was a travelling salesman and Doreen, who had read (but never quite finished) an Agatha Christie about one of these, was convinced that he was a mass murderer. Or a bigamist. One of the two. The other vehicle was the Ripley Removals pantechnicon. Ripley Bros was painted on the side in letters three feet high. It usually lived in a lock-up in Thornton Heath but sometimes the Bros drove home in it after a late job and left it in the avenue, lowering the tone.

Jane knew that something was seriously the matter the moment the car pulled up. The windows had been cleaned, the hydrangea had finally got its winter crew-cut, there were washed milk bottles on the front step (which had been gingered up with cardinal red) and there was a pot of daffodils by the path. The upstairs bedroom curtains (freshly laundered and hanging flowery side out) twitched as Jane opened the gate and June was at the front door before she got there. She was wearing a quilted nylon housecoat covered with pink cabbage roses and an apron. She looked like she'd been wallpapered.

'I didn't want you to knock, just in case she was having her nap.' She spoke in a peculiar, nursey stage whisper. The hall lino had been polished – how did you polish lino? *Why* did you polish lino? – and there was a sickly smell of baking coming from the kitchen.

You could see that June was having the time of her fucking life just by the way she wiped her hands on her pinny. She washed them all the time: it was the nursiest thing she could think of – short of pinning a watch to her chest and walking up and down the stairs with a jug of warm piss. The pinny – pin tucks, pleats, gathers, drawn-thread embroidery, satin-stitch initials, you name it, Georgette had splashed Ribena on it – represented her last term's work at school. She got a certificate for it.

'How's college?'

College was just fine. The Old Doreen would have far rather June went out and got a job to pay for her keep (particularly now that Jane's leaving had left the housekeeping forty bob short) but she had quite liked the idea of a 'daughter' who was a teacher.

The very thought of it had got June an automatic upgrade from 'my late sister's girl'. The New Doreen didn't know what bloody day it was.

June didn't want to chat.

'I'll get the kettle on. She's in here.' And, bold as brass, June opened the door to the front room which was now home to the telly (much better ITV reception on the street side of the house), several migrant pouffes and June's entire glass animal collection tricked out across the mantelshelf. Every now and then she'd come home with a new specimen tenderly wrapped in newspaper but they all looked like the bastard children of a gazelle and a giraffe. Jane reckoned they fiddled with the glass first then made up the animal afterwards. Like those poodly things made of skinny pink balloons you got at funfairs.

In the corner lurked an enormous wooden playpen where Georgette sat on her fat plastic backside, furiously whacking at a celluloid clown contraption. She wanted it to lie down and shut up but the painted smile kept lurching upright again, dongling cheerily as it rolled with each punch. Eventually, Georgette pushed it flat and laid the puzzle-bricks box on top of it.

'Night-night,' she said firmly. She was her mother's daughter.

No one took a blind bit of notice.

Uncle George didn't hold with the play pen – 'She's not a wild animal. You ought to let her run about more' – but he didn't want her running about anywhere near him. He'd sneaked off down the end of the garden before June could get Georgette into her coat and boots for a bit of fresh air so she just popped her back in her cage. She was all right. Still wasn't talking, mind you. The only words so far were 'June', 'Wibena', 'night-night' and 'wee-wee'. June was a bit worried about this – they were doing Child Development at college this term.

Doreen looked like death warmed up. There was a good inch of grey roots on her lazy twist of Golden Amber hair. She was dressed but June had made her wear a fluffy pink bed jacket over her clothes as if to show she wasn't quite the ticket. She was sat on the settee sucking thoughtfully on a banana. It still had the skin on.

Half an hour was going to be more than enough, Jane decided. Even when you went to see someone in hospital (one of Doreen's few hobbies) you never stayed longer than that, so as not to tire the patient and before you yourself got tired of sitting there, sneaking grapes and promising them their old selves.

Doreen was definitely not her old self but maybe she didn't want her old self. As soon as she recognised Jane (which took a bit of time: she had to take the mink hat off) she cracked open her face to show all her own teeth.

'Don't you look nice? Lovely colour. Don't she look nice, June? Lovely colour on you. What colour would you call that?'

'Purple?' June was clueless about colours.

'Purple?'

'Purple.'

'Lovely purple colour.'

Doreen had so seldom sat down in the front room – even at Christmas she was always in and out to the kitchen moaning about not having had a chance to take the weight off her feet – that she thought she was staying somewhere else. Somewhere a bit posh to judge from all the tea trays and doilies June kept serving up. The kettle whistled and June dived back into the kitchen.

'Nice here, innit?' she whispered, chummily.

She was wearing pale blue bedroom slippers. These seemed to bother her slightly. None of the other guests had slippers on. Did they let you wear slippers in the lounge?

'Next time I come here I'll wear my tan pumps. Bit smarter.'

She caught sight of Jane again and smiled a bit more. Her face ached with the unfamiliar exercise.

'You *do* look smart. Lovely colour. What colour would you call that?'

Christ on a bike.

June came back in with a tray. The second-best tea set, which had only ever had one (disastrous) outing from the china cabinet to the best of Jane's knowledge, suddenly appeared, complete with a new cake plate and a doily and a pile of slightly burnt-looking cupcakes decorated with what looked like bits of red and green plastic – *fun to make, ten minutes to bake*.

June had taken to making tea all the time and packet-mix cakes which she was convinced were more convenient (it said so on the box). Her new best friend Valerie's mother had a two-tiered cake plate with doilies. And a biscuit barrel. And jam in a cut-glass pot. June had bought Doreen a cake plate for her birthday in February so that there'd be something nice on the table when Valerie came round but Doreen (this was before The Turn) took it back to the department store and exchanged it for a waterproof sheet for Georgette and a pair of support stockings. June could buy all the cake plates she wanted now.

June's new mumsy manner had got into her conversation. Jane looked very smart. The buses could be murder. Had she had a good journey down?

Oh thank you, God.

'Oh June, thank goodness you've reminded me. I ought to take a cup out to my driver. He's waiting in the car.' (She didn't say 'Bentley' in case they didn't know what it was.)

Time was when Doreen's fat blue and white hand would have broken the handle off the teacup on hearing such a pile of swank but the new, improved Doreen looked up, and her face cracked into another dazzling black smile.

'Car?'

A nicer person than Jane would have offered to take her out for a ride but then a nicer person would have come on the bloody bus.

June covered her surprise by faffing about getting another cup and saucer – being careful not to get the one with the glued handle. 'Did you hire one of them mini cabs then?' June simply couldn't make out what Jane was doing with a driver.

'He works for some friends of mine. They didn't need the car today.'

'Nice friends you got.'

Bob was curled up with *Titbits – Nudity on Our Stages: does it go too far?* – smoking his way through a pack of ten Player's Navy Cut. His cap was pulled low over his eyes against the morning sun. He looked very sexy suddenly. She passed his tea (two sugars) and cupcakes (just add an egg) through the window of the Bentley. She knitted him a brave little smile.

'I'm *so* glad you're here. I shan't be too much longer.'

A dozen net curtains twitched back into place as she modelled her way back up the front garden path; Jane is wearing a Vision in Violet in a cunningly cut lightweight worsted bouclé lined with pure silk and it cost more than your last bloody rates bill.

Doreen got a big kick out of the tea tray but she was convinced that the hotel waitresses were watching her every move so she came over all genteel, sticking her little finger out sideways as she stirred in the sugar and passing the cake plate to Jane.

'*Do* have another sandbag.'

Sister June weighed in with her two pennyworth.

'She forgets words. Doctor' ('Doctor': Dr What? Like there was only one) 'says you have to expect that in her condition. But we try to keep her Mentally Alert.'

This basically involved getting Doreen her first ever library book. A large-print edition of Phyllis Matthewman's *Wife on Approval* was on the table beside her, the polythene cover all tacky with handling. Doreen seemed to thoroughly enjoy it – 'Charles Trevor's career depended on his being married, and quickly'. June had taken it back to the library one Saturday afternoon after Doreen had finally finished it.

'Where's my book?'

'I got you a new one, *Cupid in Mayfair*. It's the same writer. I'm sure you'll like it.'

'No, but where's *my* book? My book I was reading.'

Sunday was murder but June had managed to get to the library on Monday lunchtime and get Doreen's old book back again. She must have read it twenty times over by now but she always cried in exactly the same place: 'He held her closely, murmuring incoherent love words.'

Kenneth had just got back after a morning spent lurking in a record shop on Streatham High Road. He never bought anything (George and Doreen didn't have a gramophone) but the shop had booths where you could listen and Kenneth and his friend Simon would take it in turns to ask for different Charlie Parker records.

Kenneth was fascinated by Jane's mink hat. Apparently the mink was one of the weasel family and when it had killed its prey it ate the brain first followed by the contents of the stomach. It was in one of his Wonder Books of Knowledge. Apparently mink farmers usually fed them on diseased liver. Fuck off, Kenneth.

Uncle George came in just as June was clearing away the teacups. He'd been down at the bottom of the garden, poking bare earth with a hoe, and he'd have been there still, only he thought Jane would have left by now. He seemed embarrassed.

'Hello Jane, love. I didn't know you were here. You look very nice. Doesn't she look nice, Reen?'

'Don't she look nice! Lovely colour. What colour would you call that?'

Oh fuck, here we go again.

Doreen took her husband's hand and stroked it against her face, smearing the leaking tears across her purple cheeks. Uncle George tried to think of something else to say.

'Your friend got her flat then? June says you've got a Mayfair exchange.' Uncle George said this with a likely-story smile, as if Jane had pulled it off by hanging round outside a Park Lane call box waiting for the phone to ring. Even if she was really living there it was sure to end in tears. They might promise you a flat in Mayfair but you ended up dead in some back-street abortionist's or on the game in Port Said. The *News of the World* was quite clear on this point. When she told him that Suzy's uncle had bought the flat for her it was obvious he didn't believe a word.

'We've been getting quite a lot of modelling work. Suzy and I are in all the magazines this month, look.'

She showed him the Frockways ad. That wrong-footed him. Models made a nice few bob. But he still looked uneasy.

Jane left the *Vogue* on one of the pouffes then tailed her sister out to the kitchen where the Fairy June had obviously been hard at work. She'd borrowed Valerie's mother's sewing machine and made a new curtain for under the sink out of Jane's orange gingham summer dress; she'd polished the lino in here as well and wrecked the enamel top of the kitchen table with a sheet of Fablon gaily covered in orange and yellow saucepans. *If you can accustom yourself to doing household tasks with a smile, you'll have come a long way towards being prepared for married life and motherhood.*

'This looks a lot brighter.' What else could you say?

'Auntie was never very interested in home-making.' The smug, stupid voice of someone who knew how to get candle wax out of velvet (only she didn't own any velvet). If this was home-making you could hardly blame Doreen for losing interest.

In the corner next to the Utility dresser was a sparkling new fridge. It looked very strange and futuristic in Doreen's old back kitchen. The handbook was still on top of it with a picture of some overdressed bint in a cocktail frock drunkenly hugging her new Electrolux which was packed with chickens and wine bottles and cans of Long Life lager.

'We had to get it on the never-never. It'll cost over eighty pounds when it's finally paid for but it was a necessity really. I can't go shopping every day like Auntie used to.'

'What do you do about her and Georgette while you're at college?'

'We manage.' Which was just code for 'no thanks to you'. 'Georgette goes to the nursery round the corner every morning and Mrs Barton down the road picks her up and minds her till I come and fetch her. She wants thirty bob a week but we've no choice. I've been doing my teaching experience at our old junior school all this term so I can nip home to give Auntie her lunch. She's not too bad really. She can use the toilet all right at least. The main thing is to stop her going out.'

'The traffic must be a worry.'

'It's not that so much. It's just that she will keep' – dramatic whisper – '*showing herself* to people. I've had to have another lock put on the front door. But she does it everywhere – at The Doctor's even. I bought her some new panties from Vanda's – she can't have had a new pair in donkey's years and I didn't want people saying we didn't look after her properly – but of course that's only made things worse.'

They'd moved into the back room by now and June was laying the table for 'lunch'. It was Scotch eggs and salad. *Home Made* Scotch eggs and salad. June had once made Uncle George some Scotch eggs in Home Economics not realising that pork sausagemeat was pretty well top of his blacklist of mystery foods. After the first bite he'd wrapped it in his hanky, hidden it in his trouser pocket and then chucked it in the dustbin. Trouble was, he had been so complimentary about the bloody thing that she made them all the time now.

'Pass me those serviettes, would you?'

June had made a poxy little set of embroidered napkins to go in the Bakelite rings from the sideboard (a good wipe down with spirit vinegar had seen off the silverfish). Georgette was already wedged into her high chair. She was too big for it really but it was that or let her run round the room rubbing rusk into everything. June was only laying the table for four so Jane obviously wasn't welcome.

'You'll make someone a wonderful little wife, June.'

A lifetime of envy and resentment was concentrated in the look that June fired at her.

'Oh yeah? And what will you make them, Jane?'

It was like getting a bite from a pyjama case. Saucy cat.

June walked her sister out into the hall. Jane made a show of pressing some pound notes into her damp, fat little hands and June told her not to be silly just as Jane knew she would.

Jane put her mink hat back on and popped back into the front room to say goodbye. Doreen was sat next to George on the settee murmuring incoherent love words and watching the racing from Sandown. One hand was holding her husband's and the other was down the front of her lacy yellow nylon knickers.

Jane sat in the back of the Bentley and dabbed the tears of laughter from her eyes, taking care not to smudge her mascara, enjoying Bob's silent sympathy.

'Where to now, miss?'

She looked at her lovely little wristwatch. Exactly one o'clock. She'd be just late enough.

'I have to meet my cousins at the hotel we passed on the main road. I'll only be about half an hour. I'll be in the lounge but the bar's supposed to be quite nice if you want to wait for me in there.'

One last check in the mirror. The perfect make-up prettily framed by the glossy little black mink hat. She slid from the car, feeling Bob's eyes on the inches of thigh she had taught herself to show, and then she walked the walk – on full power – through the revolving door, across the busy red Axminster and into the lounge of the Nelson Hotel. The room was a riot of smoked oak and button-backed furniture and it was inhabited by a dozen or so drinkers. Friday lunchtime was quite busy at the Nelson. Men in navy blazers and women in knitted two-pieces (no slacks allowed) and pratty little half-hats that clung on to the sides of their permed heads like satin claws.

The volume of drivel dropped as Jane came in while half the eyes registered her figure and the other half priced her costume. Joy, Carol and Eileen were gathered nervously at a corner table, giggling over their drinks. Carol and Eileen were now working full time on their weddings but Joy was at a funeral as far as the typing pool was concerned. Joy and Eileen had never been in the hotel before. Carol had because her mum and dad had had their Silver Wedding do there. Carol was wearing a home-knitted yellow angora number that made you sneeze just to look at it and a new Gor-Ray skirt – 130 colours to choose from and Carol picked olive green. She was trying out different hair-dos for the Big Day and she'd been stuck in her mum's room all morning having it lacquered into big stiff flick-ups like the moat round a shiny peroxide sandcastle.

Joy and Carol were both having gin and orange because this was what their mums always had but Eileen was letting the side down with a Babycham. Only prats drank Babycham. They looked up nervously as Jane approached. They didn't recognise her – if they had she'd have shot herself.

The waiter reached the table almost before she did.

'Dry gin and tonic, please, with ice and lemon.' Only there wasn't any ice and the lemon slice came out of a jar. 'Oh, and do you think we could have some nuts or olives or something? Thanks.' Big, only-you-can-make-today-perfect smile. A cut-glass four-leaf clover arrived filled with Twiglets and bloody cheese footballs. Huntley and Palmers were taking over the bloody world.

'These are nice.' Carol's hand was already loading Cheeselets into her mouth. She'd put on so much weight that her mother had had to exchange the French brocade wedding dress for a sixteen. You could see her fat round knees when she crossed her legs. Scorch marks from a winter spent hogging the coal-effect two-bar fire showed through her stockings like scar tissue.

Norma hadn't been able to come. Her sister was getting married that afternoon to a quantity surveyor from Maidenhead and she was maid of honour – primrose Vilene complete with flower basket. She looked like a little fat haystack. Her sister (purest white Charmaine, gently lifted in front) hadn't actually planned on a March wedding in Croydon Register Office on a Friday but her sister was in no condition to argue apparently.

No one said anything about Jane but saying nothing said it all really. They had to keep talking about themselves in case one of the unasked questions slipped out – Did it hurt? Did they respect you afterwards? Did you have to keep the lights on? How did she stop the eyelashes falling off?

Carol steered them safely on to kitchenware and there they stayed. Her new kitchen in Crawley was going to be pale-blue Formica and could she find canisters in the same blue? Could she fuck. When she'd stretched this topic twice as far as it would decently go, she revealed that there was a very economical recipe for ox-liver casserole and a lovely pattern for a hostess apron in this month's *Woman's Moan*. Carol had graduated from *True Love* now, putting away childish things like make-up and petticoats and Billy Fury. She was only eighteen, for God's sake, but then Carol had been in training for a life of domestic service since the moment she got engaged. She hardly bought clothes any more but filled her bottom drawer instead: lacy pillow cases; fancy tablecloths; even baby clothes. When trying on winter coats she'd been spotted pulling out the front to see if they'd 'be suitable'.

Jane slowly took a Cocktail Sobranie from her enamel case – a bit on top with tweeds but this lot weren't to know that and besides, the lilac ones almost matched her dress. One of the men at the next table was at her side in a moment – 'allow me' – which meant she could give the girls the Suzy St John masterclass in flirting your cigarette alight.

'Haven't seen you in here before.'

He had dark hair and had done his level best to grow a moustache. He was wearing an Old Whitgiftian tie although only another Old Whitgiftian would have known this (and you wouldn't put money on all of them knowing, quite honestly). It was like a film. You could practically hear the wiggle of the clarinet as his eyes ran appreciatively down her professionally-crossed legs.

'I'm just down for the day.' 'Down' was nice. Screamed 'Flat in Town'. She smiled and turned back to the table. Carol was going to have a candlewick bedspread – *Dream rooms begin with Candlewick* – and brushed-nylon sheets apparently. Ten pounds seven shillings the pair was a Big Investment but they Saved Work. She could have bought herself a nice little outfit for that kind of money. Or put a down payment on a nice little Co-op funeral and have done with it. Jane could feel her face congealing into contempt and she had to watch herself from the chaps' table to keep her eyes bright, her smile serene. As if Carol Norton's kitchen curtains were holding her spellbound.

Finally Joy cracked.

'So. Jane. Tell us what you've been doing with yourself. You've got a little flat up in town, so June says.' 'Little'. Bitch.

And out it all came. Very casually. And God had put this month's *Vogue* on one of the hotel coffee tables and Jane sat back while they tried not to look impressed.

'Is that you in the red?'

'Yes.' Well it could easily have been.

'We've got that typewriter in the office,' boasted Joy.

Jane let another cigarette be lit. The Old Whitgiftian and his pals had been lying in wait but the waiter beat them to it this time. And then Henry's Bill's Bob arrived in his chauffeur's cap to ice the morning's cake and she kissed their cheaply powdered cheeks goodbye, smiled vaguely at the men at the next table, paid the bill with a ten-bob note – 'keep the change' – then back into the Bentley, warmed by admiring eyes.

They oozed back through South London and home to Mayfair and the bloody double date.

Chapter 22

> *Your lift home may have its*
> *own perils in store.*

Jane had been planning to give Henry's Bill's Bob ten shillings but from the way he'd been eyeing her up in the rear-view mirror, she decided to economise.

'Can you do me a huge favour, Bob? And see me up to the front door? The key sticks sometimes and my flatmate might be out.'

He still had that sexy little peaked cap on. She waited for the lift to start – it always got going with a lurch – and she pretended to stagger slightly on her pointy shoes. He put out his hands to steady her and suddenly she was in his arms being passionately kissed. He'd obviously had plenty of practice back in Ilford, pretty boy like that. He'd already copped a feel of her breasts and started hitching up her dress. He'd bathed specially and his soft almost girlish skin still smelled of his mother's cheap yellow soap and medicated shampoo. The lift shuddered to a stop at the fifth floor and she pulled away sharply as if he had been forcing himself on her, checking their reflection in the lift mirror: the pretty uniformed boy, the glimpse of black lace suspenders. She straightened her skirt with trembling fingers. Tears squeezed easily to the rim of her eyelids (any further and she'd have to re-do her mascara) and she flashed him a reproachful look.

'I'm sorry.'

He didn't know what had come over him. Jane bloody did, though. You never knew when you might need a lift somewhere.

Henry and Suzy had spent the morning wandering around Mayfair arm in arm, mostly in Fortnum's and Simpsons. Henry usually only bought Suzy evening things and shortie nighties – given that was all he was ever going to see – but he'd switched to suede and cashmere and tweed all of a sudden. They had lunched around the corner at the Connaught and by the time they got back all the deliveries had arrived and the pink bedroom was full of fancy cardboard boxes – one was from Drayke's (more commission for Brigitta). Suzy had put 'A Pretty Girl is Like a Melody' on the gramophone and given Henry a one-woman dress show and a very big thank you. Henry was now fast asleep on the big pink bed and Suzy was lying all anyhow on the sitting-room sofa, wearing pedal pushers and a gingham blouse, munching hothouse grapes and watching the afternoon dog racing. She switched it off as Jane came in.

'How did it go, darling?'

Jane was still so full of how the mink hat had gone down in the Nelson Hotel that her brain had to work fast to find the right answer. The right face to wear.

'She's quite poorly. They won't really tell me anything but I think it was some kind of stroke.'

A look like pain winced through Suzy's eyes but a jerk of her chin and a tiny sniff soon wiped it clean. She leaned across and took Jane's hand.

'Poor you. Daddy had something like that.'

But not quite like that. Daddy, who could walk into any half-decent bar in the West End and safely order 'the usual' (double brandy, easy on the ginger), bled to death internally in a small flat in the Pimlico Road.

'Will she get better, do you think?'

Tricky one. On balance Jane thought it would be easier for all concerned if June rang (while Suzy and Annie were out, obviously) to say that her aunt had passed away and let that be the end of it. Otherwise they'd be offering her rides to bloody Norbury once a week: the dutiful niece, all that rubbish.

'She's in a rather bad way. I think it's only a matter of time.' Then she (bravely) changed the subject. 'Looks like you had fun this morning.'

The sitting room was still prettily littered with monogrammed tissue paper.

'Henry didn't think I had enough day clothes. He's taking me to Paris on Thursday to get some things for the Grand National. We're going to be spending the weekend with some people he knows up north somewhere. He's told them about me so I've got to look decent. Nothing too popsified.'

Henry was married and until very recently had always looked like staying that way. He'd never made any promises about divorce. He never even said his wife didn't understand him.

Penelope Swan met Henry at a golf-club dance in Sunningdale just before the war when he was twenty-four and she was a sort of sub-deb, programmed to go to dances and tennis parties, meet eligible young men and bang one up for life in a six-bedroomed stockbroker Tudor detached in the right part of Berkshire.

Penelope (and her beady-eyed mama) wasted no time at all. She was pretty, she played tennis and bridge very nicely, she had a fetching wardrobe of dresses that artfully supplied whatever her figure was missing (*Don't, for goodness sake, let yourself appear flat-chested*) and her father owned the best part of Staines – if Staines had a best part.

Two babies and a reasonably safe corner of Virginia Water meant that Penelope had a fairly quiet war, while Henry – 'a born leader of men' – worked his way up to captain in a uniform exquisitely remodelled by his man in Savile Row (who actually farmed out this sort of thing to a jobbing tailor over the butcher's in Brewer Street). After three years' active service, Captain Swan came home with a dozen pairs of nylons, two bottles of Mitsouko liberated from a passing brothel and a nasty dose of the clap.

It was separate bedrooms after that but Penelope was a good hostess (six months being finished by the Swiss had taught her to manage menus and servants in a grand, bland manner). She was a good mother (or Nanny was, anyway) to the boy, Peter, and to Samantha, a sullen, overdressed blonde two years older than Suzy.

Samantha Swan was useful cover, Henry thought. Any present he bought Suzy (give or take the odd pair of baby dolls) could be 'for my daughter's birthday'. He didn't see the salesladies' smiles. Daughters never got nice presents like that.

Very, very occasionally someone would take Samantha out to dinner somewhere decent – as opposed to a dinner dance in some god-forgotten Berkshire country club. Her favourite places 'up in town' were Simpsons-in-the-Strand or the RAC Club in Pall Mall then Edmundo Ros for dancing afterwards so Henry was pretty safe but he and Suzy did once bump into her in the White Tower. Henry handled it very smoothly, introducing Suzy as 'Miss Massingham from the Paris office' but this was obviously codswallop, particularly as Samantha had spent most of her own dinner date clocking the pair of them, watching Suzy's whole glorious repertoire of hand-holding, fag-lighting and head-tossing, aching with envy at the way her father laughed out loud at yet another funny story. How could he? Cheap little tart – only, of course, Samantha could see that whatever kind of tart she was, she didn't come cheap. Samantha stole another glance at that ravishing gown – strapless faille with a jet-embroidered lace overblouse – at that tiny waist (twenty-one inches in a brand-new killer waspie) and Suzy herself: as lovely and confident and pettable as a pretty young cat.

Samantha, despite six months' hard finishing in Montreux and three years on the Berkshire circuit, still just looked stuck-up and sex-starved. She did get dates – Henry owned most of Hammersmith, for Christ's sake – but it was bloody hard going.

She decided not to tell Mummy. It would break Mummy's heart, she thought. She thought wrong. Mummy's main concern was that no one in Virginia Water should get wind. She knew Henry would never divorce her. It was Just Sex, she told herself, with the misplaced confidence of a woman who Just Hated It.

Nobody really liked Penelope – apart from her friends, obviously, who never actually thought about whether they liked each other or not. If you kept the talk small enough – children and delphiniums were safest although it was best to go easy on the children – she could get through a dinner party and she could complain about servants with the best of them but she had no real conversation any more and she thought the property business was a tiny bit vulgar (her mother was from Cirencester). She didn't even talk about clothes. After the pre-war mantraps by Molyneux and Schiaparelli had done their work, she retreated to her mother's dressmaker who had a rare gift for turning handsome lengths of silk and worsted into mumsy little frumps and who thought any sort of padding was common.

Just the same, Samantha did quite fancy a scene with Daddy after that chance meeting in the White Tower. She practised her lines in the dressing-table mirror, modelling herself on Deborah Kerr in *Beloved Infidel*, or possibly Jean Simmons in *Elmer Gantry*. But Henry wouldn't play. He just told her she was being cheap and provincial, that her mother knew all about it and that it was none of Samantha's bloody business.

She cried a lot, then blew her nose on Daddy's handkerchief before finessing a cheque for fifty guineas. Enough for one of those new velvet evening dresses from Debenham and Freebody and a nice suede jacket from Simpsons. Twenty-three pounds – a month's wages for the girl who sold it to her.

The velvet – they only had butterscotch left in a size fourteen – was one of eleven identical 'speciality model gowns' to pitch up at a Valentine's Day ball in some Park Lane hotel (there was quite a large party down from Manchester). Samantha was mortified and Lawrence Green was in big, big trouble with half the buyers in the West End.

So. Henry hadn't planned to marry Suzy but the *Evening News* business had rattled him. She'd seemed terribly brave and matter-of-fact about it but then he'd woken up to find her crying and decided that they weren't going to kill any more babies. Fuck Penelope. Suzy reckoned that the invitation to the National clinched it but Jane couldn't believe he'd really go through with it.

'He's not really going to marry you, is he? I thought they never did. That's what you told Lorna.'

She couldn't quite read the angry little look in Suzy's eyes. She wasn't sure she wanted to read it.

'They don't marry *Lornas*,' and Suzy leaned back against the sofa cushions and raised her chin to the afternoon sunlight, a smug little smile pinching those pink, unpainted lips.

'But wouldn't the scandal affect his business?'

'Property people won't care. They're all wide boys anyway. It's not like he's a banker or an MP or something.'

Besides which, most of Henry's business associates had 'traded the old banger in for a newer model', as one of them put it. Not Ollie, obviously. Angela still didn't seem to understand Ollie but, fortunately for her, nor did anyone else.

The only thing Henry had to worry about (and there was no need for Janey to know this) was the promised knighthood (services to the building trade) which would need to be put on hold for a year or two. Not a word about that to a soul. Penelope would have liked to have been Lady Swan and she'd do anything she could to spoil another woman's chances.

'So. Will Henry be moving in here then?'

'Don't be daft. No. He's going to rent a nice little flat in Mount Street while the divorce goes through.'

Suzy, who already had her own nice little flat in Mayfair in the bag, was prepared to be patient about the divorce.

'God knows how long it will all take but the wife won't care so long as she can carry on as normal in her Virginia Watery way. He's told her she can have an extra twenty grand if she does as she's told. That ought to do the trick.'

She tried to imagine Suzy in an apron, Suzy shopping for groceries, Suzy pushing a pram. What she forgot to imagine was Suzy discussing menus with the cook; Suzy planning drinks parties; Suzy arranging flowers by the French windows in the drawing room or Suzy playing the grand piano – all the things Suzy imagined. Almost the identical fantasy Penelope had had when she married Henry twenty-five years earlier. Suzy couldn't really play the piano but she'd had lessons when she was very small and years ago a friend of her father's had taught her to bash out 'Liebestraum' and 'Sweet Georgia Brown' which seemed to cover most situations.

'I didn't think you wanted to get married.'

'Whatever gave you that idea? Of course I want to get married. I told you, darling. You can't live on Nice Little Presents all your life.'

'I'll have to find another flat.' Aha. So it wasn't about marriage at all. It was about somewhere for Jane to sleep. Still, you couldn't really blame her.

'You'll be all right here for a while. Divorces take for ever. And you'll be good cover.' Oh thanks a lot. Two years listening to the pink velour bedhead banging just so Henry and Suzy could have 'good cover'.

'Anyway, you might change your mind and marry the lovely Johnny.'

Lovely, was he?

'You fancy him, don't you? You've always had a soft spot for Johnny.'

That put the wind up her. She was avoiding Jane's eyes.

'Not enough to do any damage, darling.' She selected a violet cream from the box on the table and tried to look casual. 'You haven't slept with him, have you?' Like she didn't want her to.

'No. I was in two minds but I decided not to risk it. It didn't do the fiancée any good.'

'Didn't you ever just *want* to?'

Suzy wanted to. You could tell. Maybe she really did like it. But did she like it with Henry? Heavy, jowly, cigar-smelly Henry?

'Do you love Henry? Do you actually fancy Henry?'

Suzy looked very posh all of a sudden. As if Jane had left a dead mouse on her breakfast tray. A girl who arranged abortions through the personal columns getting on her high horse because someone had the brass neck to ask her a personal question.

'He loves me and I'm going to make him a wonderful wife.' She turned on Jane. 'And what about Johnny? Do you love him? Do you even like him? What colour eyes does he have, Janey?'

What? What was she talking about?

'Ties?' Ties she could do. He'd been wearing a nice navy silk motif tie last time she saw him. Tiny pink elephants on it.

'*Eyes.* What colour are his eyes? You don't know, do you? You're too busy checking what he thinks about you to actually look at him.'

Suzy, sweet, soft little Suzy, seemed to have gone on the turn all of a sudden. Maybe Jane would be better off living somewhere else. Maybe Sergio could sort something out. Jane pulled a grape from the bunch. What colour were his eyes? She could picture them looking at her: amusement; desire; disappointment sometimes. All kinds of looks, but she could only remember them in black and white. Proposing a toast with a saucer of champagne; admiring her work in the cigarette-lighting routine; swallowing a smile when she used one of Suzy's lines. Laughing eyes, sad eyes but what bloody colour were they?

'They're blue,' Suzy answered her own question, 'Dior blue.' And the silly bitch started to cry.

Chapter 23

> *A single unguarded moment and all may be lost. Serve a slovenly lunch-tray, bolt your food, neglect to use a napkin and you undermine the certainty of behaving perfectly when dining under the scrutiny of others.*

The lease on Henry's flat in Mount Street didn't start until the first of April so a handsome monogrammed suitcase had arrived with two Savile Row suits, a dozen Jermyn Street shirts and ties, a beautiful Sulka dressing gown and no pyjamas (dirty old bugger). He was in the pink bathroom, shaving. He always shaved (or had himself shaved) twice a day. Either he was very considerate (so Suzy said) or he just liked shaving. Suzy was using the blue bathroom while Jane began to get ready. Jane had dug out the red velvet – he liked it last time – but Suzy advised against.

'None of my business, obviously darling, but he'll *never* propose to you in that.' (*Men might whistle at the girl with the plunging scarlet neckline but it's the demure little miss in blue that they ask for a date.*)

Jane didn't say a word but she put the dress back on its padded hanger. No sense burning her bridges. There was a blob of icing on the bodice anyway. She'd been having dinner in Sergio's suite and he wanted to eat *petits fours* from her cleavage. Fortunately it was bang in the middle so she could put a diamanté brooch over it.

'Is the navy grosgrain fixed?'

'Yes. Annie got it back from the cleaner's yesterday. That stain came out completely. Do you have to wear that one?'

'Not if you want to wear it.'

'No but I was thinking of wearing the old blue velvet.' Suzy had gone very debby and demure since Henry's proposal – still didn't wear any drawers, mind you.

'So? Does it matter?'

'No. No. That'll be fine. We haven't pulled that stunt for ages.'

Suzy secretly quite liked the double-act routine because Henry always used to play spot-the-difference afterwards: how much prettier Suzy was; how much funnier; how much sexier; how much classier. Henry was actually getting a bit fed up with Janey. The girl had absolutely nothing to say for herself. She *could* talk, he'd heard her do it, with the various men he'd found for her. Pale copies of Suzy's witty chatter but Henry was already spoken for and so she made no effort at all at normal conversation – as if she'd taken her batteries out to save power. Henry would have called her a tart – only what would that have made him?

Suzy was sat in state in midnight-blue velvet on the sitting-room sofa flicking through a copy of *Architectural Review* – just as Penelope Swan used to do when she first met Henry. Suzy was obviously in training for the bloody Grand National. You could bet your life she'd have Annie serving tea all week so she could practise being mother.

Suzy slipped her magazine down the back of the sofa before a dinner-jacketed Henry came in brandishing a bottle of Moët and a fistful of champagne glasses.

'Hello, Janey. How was your aunt? Young Bob get you there all right?'

Very nice manners and all that but he didn't stop for any answers.

'Suzy may have told you, Janey, that we're having a bit of a celebration.' He thumbed open the bottle, poured them each a glass and then proposed the toast.

'To Suzy Swan.'

So it was true. But Suzy's fingers were crossed as she drained her saucer just the same.

Jane had hardly finished her first glass (Suzy had had two in the time) when Johnny arrived. Jane answered the door (Annie was spending the night in the Fitzroy). She closed the door behind him, put her arms around his neck for a long, hot kiss, all the while checking their reflection in the hall mirror. He pulled away to look at her. They were blue but more Lovat than Dior really.

They hadn't been out together for over a week. He'd rung several times but she'd kept finding excuses.

'What happened to the Alice-blue gown? And who was the callow youth?'

'A girl's got to eat, darling.'

It was the kind of thing Suzy said but it just sounded cheap when Jane said it.

They joined the other two in the sitting room but after a quick hello Henry had gone back into the bedroom to make a phone call. He'd been trying to get hold of Penelope all day and he didn't like leaving a message. You couldn't always trust Samantha to pass them on.

Jane sat down next to Suzy, their skirts filling the whole width of the sofa, the blue fabrics glowing in the creamy silk light of the table lamps. Johnny downed another glass of champagne and knelt on the carpet in front of them; his blue eyes looked from one to the other but it was Jane he spoke to.

'I know I keep asking this, my love, but what are you doing here?'

He held her hand in his but he had suddenly stuck the other hand up Suzy's velvet skirt without even looking at her. She wriggled a bit and puffed nervously on her cigarette holder but she didn't push his hand away. Johnny carried right on talking to Jane.

'When I very first met you, you were a pretty girl of eighteen. Now look at you: nineteen going on thirty-nine.'

Suzy was still squirming and there was a frightened look in her eyes. 'You could marry me and live happily ever after or you could end up like this lovely little slag with her Mayfair flat and her middle-aged minder.'

The Dior-blue eyes flicked across to Suzy's panic-stricken face. 'Or does old Harry turn you on? Who knows? Maybe she actually likes it. Maybe she actually likes fat, droopy old men. Do you, Suzy?'

This was a lot more than two glasses of champagne talking. Johnny had been back to Gloucester Road to dress but he'd obviously been killing time in some Curzon Street drinking club for the last hour.

'Suzy here's a beautiful girl, aren't you, Suzy? Clever, kind, sexy – very sexy – but she's not really a model, Janey my love. She's a tart. A Very Smart Tart. She sleeps with old men to have a nice Mayfair roof over her head. You have to get away from all this.'

Jane half expected Suzy to rat on her about Sergio and the Mutation Mink man and the others (Jane would have) but she sat tight saying nothing, wriggling uneasily at the pressure of his fingers. For a moment she looked as if she were going to cry again. Her eyes had been glumly cast down but as the bedroom door clicked shut she flashed Johnny a look. Reproach? Hatred? Desire? A little of each, Jane suspected.

Johnny pulled his arm out from beneath Suzy's petticoats, carefully wiping his fingers on her stocking as Henry came back in.

As they all somehow crammed into the lift Johnny suggested they go for a spin in the car he'd borrowed. Sports model.

Suzy appeared to have made a complete recovery. 'Oh you lucky thing! Henry says I can't have a little runabout until I've passed my test but I can't very well practise in the Bentley, can I?

I'll never get a licence at this rate. What breed is it, darling? Is it small enough for me and Janey to have a go in?'

'If you don't mind left-hand drive.'

It was a brand-new red Volvo that belonged to a chap in the overseas department who had gone back to Stockholm for a fortnight's holiday. The girls managed to bundle into the back but it was a bit on the small side and poor old Henry looked suddenly very big and old and stiff, cooped up in the passenger seat, rather than stretched out at the wheel of his Bentley. He'd got his arm caught in one of the straps at the side of the seat.

'What's this supposed to be?' You could tell he was getting fed up.

'Safety belts. It's a new thing. All the new Volvos have got them.'

'Bloody Swedes. I don't see why we can't just take a cab. Or walk. It's only a few hundred yards, for God's sake.'

Suzy pulled a face. She hated arriving anywhere on foot. It looked cheap. And Henry was starting to sound like someone's dad. He'd be talking about petrol coupons next.

The restaurant was crowded with out-of-towners but they were shown to a decent table anyway (waiters clearly had a sixth sense about good tippers). The girls got their usual admiring stares only now there was the odd whisper to go with them – Suzy might be right about Frockways. There was even some poor deluded cow wearing one of the bloody things – even the black with gold lamé wasn't nearly dressy enough for the Coq d'Or.

They'd all ordered oysters except Johnny but when his soup came he called the waiter over and complained that it was cold.

'It's vichyssoise, sir,' he hissed, happily. He always enjoyed this one.

'I don't care what it's supposed to be. It's stone cold.'

The waiter stayed dead pan and whisked the soup away, planning the usual kitchen revenge. Henry and Suzy had hardly noticed but Jane felt sick with embarrassment. Johnny's soup came back hot but he had more sense than to drink it. Instead he began cutting up his bread roll with his butter knife. An old bitch in beige lace at the next table eyed him with utter contempt. Models. What could you expect?

When Johnny's steak arrived he took a sip of Chablis, tucked his napkin into his collar and began sawing away at it, holding his knife like a pen.

It was more like two tables for two than a foursome. Suzy had angled her body away from Johnny and seemed determined to keep talking – or get Henry talking – anything to keep Johnny quiet. Henry was telling Suzy about a property he'd just acquired in South Kensington somewhere – a friendly little bargain he'd struck with Jane's Mr Mutation so maybe the girl wasn't such a bad idea after all. The house was a complete wreck at the moment, all carved up into poky little bedsits, but it would be ideal, apparently. Ideal for what?

'I wouldn't care where it was.' Which was sort of true. Eaton Square would have been fine too.

Johnny had dropped his napkin and was asking the waiter for another serviette.

'Why are you doing this?' hissed Jane.

He looked at her hard and drained another glass.

'Doing what, Janey? What am I doing exactly?'

'You know perfectly well what you're doing.'

Oh God. *Don't whatever you do complain. You sound your shrillest and look your worst when you do.* She'd better keep that note out of her voice. Only married women could afford to take that tone. 'You can't see the look on the waiter's face.'

'I don't want to see the look on the waiter's bloody face, Janey darling. He could be stood there dolled up like Marlene bloody Dietrich for all I care, Janey darling. He's there to bring my food. When I want his opinion of my manners, I'll jolly well ask for it.'

Christ. The beige woman was staring now and the bad language meant that her husband would have to gear himself up to complain. Last thing he wanted. It was their wedding anniversary. Twenty-eight years and she'd still never actually touched it.

Johnny called the waiter over before the man could start.

'Excuse me, *garçon*, could you direct me to your smallest room?'

Suzy thought this was very funny but then Suzy had had half a bottle of Moët and three glasses of Chablis. The woman at the next table set her off laughing again. It was an attractive laugh. But loud.

'Do you know,' announced Suzy, in what she thought was a whisper, 'I thought for one terrible moment that that woman was starkers. Her dress is exactly the same colour as her skin. Couldn't work out why she had ruched tits.'

By the time the baked Alaska arrived, they were all four of them plastered.

The manager (who'd been put in the picture by the head waiter) came over for a quick ooze.

'Was everything all right this evening, sir?' Johnny might have made the booking but it was still Henry they spoke to.

Henry, who was busy stroking the hand of the second Mrs Swan-to-be, looked up crossly.

'What?'

'Is everything all right, sir?' He looked pointedly in Johnny's direction. Johnny was holding his coffee cup in a very poncey way. Suzy went to powder her nose without waiting for Jane like she normally did. She hadn't said one word to her all evening. Henry got up and headed off in the direction of the Gents'.

'Why are you doing this?'

He looked sharply at her.

'You can't stand it when people break the rules, can you, Jane? But only the little rules. Suzy can sleep with another woman's husband so long as she doesn't drink red wine with fish. That's it, isn't it?'

Hard to know how to play that one for the best. Nothing fancy. Just a tear or two and a broken whisper.

'She's my friend, Johnny.' Was she?

Piece of cake. He took her hand.

'I know. I know. I'm sorry. Why won't you let me take care of you?'

Buildings had caretakers. Men with overalls and buckets keeping everything tidy and disinfected and locked up securely after dark. Why would a girl want taking care of?

Johnny paid the bill while the girls tripped outside and bundled into the back of the borrowed Volvo, their frilly petticoats bunched up around them like a pair of matching dollies packed in tissue paper. Henry, by now in a bad mood, had remembered he ought to phone the wife and tell her he was staying at his club after a late business meeting (she'd get his lawyer's letter on Monday). He refused to be trussed back into the passenger seat and insisted on walking back to the flat on his own. It took the drunken Johnny so long to figure out the safety strap that Henry had already disappeared upstairs to ring Penelope by the time they eventually pulled into the forecourt.

Penelope was on the phone to her sister in Cirencester. No, she didn't think there was Another Woman as such, no one serious anyway, but Henry was at that very difficult age. Her sister hooked the phone into her right shoulder and reached for her copy of *Vogue*. Henry listened to the engaged signal for a few furious seconds then dialled again, pulling the sitting-room curtain back to see what the other three were up to down below.

Suzy was in the mood for a test drive.

'Johnny, darling.' *Darling*. Fucking cheek. 'You did say Janey and I could have a spot of practice while you still had the car?'

Johnny chucked the keys over his shoulder then staggered out of the driver's seat, propped himself up against the wall by the entrance and lit one of Henry's half coronas.

The girls climbed into the front of the car.

'Once round Berkeley Square and back,' cried Suzy.

'Drive carefully!'

'We will, darling! Very carefully indeed. Safety belts and everything.'

The red car roared back down the forecourt and reversed blindly into the side road and off into Curzon Street. There wasn't much traffic around (most of Mayfair was in the country for the weekend) and a couple of minutes later the car was zooming back round the flowerbed in front of the main entrance. Henry peered out of the fifth-floor window as the two girls danced round the car, sitting on the bonnet and posing pertly like dolly birds at a motor show. One of them waved up at him – he couldn't tell which – before they climbed back in on opposite sides and roared off again for another run round the block.

Johnny was starting to nod off against the wall but he was woken by the sound of tyre on tarmac as the speeding car pulled off Curzon Street a second time and back into the home straight. His bleary eyes looked up at the two dark heads above the goofy round headlights, at the gleaming chrome of the radiator, picturing the damage about to be done to the brake linings, waiting for the moment when the engine stalled to a halt once more.

The moment never came. Instead a ton of Swedish engineering carried right on accelerating into the wall where he stood, squashing his lower body like a wasp on a window pane.

Part Three

Chapter 24

> *Your allure is a science. Take control of your movements. Make them slow. Make them graceful. Monitor every pose, every gesture, so that nothing is ever left to chance.*

The policemen were quite chummy first off, sitting the pair of them down on a settee by the main door and telling them not to worry. The central heating went off at eleven and it was freezing in the foyer. There was an old paraffin stove behind the porter's desk but its heat didn't seem to reach any further than his knees.

One of the upholstery pins on the settee had torn a tiny hole in Jane's stocking and she could feel the ladder tickling its way up the side of her leg every time she moved.

When the ambulance men had finished outside one of them came over and asked if they were all right and was either of them a relation? He stank of disinfectant. That and the smell of floor polish and the dusty spray of plastic carnations in the vase on the front desk made Jane feel like she was in hospital. He asked again if either of them had been hurt in the crash.

'We're both fine,' insisted Suzy in her very best hockey-captain tones, 'completely unscathed.'

Unless you counted the bruised feeling across the chest from those rotten safety straps, thought Jane, but she said nothing.

'Your hand's like ice.'

He walked back to the desk to say something to one of the patrol-car policemen then drove away in the ambulance. No need for the siren.

The nosey old bitch on the ground floor had been woken up by the crash but she'd missed the ambulance coming and going because of the time it took to get her curlers out and change into her best housecoat (quilted nylon, *much* too long on her). She said they ought to have hot, sweet tea, like in the Blitz. It wasn't proper tea, though. It was that perfumed gnat's piss they all pretended to like. Very friendly all of a sudden but she served it in the kitchen china just the same and she didn't offer any to the policemen.

One of them came over. Did either of them know the deceased and where did his family reside? *Reside*. Pillock. Then he went back over to the porter's desk to arrange for some poor sod from the Putney branch to wake Old Mother Hullavington with the glad tidings.

'What the bloody hell happened to Henry?' whispered Jane.

Henry had been watching the whole thing from the sitting-room window upstairs while he was trying to get through to the wife. Once he'd seen the girls safely out of the car he sloped off down the fire escape to the garage where he kept the Bentley. The A30 was clean as a whistle and he was back in Virginia Water by midnight. Penelope was alone in the house when he got back, having waited up with a bottle of Cointreau. Penelope wanted to know what time he called this so he called it half past ten – just in case he needed an alibi.

The phone on the desk rang while the policemen were outside inspecting the front of the Volvo. Jim the porter answered it, nodded and yes-sirred a few times then signalled to Suzy who had started to cry. Whoever it was didn't have a lot to say and she was back on the settee before the policemen had even noticed her get up.

'Was that him?' whispered Jane.

'He wasn't here, all right? He'll sort everything out.' Suzy spoke very quietly, without moving her lips.

It was all shaping up like a tragic accident – Careless Driving at a pinch – until the police started taking statements from people and Jim the porter told them he'd seen the car deliberately accelerate into the wall. Thanks, Jim. And then the other nosey old bitch – the one who had the flat on the other side of the main door where the crash was – went and stuck her oar in. Mrs Kowalski, her name was. Foreign.

Mrs Kowalski had seen the whole bloody thing and she'd tottered out into the front hall and started shooting her mouth off. She had a ginger wig stuck on all anyhow and a white space at the front of her head where her face ought to have been: no eyebrows; no eyelashes; no cheeks; no lips. Without Max Factor there was nobody there. They took her statement over by the porter's desk but she was stone deaf so you could hear every word. Young women in motor cars at all hours driving. Decent people asleep. And not the first time flat fifty-two a nuisance made. The policeman's ears pricked up. What flat number did she say? He finished taking her statement and was just nipping out to have a word with the radio bloke in the police car when he heard the clang of a tin pail on the tarmac outside. While he'd been busy with Mrs K, Jim the porter had wandered off to his little glory hole under the main stairs to get a mop and a bucket and a bottle of Jeyes Fluid and had calmly trotted outside to wash all that mess off the stonework. What was his game? More to the point, what were the CID going to say?

The CID pulled up a few minutes later in a shiny black Humber. The detective sergeant had a few words with the constable then strolled over to the settee. Carefully combed hair, dandruff (*if allowed to run riot, dandruff can even lead to baldness*), shiny blue suit. Married. He even smelled married: a nasty mixture of pipe tobacco and cough sweets and meat pie. Jane tried to picture the wife: a carrot-topped, pear-shaped, apple-cheeked housewife in a floral apron and K Skips baking bloody biscuits in Barnet.

Something about the magic number fifty-two had got them talking about accompanying them down to the station. No charge or anything. No taking down and using in evidence or any of that *Dixon of Dock Green* malarkey but they didn't seem to have much choice about it just the same.

Suzy looked down at her blue velvet and then up at the copper. 'The police station? Like this?'

Her voice had gone very Darjeeling all of a sudden and she'd tried to turn the charm up a notch or two, pursing her lips and batting her eyelashes down (to the frock) and back up again (to the detective) but those strokes didn't cut much ice when your mascara was all down your face and you'd left most of your lipstick on the rim of a teacup. Jane surreptitiously wiped her lipstick on to a crusty old paper hanky she found in her jacket pocket. Crusty with what?

The policeman obviously hadn't heard of dressing for the occasion.

'Don't try to be funny, miss. Just you go along with the sergeant here. We'll take the other young lady in the Humber, Wilkins.' It was Wilkins who had told Johnny Hullavington that the ambulance was on its way as his life's blood trickled neatly down a nearby drain.

They might not let them change into formal daywear but they couldn't very well refuse to let them go to the bloody toilet. Mrs Kowalski's toilet. Suzy was gone nearly twelve minutes – time to put a whole new face on – but it wasn't the brightest idea she'd ever had. Mrs Kowalski only had a thirty-watt bulb in her bathroom and the thick peachy powder and Plum Crazy lipstick were much too after six. *And* she'd got lipstick on her teeth.

Jane was in and out in half the time. She peeled off her eyelashes and left them in the soap dish then washed off what was left of her make-up. No sense looking like a slag. She quickly took Sergio's bracelet off and looped it round the middle of her bra. Might give the filth the wrong idea. When she came out Mrs K was hovering in the hallway with a pair of rubber gloves and a bottle of Parazone, ready to disinfect the toilet seat. Cheek.

Chapter 25

> *Constant vigilance is required to form*
> *and maintain pleasant facial habits.*

There were a few drunks lurching pleasantly out of clubs in Curzon Street and Berkeley Square but there were no cars about and they got to Savile Row in about five minutes. They drove in round the back entrance and the uniformed man marched them along the gloss-painted corridors and up the stairs to the first floor.

Everyone was shouting and carrying on and a tone-deaf tramp was belting out 'Who's Sorry Now?' from a faraway cell. It was obviously rush hour: tarts; pimps; poofs; toughs and one very drunk, very disorderly old bag with no front teeth and a greasy tweed skirt. She squinted cross-eyed at the pair of them in their French pleats and French navy.

'Fuck me! If it isn't the lady with the alligator purse!'

A big hello from an old soak like her didn't do them any favours with the filth. Not exactly a character witness.

'Friend of yours?'

They fingerprinted them both then put them in separate rooms. Jane's had a bench against the wall and a table and chairs in the middle. She sat down on one of the chairs. The green paint, the smell of bleach and cabbage and the tiny shrivelled brains of chewing gum under the rim of the table made it a lot like being back at school.

There was a window in the room but it was so close to the wall of the office block behind that no light at all could get in and the ailing fluorescent striplight buzzed away day and night. It was hot and stuffy but she didn't take off her mink – might get nicked. They left her there for over an hour before the detective came back and started asking questions while a hatchet-faced old dyke in a blue serge dress and one of those upside-down nurse's-outfit watches sat in as silent chaperone.

Had she been driving the car? No, she was not driving the bloody car. How long had she known the deceased? How fast had the car been going? Did she possess a current driving licence? Did she know it was an offence to drive a car without a licence?

'I wasn't driving.'

Soothing suddenly. They knew it was an accident. Foot on the accelerator rather than the brake? Happens all the time. The jury would understand. Careless driving. Driving without a licence. First offence? There'd be a fine, obviously. But prison was unlikely. Six months tops.

'I wasn't driving.'

It was like talking to your bloody self.

They tried a different tack. What had she seen exactly? How did Johnny look when the Volvo hit him? Jane's fingernails picked silently at the little brains under the table. She had a mental snapshot of the funny, confused expression as those Dior-blue eyes looked up from his scrounged cigar to the oncoming car. She remembered the softish, queasy feeling as they slammed into the wall and the jerk of pain as the strap thingy dug into her shoulder. She rubbed at the bruise.

'Tell me about your evening. How many drinks did you have?'

She answered very slowly. A bit tipsy. A tiny bit slow on the uptake. Mr Hullavington was drinking Nwee. Nwee something. But Jane had wanted Whywine. Always Whywine with fish. Not too slurred. Her accent was edging steadily down the A3, mouth slightly ajar, a bit of a wobble to the head, letting her chin stroke the collar of her mutation mink.

Wouldn't she like to give Mum and Dad a ring? Let them know where she was? The detective came into sharper focus when she filled her eyes with tears. He had really bad skin.

'They died. I moved up to London.'

As usual, nobody thought to ask for dates.

How long had she known her fiancé? Turned out he'd been having a word with old Mrs Whatsit down in Putney so that suddenly a run-of-the-mill Death by Dangerous Driving was shaping up into a nice little murder inquiry.

'He wasn't my fiancé.' She gave the word a tiny lick of French polish. The way Suzy always said it.

Oh yes he was.

Oh no he wasn't.

'Oh yes he was. Your flatmate says he was.'

Did she now? Thank you, Suzy.

And then he pulled a small green leather box out of his pocket. There was a dark stain on one side.

'This was found on the deceased.'

The detective flicked the box open with his bitten thumb and held it out to her, tilting it from side to side, trying his best to make the stones twinkle in the dead fluorescent light, as if offering her three thousand a year plus five bedrooms and a garage in Putney.

Jane stared at the ring with its dirty blue and white stones. It would go nicely with the bracelet. Gin was good for cleaning jewellery.

Doreen's engagement ring was very cheap-looking. A nine-carat Princess setting for a dull ruby and two tiny chips of rose-cut diamond. They'd had one just like it in the window of the pawnshop in Croydon. You could see it wasn't worth two bob but Doreen always wore it swivelled to the inside of her hand just the same – in case somebody took a fancy to it. She used to twitch it round by flicking it with her little finger which always had scratches on the knuckle from the crudely-made claws holding the stones.

Carol's was no better. 'Illusion-setting solitaire', she called it, but there was more setting than diamond with shiny white metal bits all round the crappy little tenth of a carat to make it look flashier than it was.

Johnny's ring wasn't like that. A bit old-fashioned but good stones. His mother's probably – *her* mother's even. Jane glanced down at the ringless fingers in her lap, unconsciously fanning them out to imagine sapphires against the navy grosgrain, but the effect was spoilt by a big blob of fingerprinting ink under one of her Persian Pink nails. She'd need turps to get that off. Fingerprints, honestly. Blue-satin evening gloves and a red velvet steering wheel cosy and the berks were looking for fingerprints.

So. Had she and her fiancé quarrelled? He wasn't her bloody fiancé, how many more times? He obviously didn't believe her. She'd met the mother? Yes. Seen the house? (He knew those big houses in Putney.) A twopenny-halfpenny mannequin like her wasn't going to turn down a public-school meal ticket like John Frederick Hullavington. Of course she bloody said Yes. What had the row been about? Had she ever driven a left-hand drive before? Left-hand what? A foreign car. A car where the steering wheel was on the left-hand side. She looked dimly back at him. Where was it supposed to be?

They left her on her own for a while and she put her head down on the table. She woke up when the door clicked open again and she looked up at the man who came in. Her face was flushed with sleep and her wristwatch had left a funny pattern on her cheek. It was a new policeman: not married; smarter suit; posher voice; better barber. Jane swivelled slightly in the chair so that the ladder in her stocking wouldn't show.

He was a Detective Inspector – sounded like two jobs. He sat down opposite, eyeing her up, but she couldn't hear any clarinets playing. He didn't swallow hard or check his tie. Nothing. Without her face on she was invisible – like Mrs Kowalski. Being old must be like this.

'So. What is a nice girl like you doing in a place like this?'

That old line again. The matron, MacDonald her name was, settled back on the bench like an old dear up the pictures. All she needed was a bag of sherbet lemons. She loved it when they sweet-talked them first.

He leaned forward, his eyebrows repeating the question. He didn't half fancy himself. She tried to imagine him in a nice eleven-ounce navy worsted but he would never clean up as well as Tony – not with those teeth.

The detective inspector leaned back in his chair again and looked her over with squinty eyes the colour of dogfood.

'We know it wasn't you behind the wheel, Suzy. What did your friend and her fiancé quarrel about?'

Whoops. Wrong room.

There was a sharp sniff from matron but he took no notice.

'Our witnesses know it wasn't you. The downstairs neighbour is willing to swear that it was you, not your friend Jane, in the passenger seat.'

You could almost feel sorry for the poor, stupid sod. The matron gave a warning cough – she even coughed in a Scotch accent – but it was far too late by then. He'd got the wrong room and the wrong girl. He opened his mouth to speak but thought better of it.

'Excuse me a moment.' He picked up the telephone. 'Tell Cotton I need to speak to him downstairs. If you could keep an eye on Miss, er . . .'

'James.' Jane supplied the missing surname in a carefully flat voice.

'On Miss *James*, matron. I shouldn't be too long.'

That little fiasco, plus the fact that their other key witness, Jim the porter, had previous form for perjury, seemed to take the wind out of the detective inspector's sails. The deceased's mother was no bloody help, crying and carrying on. Yes, her son had been about to get engaged. Nice gel. Very well turned out. Dark hair. Name? Definitely not an Amanda. Jenny? Jilly? Yes, it might have been Suzy. The girl in the other detention room, whatever her bloody name was, the posh one with all the lipstick, not only swore blind she wasn't driving but insisted that she had seen the deceased step in front of the car – which given the amount of alcohol in his blood was a distinct possibility. The inspector had felt quite optimistic about the posh girl at first – no actual form but she was 'known to the police'. Unfortunately she was also known to a bloody good solicitor who'd kicked up a right stink and dropped hints about friends in high places. They'd have to let her go without charge. Their only hope had been a confession and there was fat chance of that now the DI had shown his hand.

It was daylight outside and a fried-bacon smell was sidling up from the canteen. Someone brought Jane a cold cup of stewed tea that left nigger-brown tide marks on the inside of the cup as she drank it. There was a very old cheese sandwich on the tray. She left the bread out of habit.

The superintendent had told his men not to waste any more time but they strung her along for another hour or two, filling in forms, before the smarmy detective inspector grudgingly conceded that Miss James was free to go – for the time being. He did his best to make it sound like a threat and muttered something about not changing her address. He held the door of the interview room open but Jane just sat glumly in the chair. The matron thought the tears in her eyes were delayed shock but it was just Jane remembering the last time she'd had to make her way through Mayfair in a model gown in broad daylight. The ladder in her stocking was all the way down to her shoe and she didn't have the price of a cab in her little beaded bag. The copper (the married one this time) gave her a tissue and said he'd find a car to run her home. An unmarked car.

Chapter 26

> *Relax in your bath tub and try to imagine*
> *yourself in different difficult situations.*

The Volvo was under a tarpaulin waiting to be towed away and a man from the station with a clipboard and a measuring tape was drawing a plan of the accident when the police car pulled up in the forecourt of Massingham House. Mrs Kowalski's curtain twitched but there was no one behind the front desk.

The flat smelled of stale cigarette smoke from the evening before but there was no sign of Suzy, no sign of anything belonging to Suzy. The hangers in her wardrobe were all empty and the only stitch of clothing she'd missed was her navy and beige reversible swing coat in the hall cupboard and the fuchsia-pink Harry Popper suit which was still hanging on the back of the kitchen door where Annie had left it. No sign of Annie either and no answer to the maid's room telephone. Jane lifted the receiver on the phone by the sitting-room window and laid it down on the side table.

She was woken by the rustle of an *Evening News* being stuffed under the front door. It was all foreign stuff on the front but someone had folded it round to an inside page.

There was a photo of Massingham House and a column of copy cobbled together from the morning's post-mortem and what they'd been able to winkle out of Jim the porter.

Stockbroker crushed by Swedish car

John Hullavington, a stockbroker of Gloucester Road, Kensington, was crushed to death last night in a freak accident with his car in the forecourt of a Mayfair luxury block. An ambulance was summoned but Mr Hullavington was pronounced dead on arrival at St George's Hospital, Hyde Park.

The Swedish-made car, a Volvo PV544, was being driven by one of his two female companions, Susan St John (20) and Jane James (19), both of Massingham House, Mayfair. Savile Row police have, as yet, been unable to determine which of the two brunettes – both of whom are believed to work as glamour models – was behind the wheel when the accident occurred.

Mr Hullavington, an Oxford graduate, was a junior partner in the stockbroking firm of Banning and Holt. He was 31 and unmarried.

'Glamour model'. Fucking cheek. Made her sound like a tart.

The phone started to ring the minute she put it back on the hook.

'Welcome back, Janey love,' whispered Jim. No 'Miss James' now. 'Couple of gents down here say they're from the *News of the World*.'

She peeped round the edge of the silk curtains and saw a man in a Burberry looking up at the front of the block. She could see flashbulbs going off, as if there was a model posing in the doorway.

'Tell them I'm out.'

She took the phone back off the hook and ran a bath while she had a look in the fridge. Apart from some grapes and peaches in the fruit bowl there was nothing to eat in the place but a tin of shortbread, a box of marrons glacés and half a bottle of flat champagne. She had the lot then soaked in a bath of Jasmine for an hour, to wash away the smells of the night before crawling back into her unmade bed.

* * *

The *Sunday Times* and the *Observer* were in the service hatch as usual the next morning. Nothing in either of them. She put her reversible silk raincoat over her nightie, tied on a headscarf, slipped on a pair of matching kid pumps and went downstairs. *Even if you are only popping out for some cigarettes, there is no excuse for dressing all anyhow.* She had a quick peep through the window in the lift door when the cage clunked to a halt at the bottom of the shaft. There was no Jim at the desk but there were still two men in raincoats hanging round the main entrance, so Jane went back up to the fifth floor, left the flat by the kitchen fire escape (the two exits had come in handy after all) and ran down to the stall on Park Lane for a *News of the World*. She didn't dare open it till she was back indoors.

Christ. About half of page six. Double Date Dollies Deny Death Drive. The reporters had dug out the Frockways ad and somehow got their hands on some studio shots taken by a mate of Terry's, designed to play up the twins gimmick.

There was a photograph of Johnny, looking very handsome and very posh in cricket whites at an old boys' match somewhere. There was a picture of his poor widowed old mother wearing a black frock, the three strings of fake pearls and a bewildered snapshot smile in the drive of the villa in Putney. Amanda, who was reading it all over breakfast with Mummy down in the country, thought the house looked a lot nicer than she remembered it. He was the only son. There was a sister, it turned out, but she'd joined a silent order on the Isle of Wight and they never spoke about her.

The medical correspondent explained matter-of-factly that after the femoral artery was severed the victim would have bled to death in eight minutes, less time than it took the ambulance to nee-naw the short drive from St George's Hospital to Massingham House. The motoring correspondent managed to get in two paragraphs on the irony of being killed by a car designed for safety and how James and St John emerged without a scratch, safely inside the torsional wossname and the revolutionary three-point seat belt. He'd written another paragraph boring on about the four-speed gearbox but the sub-editors cut it out. The legal desk explained that if both girls denied driving there was nothing the police could do about it because one of them was telling the truth and had committed no offence. The news reporters then laid it on good and thick about how, as he slumped in the doorway of Suzy St John's luxury Mayfair block, Johnny Hullavington, 31, felt his young life slipping away, staining the Portland Stone façade with his heart's blood and other claptrap. There wasn't a bloody stain, not after Jim had been round with the Jeyes Fluid.

Jane risked putting the telephone receiver back on the cradle but she had hardly done so when it rang. Jim was back on duty.

'There's a young man down here says he's your brother.'

She looked around her. The flat was in a right state. The champagne glasses still hadn't been cleared away. The ashtrays were full of fag ends and half-eaten hard centres.

'Let me speak to him.'

She arranged to meet him in the lounge bar of a pub in Shepherd Market, making sure he knew not to say a word to the men waiting outside. She had just enough time to fix her hair and face, wriggle into Suzy's fuchsia suit and Glenda's navy winkle-pickers and nip down the back stairs, her high heels echoing strangely on the cast-iron steps – *Smart girls know how to change from one outfit to another in double-quick time without ever looking as if they responded to a recent fire alarm.* Kenneth was sat like a lemon in the corner of the bar in his green tie holding tight to an unopened packet of crisps. He reeked of Norbury.

'You didn't waste much time. Who put you up to it? Uncle George?'

Kenneth salted his crisps nervously.

'June's in a right state.'

'Don't tell lies, Kenneth. She wouldn't rotten well care. Besides, it's not her precious name in the papers, is it?'

'She's very upset just the same. She couldn't get away what with Mum and Georgette and everything. She hasn't dared tell Mum' – as if she'd understand a blind word anyone said to her – 'but she says you've broken Dad's heart and it's a blessing you weren't using the name of Deeks. Croydon Education Committee can be very particular, she says.'

Unhappily for June, the CEC turned out to be equally picky when a Mrs Doreen Deeks of Pamfield Avenue, SW16 was arrested at Thornton Heath Pond later that month after asking a succession of passers-by whether they liked her nice new pink ones.

Jane went over to the bar. It was only just gone twelve but there was already a handful of regulars in: clerical workers from the big hotels clocking off after a shift and a couple of old blondes cackling into their ports and lemon. Nicely turned out, but you could tell they were on the game: hair too yellow; eyelids too blue.

An old drunk in the far corner was making a silver paper cup from the remains of an empty fag packet he had found. Jane watched as his peeling red fingertips delicately separated the silver foil from its tissue backing and moulded the goblet round his little finger. He then gummed the paper to a sticky pulp which he squished into the base before expertly firing it at the ceiling where it joined the hundreds of others that covered the smoke-browned paint like shiny little barnacles.

Jane ordered a gin and tonic and a lemonade. She could see the landlady clocking the pink suit and trying to work out where Kenneth fitted in.

'That your brother, dearie?'

'That's right, up from Bournemouth for the day.' Why Bournemouth, for heaven's sake? Must be something about that car coat. 'He is sixteen.'

'Course he is, love. Looks like a nice boy.' No he bloody didn't.

Back at the table Kenneth put down the paper and began to tell Jane the news of his own world.

'Your friend Carol phoned at the crack of dawn. Wanted to know if it was really you. She'd recognised that Double Dates picture. She asked for your full address but we said we didn't know where you'd be living. Then about an hour after breakfast her dad's car pulled up outside and this came through the letterbox.'

It was written on that peculiar paper with the chewed edges in Carol's babyish, Marion Richardson handwriting. She was buying back Jane's invitation to the May wedding. 'If it was up to me,' she said – so tidily that she must have written it out in rough first – 'I would have been more than happy to let an old friend join Alan and I on our Big Day but the *Gazette* will be covering the wedding and are sending a photographer and Mum feels it would be better not.' Carol managed, casually, to drop in the fact that they had decided to plump for the Royal Worcester as their best china and that they were still missing the six salad plates and that they had them in Allders. Alan didn't even like salad. She also thought that Jane would be interested to know what fucking hymns they'd both chosen. She'd decided that she was going to obey Alan which was going to be a fairly safe promise as there was next to no chance of poor Alan ever, in his wildest dreams, daring to tell Carol to do anything. Once the letter was safely over the page Carol wound things up pretty sharpish, hoping this found Jane as it left Carol who was hers truly. 'Sincerely' would have been pushing it and 'faithfully' would have been a black lie in the circumstances.

'What are the police going to do?'

'Nothing they can do.'

Kenneth, being an expert on bloody everything, said that it was a classic Cut-throat Defence and that so long as they stuck to their story the police wouldn't be able to touch them.

'You've got a right bloody cheek, Kenneth Deeks.' Kenneth cringed with embarrassment as the other drinkers turned to look. 'Stick to what story?' hissed Jane. 'I wasn't bloody driving.'

She flounced off to the Ladies'. It was a pigsty. There was an unfolded cardboard box on the floor to cover the holes in the lino. The toilet was blocked, the cracked yellow soap was striped with grime and there was a used French letter draped over the edge of the basin.

No well-bred girl ever paints her face at table, in the street or at the theatre. Sod that. Jane went back to the bar and made up while Kenneth reread the *News of the World*: *He made sheep's eyes at farmer's daughter: when she got home she had lost her upper dentures, one of her gloves and her handbag. Happily she had retained her virginity.* Didn't say what sort of handbag.

Jane wiped her face over with a pressed powder puff (Honey Veil), gave her eyes a lick of brown-black pencil and transformed her lips into a big fat kiss of Persian Pink – an exact match for the suit.

Kenneth looked up.

'You don't need all that make-up. You're pretty enough without.' Pretty enough for what?

She took one last look at the girl in the mirror: glossy; glamorous; finished.

'Why don't you piss off back to Norbury, darling?'

She uncrossed her legs and carefully squirmed out from behind the table. She could feel bloodshot boozers' eyes slithering over her knees. She shuddered with disgust and pulled her skirt down.

She catwalked back round the corner to the front entrance of Massingham House. There was a photographer and his spotty young sidekick lurking by the desk discussing football with Jim (who was making a small fortune in tips). The porter looked up in surprise when he saw the pink-suited figure open the door and sail into the foyer.

'We weren't expecting you back, Miss St John.' He scuttled across the room to call the lift.

'I know, darling,' purred Jane, chin held nice and high for the photographs, 'but I forgot something. I'll be back down in a minute.'

The sidekick tore off back to get the reporter out of the pub where they'd left him and to take the film back to Fleet Street. The photographer settled down on the settee until one or both of the girls came out again. He'd have a bloody long wait.

Jane was stuffing knickers and stockings and her sapphire bracelet into her overnight bag. She could only find one of Glenda's black patent stilettos. Pity about the sapphire ring really. The phone rang. The call came from a phone box and the voice on the other end had a peculiar, open-air sound.

'Is that you?' said the voice. It was Henry but it didn't say it was Henry.

'Yes.'

'What are your plans?'

The police had said not to change address. Safest to be vague.

'I thought I might go and see Lorna.'

'Very good idea. Excellent.'

And he hung up.

Suzy hadn't been driving either of course. She said so and Henry believed her. She had been whisked away from the police station and taken to a borrowed flat in St John's Wood where Big Terry was waiting with a new short hairdo and a rather racy auburn rinse – *A fresh hairstyle can make a woman feel reborn.* Henry had found her a job as a receptionist in a big firm on Western Avenue somewhere where she could sit behind a bird's-eye maple desk in tight cashmere sweaters – a whole new wardrobe of greens and blues to go with the auburn rinse – purring into telephones and flicking through her *Architectural Review.* When the divorce came through two years later and Sir Henry Swan married Susan, only child of the late Captain St John 'Brandy' Johnson, nobody made the Double Dates Death Drive connection. Henry made friends with some new maître d's and Captain Swan got some new usual tables.

*   *   *

Jane picked up the phone again and rang Lorna. There was still that funny open-air sound. Lorna no longer messed about with silly voices:

'Hello.'

'It's me.'

'Hello.'

Lorna never felt the same about Suzy after the *Evening News* affair, as if the whole sordid business – her getting pregnant; the professor not wanting to marry her; her mother being a poisonous, loveless old bitch – were all somehow Suzy's fault. She arranged for the murder of Lorna's baby, she was capable of anything as far as Lorna was concerned.

'Suzy killed him, you know. She put her foot down and drove straight into him.'

That ought to keep them busy. It had gone very quiet Lorna's end. Jane leaned back and suddenly spotted the missing black shoe peeping out from under the sofa.

'Is Glenda there?'

'No. I thought she was away. Spain.'

'I've got a feeling she'll be around later on.'

The sound of pennies dropping.

'All right.'

The line went dead.

Jane lugged the laundry box out of the airing cupboard and crammed in what she could: the navy grosgrain (unfortunate associations but still very useful); the red velvet; the blue faille; the two Hardy Amies numbers – poor old Tony; her cashmere twinsets and her tweed skirts. She remembered seeing a Junior Saleslady Required sign at a madam shop in Kensington High Street. You never knew.

She squeezed a dozen pairs of Glenda's shoes round the sides then laid the mink jacket and alligator bag on top. She should be able to get a few quid for them or she could use them as bait for a new Sergio. Always supposing she wanted a new Sergio.

She checked the contents of her old manila envelope. There was over £100 in the post office savings book and another, smaller brown envelope tightly filled with crisp five-pound notes which hadn't been there before. And there, right at the bottom, still in their wallet were the birth certificate and National Insurance gubbins of the late Mary Jane Deeks (eighteen next birthday). That and her make-up all fitted nicely into Uncle George's overnight bag.

She didn't have to be a saleslady. She might be able to just do that part time, go on day release and train as something else entirely: typist; stylist; telephonist; receptionist; chiropodist; machinist; manicurist; illusionist; contortionist; abortionist. Anything she fucking liked.

She sat at her blue dressing table and checked her make-up. The emergency paint-job might have looked all right by the light of a Fleet Street flashbulb, but in the soft, expensive glow of a Mayfair bedroom she looked suddenly very old and very cheap. She brushed her hair out of its makeshift chignon and tucked it into the old fake tortoiseshell slide. Could she still pass for a seventeen-year-old junior sales? She could if she took all that stuff off her face. She went into the blue and gold bathroom, ran the blue flannel under the hot gold tap and washed herself away.

She dragged the laundry box through the kitchen and out on to the fire escape. She had to stand on tiptoe to keep her stilettos from slipping into the square holes of the iron gridwork. Still nobody down below.

It had turned very cold all of a sudden and the March wind was cutting right through her thin mac. Suzy's reversible swing coat was still hanging on a hook in the hall cupboard. Warmer than the silk: smarter. She nipped back inside to shrug into it (beige side out), ignoring the tinkling phone and letting the fire-escape door slam behind her as she left the empty flat for the last time. The cashmere of the turned-up collar slapped softly against her face. The sweet, sickly scent of Suzy was still trapped in the fabric: smelled a bit like Joy.

ACKNOWLEDGEMENTS

A Vision of Loveliness was locked in a drawer for a number of years. It emerged thanks to a sharp prod from the *Sunday Telegraph*'s literary editor Michael Prodger and to the faith and encouragement of Paul Golding, Kyran Joughin and David Benedict (who introduced me to United Agents). Anna Webber (of UA) and Helen Garnons Williams, Alexandra Pringle, Erica Jarnes and the team at Bloomsbury have all been a joy to work with. Sarah-Jane Forder was a sharp but painless copy-editor.

June Torrance gave me the inside track on London's post-war couture showrooms and Chief Superintendent Anthony Stanley (retired) supplied priceless insights into the workings of Savile Row police station in the early Sixties. Clement Crisp and the late Pat Creed were kind enough to check the original typescript for errors and anachronisms (remaining blunders are mine).

Most of all I must thank Pete Mulvey for his love and patience.

A NOTE ON THE TYPE

The text of this book is set in Adobe Caslon, named after the English punch-cutter and type founder William Caslon I (1692–1766). Caslon's rather old-fashioned types were modelled on seventeenth-century Dutch designs, but found wide acceptance throughout the English-speaking world for much of the eighteenth century until being replaced by newer types toward the end of the century. Used in 1776 to print the Declaration of Independence, they were revived in the nineteenth century, and have been popular ever since. There are several digital versions, of which Carol Twombly's Adobe Caslon is one.